VOICES LIKE THESE

© 2025 StoryForge

All rights reserved.

This is a work of fiction. Names, characters, places, and incidents are either the product of the author's imagination or used fictitiously. Any resemblance to actual persons, living or dead, events, or locales is entirely coincidental.

ISBN 979-8-9930133-2-9 (ebook) - ISBN 979-8-9930133-0-5 (paperback) - ISBN 979-8-9930133-1-2 (hardcover)

Cover design, illustrations, formatting, and layout by Beatrice Lebrun.

Edited by Danyelle Briggs, In The Write Dyrection

First edition, 2025

VOICES
LIKE THESE

A STORYFORGE ANTHOLOGY

Foreword

"Oh, I'm not a writer."

That's what someone told me in one of the first writing groups I ever joined. This woman had been crafting new material every week for half of my life, but in her mind, she wasn't a writer. I think for her, publication was the ultimate stamp of approval that would make her an official writer.

It still makes me sad, because that's a dumb distinction. She writes, so she's a writer. And if you write, you're a writer too.

There are a lot of voices we don't get to hear from in publishing. So many people do exactly what that old lady did, and give up on writing – on being a writer – before they even begin.

I founded StoryForge to make publishing more accessible. She might not think she's a writer, and you may not think you're a writer, but I promise you: If your words exist, they can be read. And your words might just change someone's life.

Without the inspiration of an out-of-print, little known fantasy book sitting in the basement, I wouldn't have started this company and these authors wouldn't be in this anthology, and you wouldn't be reading this foreword.

It is my absolute honor to be able to share twenty stories from twenty talented new authors who were writers and are writers and will always be writers. Their work has made me cry, and laugh, and also be so nervous I had to take a break from reading. You're in for a real treat.

If voices like these have been published – why not voices like yours?

Sabrina Rucker
StoryForge CEO

StoryForge has a different feel from other writing platforms because all of the things in StoryForge come from different universes where the stories take place.

Each story is a window into that universe that an author has opened for you.

This anthology is a collection of those windows that we're excited for you to look through.

Try not to leave prints on the glass, please.

Table of Contents

Rise to the Occasion 13

The Destruction of the Sage 25

A Mere Moment and an Eternal Red Light 35

Fairy Circles 45

The Adventures of Chuff and the Janitor 59

Anesthesia 105

The Obituary of a Planet 113

Christ's Blood 125

Saving Daisy 141

I Am A Button 159

Shadows of the Mountain 173

A Fair Price 199

The Light that Draws the Eye 213

Ashes of the Silver Flame 227

Beautiful Evil Thing 271

Boy Scout Camp 283

Guided by the Lost 295

Lehol 305

Haint Blue 321

Under the New Moon 337

RISE TO THE OCCASION

A SHORT STORY BY
AMY WESTRICK

*Dedicated to every "aspiring mage" who is
working to bring their dreams to life!*

Rise to the Occasion

"**N**ow this will get ya through a long winter's night!" Eliza remarked to herself as she pulled her third tray of cinnamon rolls from her small wood-fired oven. She didn't think of herself as much of a baker, though her cottage's lack of surface space—due to the copious number of pies, strudels, and rolls—would beg to differ. Stress baking had been her comfort over the past decade of mage studies, and as The Longest Night approached, Eliza felt a looming pressure.

She plopped the steaming buns down to cool with a huff and crossed the floor to her workbench, approaching a large, worn book. Eliza's grimoire was open to the same chapter it always was this time of year. She sighed deeply, closing her eyes as she ran her fingers over the well-worn page, and recited by memory:

To become a mage of substance
One must pass a simple test.
Summon a Familiar to bond,
And they will do the rest.

First, build a body, fine and fit,
From natural materials.
Then coax a Spirit from the Everplane
To make real from the ethereal.

If your ways are true and right—
The Spirit will decide—
To bring your crafted form to life
And live forever by your side.

There's but one chance a year to summon
When the veil between worlds is thin.
Betwixt dusk and dawn on The Longest Night
May you call your Familiar in!

Tonight marked her seventh attempt to earn her standing as a full practitioner of the arcane arts. She had dreamt of joining the prestigious ranks of her kingdom's magery for as long as she could remember—and ever since she'd reached summoning age, she'd been trying. Year after year, she'd tried, and year after year her attempts had ended in disaster. A bit of a late bloomer by mage standards, Eliza had begun to wonder if she should just call it quits and stick to the simple magics.

But no, she was determined!

"Tonight's the night!" She spoke aloud to the empty room. Her large oak table was cleared with a sweep of her arm, stray muffins toppling onto a shabby, rumpled rug below.

"No time to worry about that, I'll fix it later!" She chirped as she paced from table to cupboards to workbench and back again, collecting all the necessities for the long night ahead. Eliza snatched a kettle from the roaring fire of the hearth and used the spout to nudge cluttered trinkets aside to pour its boiling contents into a ceramic mug. She plunked a satchel of tea in the cup and set it aside by her worn velvet armchair to continue her preparations.

Her arms cradled a precariously growing stack of supplies, which tumbled across the tabletop as her foot caught the upturned rug on the way back.

"Oh gobbets!" She exclaimed, picking herself up from the floor. Dusting herself off, she began sorting the pile of objects before her.

"Let's see, I've got my tea for staying awake, candles to keep things illuminated, and plenty of snacks. But most importantly, a body fit for a Familiar," she spoke as she delicately unwrapped the protective cloth from the creature-form before her.

Oh, the hours she'd spent building a body—truly, a home—for her Familiar. It was remarkable! Eliza had crafted the form of a wiry terrier from strong mahogany wood. It had sharp, pointed ears, a keen snout, and perfectly articulated joints with dowel pins sanded flush. She stroked its back adoringly, running her fingers over the quill-width grooves of spell work carved across its sides.

She stared into the depths of the eyes, small, dripped pools of amber resin reflecting back at her. After tonight, this perfect wooden body would become flesh and blood, Everplane willing. She felt more ready tonight than ever, though she felt a tinge of wistfulness realizing she might never get to admire her handiwork quite like this again.

"Just breathe, you've got this," Eliza whispered as she eyed the sun slipping past the horizon. It was time to begin. Her fingers glided across the polished surface of the wooden animal's body as her whispered incantations lit up the curling script.

As Eliza's recitations grew stronger in her convictions, the atmosphere within her cottage home began to shift. The arching tops of the walls and ceiling above faded away, as if dissolving into the sky above. An iridescent fog seemed to collect in the air above her, barely separating Eliza's mundane living quarters from the font of boundless magic that was the Everplane. Her eyes widened as she gazed at the glowing light above the ethereal barrier.

A small gasp escaped her as she realized that light was a figure. It was coming closer.

At first, in an amorphous form, the light figure tentatively reached out as it approached the glossy film above. That stretching light shifted, and suddenly was the form of a leg delicately passing through the fog as if submerging into a pool of water. The foot dangled above Eliza, then came a second, a third, a fourth, and finally the blob of a body attached as the four-legged ball of light began to float down through her living room.

Despite the Spirit being a leggy blob of light, Eliza already began to recognize a bit of personality. The light-figure descended with a tentative curiosity, hesitating slightly, bobbing from here to there before softly landing in front of Eliza's constructed creature-form.

In all her years of summoning attempts, Eliza had never seen an Everplane spirit this close. It was glorious—pure magic. A brilliant mote of potential.

"I hope you like it," she whispered in awe, stepping back to allow the spirit space to investigate the body before it. "I've worked so long on this one, I really think it's quite per—

"OUCH!" Eliza exclaimed as she stumbled, having caught her foot on the rug again.

She reached out to catch her balance, only to bump the table, sending the wooden figurine flying into the air. Eliza lurched forward to catch it, only to come up empty-handed as the wooden dog crashed to the floor, skidding straight into the hearth's flames.

It was gone before she could utter a word.

Her eyes widened in shock and dismay. "No, no, it wasn't supposed to happen like this! I had everything right!"

Distraught, Eliza scanned the room for the Spirit. "Hello? Oh please, don't go…" Her voice trailed off as her eyes completed their sweep of the cottage without a sign of the light figure.

Defeated, Eliza grabbed the nearest pastry and tea mug as she slumped on the floor in front of her armchair. "Well, I suppose there's always next year," she sighed, glancing forlornly at the deep, starry night outside.

She was immersed in her snacks when she noticed the faintest glimmer of light flickering from behind the table leg, almost as if it was… peeking at her.

"You—you're still here?"

The glowing Spirit crept out from the protection of the table, approaching the fireplace. It paused before the warm, glowing fire, then leapt in front of Eliza to land on the plush armchair she was leaning against. The hopeful mage followed the Spirit's movements and, unbelievably, body language, despite not having a body of its own. It circled the cushion several times before settling with a flop over the armrest. It leaned over the edge of the chair, peering past Eliza's shoulder to the collection of snacks in her lap.

"You're interested in… This?" Eliza gently lifted her hand to the creature, cradling a teacake. She watched as the warm glow of what must be a paw reached out, only to pass right through her hand and the treat with a tingly whoosh. The paw retracted in disappointment as the mass of the Spirit seemed to deflate ever so slightly.

"Oh…" Realization swept over her. "You can't have it like this, can you? You need a body first…Arrghhh!" She exhaled in frustration, "The body I built you took ages, I'll never be able to craft another before sunrise!"

She half expected the Spirit to leave then and there, but it still sat expectantly.

"Think, Eliza, think," she muttered as she stood up to pace the cottage. "Something natural, something living, something…soft?" Eliza's eyes had landed on the large jars of flour, salt, and the yeasty starter on her countertop. "That's it!"

With this spark of inspiration, Eliza brought a large bowl to the countertop and began to add scoops of flour, water, and bubbling starter to form a shaggy dough. Then she began to knead.

The Spirit crept closer, weaving between Eliza's legs as she darted around the kitchen, even floating up to the countertops to closely investigate the dough. Eliza welcomed the company, whispering incantations as she stretched and pulled the mass. Her magic manifested in stubby legs, which popped out from the soft rolls of the body she kneaded. She molded more dough to form a square head and made quick, precise incisions, drawing up small points of ears that flopped forward languidly. With a final cut, she made a large slash across the head that gently spread into the smile of a mouth.

"It may not be perfect, but I promise you'll have everything you need to enjoy this world," Eliza reassured the Spirit, glancing up to see the first hints of a warning purple sky gleaming in the distance. "Hold out just a little bit longer!" She rushed to the pantry cupboard and gathered a stack of jars containing different pickled items.

"Your eyes will be big enough to see the whole world," Eliza said as she gently placed two large stuffed olives into their sockets. "And your nose will guide you wherever you need to go," she mused as she set a dried cherry in place.

"Your tongue will let you taste all the fine things we have to offer here, and of course, you'll need teeth for chewing," she continued, placing a long slice of marinated pepper inside the mouth and neatly arranging a set of dried bean teeth. With a few dots of jelly candy to pad the feet for walking, she rolled the last bit of dough up in a tidy little tail swirl and took a step back to admire her work.

The doughy dog sagged as it relaxed, and Eliza's eyes darted between the quizzical Spirit and the growing faint flow of the coming sunrise.

"Maybe a little time to rest," Eliza sighed a she scooped the doughy creature-form up and laid it gently into its mixing bowl. With a few last whispered spell words, she drew a tea towel over the top and moved the bowl to gently warm before the fire.

Exhausted, Eliza collapsed back into her armchair and promptly fell asleep.

§

She awoke groggily to the start of winter sun warming her face.

"Huh? What happened?" She exclaimed, looking around at the mess of flour and toppled jars of ingredients strewn about the countertops. Her face fell as her gaze passed over the bowl by the fireplace. The tea towel sagged, and her suspicions were confirmed as she lifted the fabric to find the empty bowl.

"Oh goodness, oh gobbets, I must be going mad! Did I... dream that?? I could have sworn I'd made some kind of dough-creature, but there's nothing—"

Eliza's panicked rambling was abruptly interrupted by a loud SNNNNNORRRRRRGGGG of a snore, coming from below her armchair. She spun around to see that her doughy dog creation had come to life, in the body of a tawny little pug with a short, squished face and rolls beyond counting. Eliza's new Familiar stirred and looked up at her with saucer-like eyes as it yawned contentedly.

"Why, you stayed after all!" Cried Eliza as she scooped the portly Familiar up in her arms. "You're exactly perfect. After all this time, I'm so glad you're here to stay.

§

Later that day, Eliza strode proudly to the market, Familiar trailing happily along behind her. Townsfolk and mages alike stopped to stare and the waddling little creature with the cinnamon roll tail.

"My, my Eliza!" Exclaimed a shopkeeper, "What kind of a mutt is that?"

"Nonsense, good sir, this is no mutt!" She quipped in return. "He's a purebred".

Rise to the Occasion

THE DESTRUCTION OF THE SAGE

A SHORT STORY BY
ALEX BUCK

For Meg.

The Destruction of the Sage

Thrace Moonflower was at peace in his meditation and introspection room on the Sage. It was studded with Himalayan salt for humidity and focus, yellow quartz to open his crown chakra, and dozens of other crystals and healing plants strewn throughout the cabin and the hull. The hem of his tunic danced on the floor as he sat in his anti-gravity circle with legs crossed.

He found his center and aligned his energies. The vibrations of the Universe rang with him. He was powerful and could take on any challenge, and the Universe would protect him. The essential oils he ran through the jump engines helped spread positive energy through each system the Sage visited. He loved that as they traveled, they would spread the positive energy and the nice smells of eucalyptus and oregano, forgetting that odor needed air to propagate. Setting his intention and goals for the day, he ended his mediation and floated to the floor.

Thrace walked through his ship, greeting all crew members. He hated that term; it made them sound so subservient to him. They were his commune members. Brothers and sisters wearing their UniversaFit branded tunics. Working towards spreading positive energy, love, and peace, more people were added to their downline through the Universe. And even better, if they could make a pretty penny by selling the oils and crystals they bought from their upline!

They were spreading positivity after all, not poverty.

Every person he passed, he touched his forehead to theirs, "The way and energy of the Universe is within you, sister."

"And with you, Brother Moonflower," they would always answer. The Sage was not a large vessel, and he regularly had to deny members from joining. But they could still purchase his energy cleansing crystals and essential oils to help with diarrhea… or was it constipation? Either way, they promoted good gut health.

Thrace took his seat as captain and turned off the autopilot. Scanning the new system, he found a few planets with fairly sizable settlements. Plenty of settlers need the latest cleansing crystal technology. He kept scanning to find the largest collection of potential downline members and found it on the second planet. The settlement identified itself as Galant Pass. Dirty, he knew, but all he needed was a spark of desperation, and he could create the way in. The way they are buying a planet's worth of distributorships and creating a whole new downline in this sector.

The Sage landed and opened the market doors. Crystals, candles, herbs that did nothing besides make the air smell like burning plastic, and oils were presented on the shelves. Commune members began hawking the wares, promoting a quick way to fat loss or better spiritual energy. Or even better, buy into the UniversaFit family and become an independent business owner. Financial freedom was only a few hundred thousand credits away.

They sold a few fat loss supplements and essential oils, but no distributorships. Speaking to some residents, word had been getting around that UniversaFit was a pyramid scheme, and hundreds lost everything in joining. The commune members responded, "Well, if you don't work hard. You just need to work hard to make your dreams come true!"

It was unsettling to Thrace as those terrible rumors were beginning to outpace their travel to newer systems. They didn't even sell his favorite, "This candle smells like my tantric sex chamber"! It was disappointing, but they needed to move on. He had to remind his commune members that failing people did not work hard and tried to suppress their winning energy.

Taking off from Galant Pass, the Sage went into high planetary orbit. Thrace sat in the captain's chair, pondering where to go next. Alarms and flashing red lights filled the bridge as he was deep in thought. A giant ship slapped together with armor, guns, and space tape came out of hyperspace. They were being hailed.

"Hello, fellow traveler of the Universe. How can I help you on your journey?"

The man on the viewscreen was large, gruff, and barrel-chested.

"Are you that new age son of a bitch that sold my family ten different oils and a UniversaFit membership?"

"Sir, I will ask you to keep the abrasive language to a minimum. It disrupts the communication energy between us." Trace responded diplomatically.

"Get fucked."

The Destruction of the Sage

"Sir, I would ask you again. The Universe makes us friends more than enemies."

"The Universe wouldn't sell oils that make your hair fall out and a distributorship that makes half of our community go bankrupt!" The man's face reddened, and spittle shot from his lips. Thrace may not be able to talk his way out of this one. He readied the engines just in case they had to quickly exit hyperspace. In a moment, the Sage was surrounded by green energy. The angry man, now joined by others in tattered UniversaFit shirts and tunics, had trapped the Sage in a tractor beam.

Thrace had fewer options now, and none of them were good. He could attempt to jump into hyperspace, but it would risk ripping the Sage apart. The Sage was one of the best brand ambassadors he had! He could try to open fire, but his weapons were barely for defensive measures, and he had to maintain his universal peace facade. Or he could continue talking.

"Dear friends, I am so sorry you had this experience with UniversaFit and my crew," Thrace tried his best to be contrite. "I would offer you a full refund if you return the items you purchased, and the refund will be sent back to you in three to six standard months, provided there are no defects or damages to the product. Would you agree to that?"

The man's eyes widened he stared intensely at Thrace.

"Everything you sent and sold us was shit! We used half of it promoting your shitty company, and the other half went moldy in a few weeks! Three to six months for a refund? You're damn lucky we don't report you to the Galactic Trade Commission!"

That didn't scare Thrace as much as the man thought it would. The Galactic Trade Commission was toothless at best, and multiple GTC board members had spoken at UniversaFit conferences.

A smirk appeared on Thrace's mouth, enraging the man and his crew even more. They were shouting at the viewscreen, and Thrace waited for them to calm down.

"Sir, I would ask that you turn off the tractor beam before I report you to the sector authorities." Thrace was done dealing with people who have little to no work ethic.

More alarms blared and red lights flashed through the ship.

"Tell them all you want, you son of a bitch." The man and his ship were charging weapons.

VOICES LIKE THESE

As Thrace dove to engage the hyperdrive, the Sage was ripped apart by an impact mass projectile traveling near the speed of light. The Sage disappeared in a puff of burnt metal, essential oils, and all the empty dreams of down lines everywhere.

The Destruction of the Sage

A MERE MOMENT AND AN ETERNAL RED LIGHT

A SHORT STORY BY

CONSTANCE ROGERS

CONTENT WARNINGS

This story contains themes that may be distressing to some readers, including:

Mention of off-page Domestic Violence

Death

To the friends and family who have encouraged me to write and grow, who have been there when I struggled to feel like writing was something I had any right to do.

And to the people who made me feel my writing didn't matter, spite really is a good motivator to improve.

A Mere Moment and an Eternal Red Light

The light ahead was red; its hue breaking through the black tinted night to encase the battered vehicle in its demonic glow. She sat in the driver's seat with her fingers gripping the steering wheel to ground herself to this moment. The leather under her palm uttered a resisting noise as she squeezed, as if she could usher the light to change if she only tightened her grip enough.

Alexis had probably only been sitting there for a moment or two, but as the wind howled around her car and the darkened road ahead seemed to lengthen under the dimmed moonlight, she felt like hours ticked by. There was no one else out tonight in these field-enclosed roads. Her car sat solitary at the intersection. The towering corn billowed past her passenger side door. An endless expanse of flat land to her left.

The murmur of sound behind her drew her gaze to the rearview mirror. There was very little light given from the sole flickering street lamp. Its soft yellow glow melted over her car, giving the slightest bit of illumination to the car seat strapped tightly behind her. The bulky yellow knit blanket covered the seat, with the smallest face pocking out from the fabric.

Peace was written across the toddler's sleeping face. Like her mother's, her curled brown hair sat in bundles of tangles around her soft olive-toned skin. Her nose was scrunched as she fidgeted in her car seat. A restful sleep retook her, letting her features once more soften. The blossoming bruise across her cheek was an even sharper color under the harsh light of the lamp post. She cradled a ragged stuffed dog against her chest. Little Belle rested peacefully in the back seat, unaware their whole world resided in that car.

The stoplight continued to sit as a red beacon in the night.

The empty roads coasted a whistling wind down them.

Alexis continued to wait at that intersection. Her hands were tight on the wheel. Her daughter slept soundly behind her. She chose to ignore the speckling of blood that still stained her bruised skin.

A second set of lights began to overtake the night. Her heart dropped out of her ass as she raised her gaze once more to the rearview mirror. The flashing of red and blue raced rapidly down the dark, stained road. Gaze flicking back to the stop light, she begged it to change. The red light continued to rest there in the sky. It was taunting her now.

How she'd come to loath the color red. The red of the stoplight that refused to change. The red of the lipstick she'd found staining the collar of his shirt. The red of the blouse he'd ripped from her shoulder just that night. The red of the bruise that now marred their daughter's face. The red that had dripped down the staircase and pooled around his head. The red of the police car that was growing closer and closer, surely to take away the only thing she had left.

The sound of her turn signal blinking pounded against her ear. The police sirens were like a death call as the vehicle grew closer and closer. The toddler in the back continued to sleep, nestling her face into her stuffed animal. Alexis made note of her daughter's features. Made a tally of the bags that were packed around her.

The light changed. Green washed over the car. Foot lifting from the brake, she flicked her gaze back to the rearview mirror. The cop was close. Its lights were blazing against the darkness. Its siren was shattering, the sheer noise rupturing the peaceful night.

The car began to roll forward. Her eyes never left the approaching car. The green light washed further over the vehicle as she began to inch into the intersection.

There was every rational that they weren't there for her. After all, she'd only left the house an hour prior. It had been messy, what had happened that night. It had been loud. No doubt, a neighbor had heard the argument, but the neighbors always listened to the arguments. What was supposed to make them think this night had gone different? That it had escalated from the usual shouts and hits into something more than the normal.

The fight had been loud, though.

The gunshot had been even louder.

As the car rolled forward, a second siren coursed through the night. Frenzied gaze flicking to the right, she spotted a second cop car barreling out of the night. Its lights were startling, and its siren was ear-shattering. As slowly as she'd raised her foot, she pressed it back onto the brakes even harder. The car lurched to a second stop.

The movement jostled the sleeping toddler. Her stuffed dog fell from her hands as a belching wail tore from her lips. A suitcase fell forward against the passenger seat.

"It's okay. It's okay." Turning fully to tend to her daughter, she faced the cop car now upon her. Its rapidly spinning lights overtook the night. She could see nothing beyond their glow; she was unaware of the yellow light that now washed over her back. Both cars were coming upon her quickly.

"Mommy is here," reaching for the stuffed dog, she bore her eyes on her daughter and nothing but her. The encroaching red and blue meant nothing to her in that moment. It was just her and the daughter she'd do anything to comfort. The daughter she had done everything to protect.

She carefully grasped the stuffed toy and placed it within her daughter's grasp. Belle took it readily, burying her face into the fluff. Her tears began to slow, but the cry still rested in her throat. "Mommy."

"I'm here." She stretched, grasping the tip of her daughter's foot. The cop car behind them was slowing down. The approaching second car was still nearly upon her.

"Where's Daddy?"

Giving the girl's foot a squeeze, she knew there was no honest answer to give. "He's back home."

How did one tell a toddler that their father was indeed back home?

Back home, as in, left to bleed out on the hardwood flooring. Back home, where he'd dragged her mother out of bed, drunkenly projecting his own affair onto her. Back home, where he'd slammed the back of his hand against their toddler's face when she'd been awoken to their fight. Back home, where he'd pinned Alexis against the wardrobe, his demanding fingers had tried to wrench away what he thought was owed.

Back home, where she'd had enough and pulled that pistol he kept in his nightstand, and directed it at his chest. Back home, where he'd toppled down the staircase, and even though the bullet had missed, the cracking of his skull against the wooden banister had been enough to finally end his violence that night.

Back home, he would never again lay another finger on her or her daughter.

The cop car moved to a crawl.

She knew they were a sight within that vehicle: the bruised toddler, her even more battered mother, two suitcases stuffed with everything she could grab, and a smattering of blood still on her hands no matter how much she had tried to scrub them.

Still holding her hand tightly to her daughter's foot, Alexis re-positioned herself to face forward again. Her gaze moved to the once more red light that cast upon them.

A breath was pulled through her lips.

The two cop cars were feet from her now.

That breath was passed from her lungs.

The incoming cop car pulled beside her. She glanced over, taking in the two officers residing within the vehicle. The driver looked in her direction. The flashing red and blue lights were nearly blinding. The siren shattered the night air.

She inhaled, finding herself unable to let the breath go. Belle continued her sniffling from the back seat.

A mere second or two must have passed in all of this, but once more Alexis felt like she'd been dropped into that space for an eternity. The neighbors must have been worried this time and called the fight in. They must have heard the gunshot. They must have found the body and quickly pieced together the missing wife, the missing daughter, and the missing gun. They must have seen her, somehow and someway, in this dark intersection surrounded by cornfields.

They must have come to take the last thing she had in this world away from her.

Blaring sirens and flashing lights crossed the intersection before the second cop car continued to race down the road. It tore further into the night. It drove away from her. The car beside her moved to follow, its rapidly spinning lights crafting a signal through the darkness.

The empty cornfield echoed with the sound of the passing police cars.

Alexis gripped the wheel tighter, letting that breath pass from her lips. As the police disappeared into the night, she felt the sob tickling at the base of her throat. She smothered it down, quickly wiping the tears from across her face. Her ribs hurt from the shaky breathes she tried to draw. A twisted chuckle outmatched the incoming cry. With blood-stained knuckles gripped tightly against that steering wheel, she allowed that hysterical laughter to grace her lips.

"Mommy?"

The sound of her daughter's voice sobered her up instantly. She lifted her gaze to the rearview mirror. She almost expected to see another cop car come barreling upon them.

"What, honey?"

"Wanna go home?"

"I know, baby girl." She turned the radio on, hitting the preset to the lullaby CD in the bank. "Just go to sleep, honey. We'll be home when you wake up."

That was a lie. There was no going back home. The light turned green; once more, its color washed over them in a welcoming manner. Pulling her foot from the brake, Alexis rolled into the intersection and took the left turn quickly.

She could still see the flashing police lights up ahead. Following behind them slowly, she noted the vast blackness she now drove into. If there was any luck left on her side, she'd hit every incoming light on green and have them to safety before his corpse even grew cold.

FAIRY CIRCLES

A SHORT STORY BY
NICOLE NELSON

CONTENT WARNINGS

This story contains themes that may be distressing to some readers, including:

Brief child abuse

Intentional misgendering of trans person

To all the kids like me.

Fairy Circles

The day had arrived; Father was taking me into the woods to find a fairy ring. All children enter the woods at some point during primary school, and my father was determined that I would be the first in the village that year. Mother had argued against it because of the dangers of the fairy circles, but Father had insisted.

The snow crunched beneath my ill-fitting boots. I had gotten them from my brother Ted, who had gotten them from our other brother Benny. They were broken in strangely, and my feet slid around as I walked.

"Father," I said, struggling to keep up with him.

He looked down at me, and I stumbled to a stop. Father placed a sheathed dagger in my still-small hands.

"Son, this is an iron blade. Do you know why it's iron and not steel like our other weapons?"

His critical eyes bored into me, and I looked away. The dagger was heavy in my hands. I had never held one before.

"Because iron is a fairy's only weakness," I recited to him. The idea of holding this weapon, which was meant for hurting another living being, sat wrong with me. Even if it *was* for fairies.

"Stay by my side. Do exactly as I say and you'll see a fairy ring. You will be harmed if you stray even a foot from my side. We don't want to worry your mother, now do we?"

As I struggled to loop the sheathed dagger onto my belt, my father drew his own. He tossed it into the air, and I gasped when the blade arced downward on a path to impale his hand.

But he caught it deftly by the hilt and smiled at me.

Looking back, his smile was too cold, too calm, but at the time, I didn't see it. All I saw was my father, who would protect me from the evils sure to come. The view of a naïve child.

Shaking like the leaves around us, I stuck close to my father as we entered the woods. The canopy overhead swallowed us as we ventured into the menacing darkness. A bird shrieked, and I flinched, moving closer to Father.

He laughed contemptuously. "It's just a bird, son. It's not *those* you have to worry about."

"Father?" I said, not daring to raise my voice above a whisper.

"Yes, son?" He had an edge of impatience in his voice.

I could feel the weight of the dagger at my side. "Can we go home now?"

My father laughed and slapped a hand on my back like I was one of my brothers. He caught my shoulder as I fell and pulled me upright.

"Don't get cold feet now," he said. "You haven't even seen a fairy ring yet."

I wasn't sure I wanted to. Benny and Ted had talked about seeing their first fairy circle as if it were a pleasant holiday, but I found no such joy in it. However, I knew Father would get angry if I retreated, so I kept pace with him.

Just when I could go no further before my heart would burst from fear, Father stopped.

A delicate ring of moss-covered rocks sat in a small clearing in the trees. The vibrant grass around it waved in the breeze, and sunlight—the first I'd seen since we'd entered the forest—filtered through the trees and illuminated the clearing. I wondered what could possibly be so dangerous about such a pretty thing.

"Do not be deceived," my father said in a low voice, crouching to be on my level. "Step one foot in that circle and the fairies will appear. Only the pariah has ever done so and lived."

My mouth was so dry that my tongue felt nailed to the top of my mouth.

My father stood. "Do you hear me, son?" he said.

I tore my eyes away from the mushroom circle. "Yes."

We finally set back toward the village. The panicked beating of my heart was painful, and I was sure my father could hear it. I didn't want punishment for my weakness, so I set my jaw and faced forward on the path as we walked, finally unsheathing my dagger and gripping it tight.

As we left the darkness of the woods and entered the safety of the rising sun, I silently made a vow never to set foot in a fairy circle. What a promise to make.

What a promise to break.

Fairy Circles

§

As the years passed, my fear of the fairy circles in the woods gave way to reason. I graduated primary school at 17, thinking (as children that age do) that life couldn't go wrong. I was sure I was the smartest kid in the village, maybe even smarter than Teacher. I knew nothing could hurt me, not even fairy circles. I was *invincible*.

Until I was walking down the path past the bakery, and the baker called out, "All finished with primary school, then?"

"Today was my last day."

She clapped, and white flour plumed from her hands. "You're a young man now!"

The words hit me in the chest. A young man? I had never thought of myself that way.

To me, a young man was tall and lean, with short-cropped hair, a deep voice, and the responsibility to be a father someday. I didn't feel like any of those fit me. I wanted to stay short and soft. I liked my boyish long hair. I balked at the thought of having a deep voice.

Most of all, I wanted to be a mother, not a father. I wanted to be gentle, to be a nurturer, and to be the one person that my children would love above all. I didn't just want it, I *needed* it. The feeling ached in my chest as I thought about this new future of being a "young man."

I remembered how the boys in my class had started acting toward the girls when we started upper primary school. They started being nicer to the girls and brushing their hair before school to impress them. James had even brought flowers. It was cute.

But I despised the way the boys talked about the girls' bodies behind their backs, like the girls were objects. I had only noticed how much curvier and grown-up the girls were looking when the boys pointed it out. Even then, I hadn't understood why it was such a big deal. It wasn't like I looked much different.

Standing outside the bakery, alone, I looked down at my body. Flat as a door. Skinny to boot. When had I gotten so tall?

The air became thin, and I clutched my chest—my *flat* chest. How had I missed this? I didn't look like the girls. I was tall and lanky and *masculine*.

How could I have missed this? How? *How?*

The world tilted around me, and I ran. I made it home and collapsed against the front door frame. There were ants under my skin, especially in

49

my chest. I wanted to rip my skin off.

"Mother!" I cried, clinging to the smooth wood of the doorframe.

My father came into the room. He looked at me with a pinched expression, brows furrowed with disgust. "What's wrong with you, boy?"

The word *"boy"* hit me like a knife. I gasped, "I'm not a boy."

Father's face darkened, a storm on the horizon. Menacing and unstoppable, he grabbed me by my hair. I cried out in pain as he lifted me straight up, until I was stretched to my tiptoes. Each strand of hair he held me up with pulled at my scalp.

Father jabbed his finger between my eyes. "You are a boy," he snarled. "Do you understand?" My hands scrambled at his, trying to loosen his grip.

He lifted me higher and yelled, "Do you understand, boy?"

"Yes!" I screamed, and he released me. I crumpled like a doll—my knees collapsed under me and I hit the ground hard.

My father stepped over me. "No son of mine will be the next village pariah," he said under his breath as he left the house.

I clutched my scalp and curled into a ball, so tight that the world was shut out. I gasped for air again, trying to handle the pain. Father had never hurt me this badly. He hadn't hurt any of us this badly.

Then I heard my mother's footsteps and the crash of her basket on the ground as she rushed up the front steps to me. I looked up at her, just a silhouette against the blue sky shining through the door.

"Oh, son, what happened?" she said, gathering me into her small lap. Too small. *I'm outgrowing my mother,* I thought.

I buried my face into her shoulder. "I'm not a boy. And Father—" I choked on the words.

Mother hummed and stroked my hair gently. The pain started to fade away. The magic of mothers. I couldn't imagine why anyone would want to be a father instead of a mother. I closed my eyes and let her rock me back and forth, like I watched her do with Eli when he was a baby.

"My child," Mother said as she held me, and I felt a warmth in my chest at the phrase. Not *"my son,"* but *"my child."* I clung to her until my aching head stopped hurting, until the beat of my heart slowed.

"Mother, what do I do?"

She was quiet. Maybe her motherly magic only went so far to fix things.

"The woman on the edge of town," she said, voice low.

I shuddered. "The pariah?" The one Father hated so much.

"Yes," Mother said. "She will have a solution for you."

"What? She can help me?"

"Yes, child."

"Daughter."

"*Daughter*," Mother amended, and I smiled.

"What do I do?"

Mother stood and helped me to my feet. I looked down at her as she spoke, but somehow, I didn't feel the stress of being tall like a boy. Motherly magic really could fix it all.

Mother said, "Go to her tonight. Take your iron blade."

"My *iron* blade?" That could only mean one thing.

"Yes," Mother said, gripping my shoulder. "Be brave, daughter."

#

The old woman—the pariah—lived on the edge of town, right near the forest. I walked toward her house, treading softly the little-used path from town. I gripped my iron blade in my hand. It felt strange, since I rarely held it, and even stranger that I might use it. I didn't want to hurt anyone.

I approached the door with trepidation. I knocked, and the sound was swallowed up by the darkness pressing in on me. I swallowed hard.

The door opened slowly. A wrinkled face peered out at me. She wore a bright blue headwrap, the top of which barely reached my shoulder. She held a blue candle with a tiny, flickering flame.

"What brings you to my doorstep?" she asked. "Here, come in out of the cold."

"Wait," I said, looking down at the knife in my hand. "Are you a fairy?"

She laughed, and it was a croaky, old sound. "No, boy. You'd be dead if I were."

"Actually, about that," I said.

"Fairies?"

"No, me being a boy."

She turned around and looked at me very seriously. "Keep talking."

"I... I'm not one. I'm a girl. On the inside. Can you help me?"

She nodded. "I can."

51

§

Everyone knows about fairy rings. Whether made of mushrooms, flowers, or a ring of tree roots that's just a bit too circular, everyone knows to be wary of fairy circles when venturing into the woods.

On my 18th birthday, I knew this. I stepped foot in the woods, alone for the first time, as had every other 18-year-old on their birthday before me. It was a rite of passage, a test of courage. I was armed with my iron knife, wore my quiet leather boots, even tied my hair back to keep it from falling in my face.

There was trepidation in my heart when I entered the woods. Fairies were dangerous, and I'd always had my father to protect me before. Other people in the village entered the woods to be proven as adults. I entered to be proven as a woman.

It didn't take very long for me to find a fairy circle. It was beautiful, a circle of purple flowers grown tightly together, interweaving to create a near-perfect circle.

I stepped into it. Nothing happened.

I turned back to the path to my village, but the path was gone.

Fear rose in my throat, but I tightened my grip on my dagger. These woods would not best me. I knew what I was here for. I would not let myself fail.

The woods seemed to hear my thoughts, and they were angry. The trees around me closed over my head. Branches snapped; it sounded like someone—some*thing* was closing in on me. As I backed myself helplessly into a tree, a hand caught my arm from behind. Its nails dug into my arm, and when I tore away from it in panic, it left long, bloody gashes in my skin.

"I came to bargain!" I cried to the woods, terrified.

The woods didn't listen.

I feared for my life and prayed that my death wouldn't break my mother.

A sound, guttural and low, echoed out from the trees. The great rustling around me ceased, and the trees went still. I turned in a frantic circle, brandishing my dagger.

"Who goes there?" I called, and faint laughter rang in the air, coming from all around me, yet somehow inside me. "I have a deal!"

They were tall, lean, and imposing. I saw them step out of the shadows into the clearing, but I could not see their face under the dark hood of their cloak. I could make out claws on their hands instead of fingers, claws that were red with *my* blood.

Those claws reached up and pushed back the hood of their cloak. Thin lips pulled back into a smile, revealing wicked sharp teeth.

It was a fairy. It was taller than me, with an ashy, distorted face, like looking at a reflection in a pond.

"I have a deal," I repeated, voice shaking.

"So I heard," the fairy said, its smooth voice incongruent with its mangled features. "What can you offer me?"

I squared my shoulders. "My name," I said.

"Oh? Don't you know that most humans *avoid* giving their name to fairies?"

"Yes, but I don't want it anymore."

The fairy tilted its head. "Interesting." It paced around the fairy ring. "And just what would you be wanting from me in exchange for your name?"

I looked at it in its red eyes. "A new one."

The fairy stopped pacing. "Shiara sent you."

"The old woman?"

"I suppose she would be by now."

I stared at the fairy and gasped. "Is she like me?"

"You ask too many questions," the fairy said, annoyed.

"Can you do it for me?" I asked, hope glowing like a lantern in my chest.

"Give me your name."

I pursed my lips. "How will I know you'll return me with a new one?"

The fairy sighed. "Fine. You humans are so picky." Its eyes glowed a brilliant orange. "I swear upon my word as an immortal being of the Wilde Places that I will take this human's name and return them with a new one. I swear that no harm will come to them. I swear on my immortal power."

Their eyes faded back to red. "Your name, human."

"Nathaniel." As I spoke, the name went from something familiar to something cold and dead. It wasn't mine anymore. It belonged to this fairy.

The fairy's eyes glowed again, and it said, "Upon my immortal power, I now give this human a name by which it shall be known to all who encounter it." It looked down at me. "Are you ready for your name?"

§

I walked back into my house feeling lighter than air. My body was different—I could feel my weight in my hips now, and I had the curves of a normal woman.

My father was inside, and I tensed when he saw me. But he just waved and smiled and said, "Hello, daughter. Congratulations on finishing school." I was shaken for a moment, but Shiara had warned me that everyone unwilling to see me as I was would be forced to by the fairy magic.

I grinned at Father. "Thank you," I said. I had a grim enjoyment in the fact that he had no idea that he used to call me boy and would have died before seeing me as a girl. The stubbornness of a human, it seemed, was no match for the power of a fairy.

Mother entered the room, and when her eyes fell on me, she covered her mouth. She gasped, and I ran to her, hugging her, now standing at her height. "Hello, Mother," I said.

"Hello, daughter," she said, voice thick. She pulled back to look at me. "What shall I call you now?"

I smiled. "Faelin."

Fairy Circles

THE ADVENTURES OF CHUFF AND THE JANITOR

A SHORT STORY BY
H. W. PERFIDY

CONTENT WARNINGS

This story contains themes that may be distressing to some readers, including:

Child abuse

Child exploitation

Child experimentation

Child murder

Suicide

Violence

Blood and gore

Death and dying

The fun part of writing comedy is that the reader can't always tell if it's a joke or foreshadowing.

The Adventures of Chuff and the Janitor

ACT 1

In which Miss Finch finds her Voice

"**G**ood mooorning, New Penumbra!"

The Janitor's booming sing-song call rang across the sky's emerald expanse. It danced amidst the crooked rooftops and rapped on my windows, giggling and snickering as it went. 7 o'clock sharp, just the same as every other day.

I rolled out of bed and stumbled to the window, lifting my left leg on the fourth step to avoid the ankle-biting snap of a particularly feisty floorboard. I threw open the curtains. Cotton candy clouds streamed in through the glass. They danced and giggled, brushing over the birthmark on my arm, before dissolving into a rosy, pink light that filled my room. Outside, the crooked, lopsided buildings of the city stretched, doors slamming and roof tiles rattling as they yawned, grumbled, and settled. Suspended up high in the sky on a gilded wire, the sun beamed down on the city, licking at puffs of cotton candy as they streamed past.

I pushed open the window to let in more of the cotton candy. The sun turned to beam through the opening. Its toothy grin leered.

"Hello, darling," it said in a deep drawl.

I grimaced and stepped away from the window.

Making my way to the bathroom, I washed up in preparation for the new day. I glanced at my reflection in the mirror above the sink. The hairless face of an oddly proportioned ape looked back at me. I'd always been told I was the most unique person to ever live in New Penumbra. Sure, there were other ape-heads, but most had more hair, broader palms, longer skulls… None of them looked quite like me.

I liked that, though. It made it easier to set myself apart. Make myself recognizable. "Special is memorable", as the Janitor liked to say. And when you were the apprentice to the world's greatest detective, you wanted to look memorable. Reliable. Professional. I pulled the sleeves of my dress shirt up to cover my birthmark. The letters "E-L-E-C-T-U-S" were slowly blanketed beneath the smooth, white fabric. Reaching for the hairbrush, I pulled the odd spot of long hair on the back of my head up into a ponytail and fastened it with a ribbon.

"Looking good today, too, Chuff," my reflection leaned on the counter and winked.

"You too, Chuff," I agreed.

I was just in the middle of wrangling the squealing toothpaste onto my toothbrush when someone knocked on the bathroom door.

The Janitor was standing in the doorway. One gloved hand on the doorframe and the other on their hip, they looked the same as they did every other day. A plastic, pink spray bottle nozzle emerged below the collar of their perfectly pressed blue dress shirt, while the tips of their cap-toe shoes shone with cotton candy.

"Heeeey, Chuff, trouble with the toothpaste?" they sang. Their voice pitched high and low at unpredictable intervals, sometimes deep, sometimes shrill.

"Yeah," my reflection answered, gesturing at the screaming mess on my toothbrush. "It won't stay still."

"Allow me to remedy that," taking their hand off the doorframe, the Janitor snapped their fingers at me. In an instant, the toothpaste flopped over and crawled back onto the bristles, where it lay still once more.

"Thanks!" I gave them a thumbs up as I brushed my teeth.

"Always a pleasure," if my mentor's spray bottle head could grin, it would.

Having brushed my teeth, I followed the Janitor to the kitchen for breakfast. Today's meal was a delicious pile of flapjacks, drowned in butter and with a generous helping of rainbow sprinkles. As I puzzled over how best to dissect the gurgling, fluttering treats on my plate, the Janitor read the November 20th newspaper. After finishing, I placed my dishes in the sink and headed to the entrance hallway.

"Ready for a new day, Chuff?" the Janitor asked, standing near the blank wall at the end of the hall with their top hat in one hand. Seeing me nod, they turned to the wall. They ran their fingers over the rough plaster. There was a rumble in the woodwork. A light giggle that vibrated throughout the house, stronger and stronger until...

There was a loud whoosh of air as the wall sneezed. The front door burst into existence with a thump. A quaint wooden door in a fresh coat of white paint.

With gentle pluck, the Janitor swept the coat off the wood, settling it around their shoulders. The tiny copper bell attached to the doorframe rang merrily as they opened the door and ushered me through, setting out on our first case of the day.

Stepping out onto the streets, my senses were flooded with the overwhelming cacophony of New Penumbra. Lively, buzzing, vibrant. Buildings stretched and clattered their shutters, stealing the paint off their neighbor's walls. Cars honked angrily on the road, feathered wings fluttering as they goosed each other to move along. Cotton candy was everywhere. It drifted through the air, dusting the windows in a thin layer of sugar. Chalk numbers of rainbow colors bounced along the hopscotch tiled street.

There were plenty of pedestrians out and about despite the early morning. The fine folk of New Penumbra, with neatly combed hair and freshly pressed suits, going about their everyday business. An owl-headed civil worker hobbled past us on its way to parliament. Lying in wait next to a dumpster was a mob of kangaroo gangsters in matching fedoras and black sunglasses. We walked past a bag overflowing with cats, and a torsoless leg trying to ring a doorbell with its nonexistent arm.

There was so much to see, so much to take in. And it was like this every day.

There were a lot of citizens in New Penumbra. The number tended to fluctuate from day to day. Sometimes it was 300, sometimes it was 179. But there were always at least a hundred of them around, and none were very bright. See, when a lot of dense, air-headed people all lived together in the same crowded place, quarrels inevitably popped up. Things like whether the dress was blue or yellow, or who was the true owner of the little cotton dog... Silly little things, but New Penumbruns tended to work themselves up just on those things alone. Peacekeeping was necessary if one wanted to keep the entire city intact at the end of the day.

But there was a catch. In quarrels like these, nobody actually wanted to keep the peace. If they cared any little bit about peace, they wouldn't have been fighting over dress colors or cotton dog ownership in the first place. They just wanted to be told the "truth". The "truth" being that their stance was correct.

That was where we came in, the Janitor and I. We were the detectives, the de facto peacekeepers of New Penumbra. Every day, there was a new quarrel to resolve, and every day, we'd swoop in, figure out what happened, and sort it all out before the sun went down. And because we were detectives, no matter who was arguing would have to accept our conclusion, because detectives were the people who found the truth.

Today's case involved a certain Miss Finch who had lost her voice. Arriving at her home, the Janitor and I found ourselves ushered into a cozy little parlor by a bird-headed butler.

"Oh sweeties, sweeties! Thank goodness you're here," twittered Miss Finch, her bright red beak snapping as she bobbed her head at us. "I've lost my voice, you see. My voice, yes, my voice is missing and I can't find it."

You don't sound like you've lost your voice, I thought to myself. I didn't comment out loud. That was one of the rules of the job, after all — don't question the customer.

"Don't worry, Miss Finch," the Janitor chimed, snapping a finger in her direction. "My trusty assistant Chuff and I are on the case!"

The Janitor sat down in a nearby armchair and began questioning Miss Finch. When she had last seen her voice, what was she doing at the time, where did she put it last… While they talked, I jotted the details down in my notepad. Last seen yesterday, before dinner. She'd been warming up her voice for her concert this evening.

"Ooh, yes, I warmed it up with a nice bowl of milk," Miss Finch bobbed her head. "Very nice. Dunked it right in there for a good, warm soak. A singing voice isn't complete without a nice warm-up, as you know, sweeties. I put the bowl on the nightstand and took a wee nap… And ooh… when I woke up, it was gone! Gone by the morning! Ooh, nooo."

"How terrible," the Janitor remarked politely.

"And I went into the kitchen and asked Mr. Starling," Miss Finch gestured at her butler. "Starling, sweetie, where's my voice? And he said, 'Isn't your voice in your throat?'"

I barely suppressed a snort.

"And I said, 'Sweetie dear, this is very serious,'" Miss Finch continued. "'Don't jest at a time like this. Go find my voice!' And you know what he did?"

"What?" I blurted out.

"He went down to the kitchen and came back with a glass of warm milk, and said, 'Once you drink this, your voice will return!' Can you believe it? What nonsense! Milk is for soaking voices, not for drinking!"

I wheezed.

We spent the rest of the morning trying to interview Miss Finch. We weren't able to make much progress, however. The bird-head seemed to be thoroughly convinced that what she was referring to as her voice would be clear to everyone. So questions like "what does your voice look like", or "how big is it?" were faced with the same answer of "why, like a voice of course!"

As noon approached, the Janitor leaned over the arm of their seat to look at my notepad, "Any ideas, Chuff?"

I shook my head.

The Janitor didn't seem phased, however. They just clapped their hands and stood up.

"Either way, it's about time for lunch. Let's take a little break."

The Janitor and I left Miss Finch's abode, stepping into a nearby cafe for lunch. Lounging in the plush flesh of a window seat, I tucked into a stargazy pie with gummy sharks swimming in a raspberry nebula while the Janitor read the paper across from me. The date at the top of the column read November 20th, same as always.

We returned to the manor half an hour later to continue the case. With Miss Finch being thoroughly unhelpful, we inspected the rest of the house. Starting from the master bedroom, we worked our way through every room and hallway, trying to find clues regarding the missing voice. Other than the bowl of cold milk that had allegedly held the voice the night before, we found nothing of note.

"Maybe it dissolved in the milk," I said at last, throwing out wild ideas as a last resort. "That's why we can't find it. It's all gone in the milk."

"But why would she soak the voice in milk if it were soluble?" questioned the Janitor.

"Who knows? I think she's a bit daft," I scoffed. "What even is this voice of hers?"

The Janitor fell into deep thought, one gloved hand rubbing the base of their nozzle.

"I think there's more to this than meets the eye, Chuff," the Janitor hummed. "What do you say to a bit of magic to help us along?"

I perked up.

"Magic? Yes!"

"Righto, then," the Janitor puffed up their chest, turning towards the wall. "One magic hint coming up!"

They snapped their fingers. In an instant, all the walls in the house came down. The dividers, the load-bearing ones, the outer ones. All of them collapsed with a resounding crash. Miss Finch's house now only consisted of the first floor and the floating second one, her parlor looking out directly onto the street.

There came a startled squawk from behind me. I turned. Without the walls concealing it, a secret room once hidden behind the parlor's bookshelf was revealed. The room was filled with interconnected vats, bubbling with a sort of green fluid. Suspended inside the topmost vat was a set of dentures.

With a hiss, the fluid in the denture vat drained into the vats below it, delivering drops of the green denture fluid into a collection of tiny glass vials. And sitting amidst all this was the butler, Mr. Starling.

"Drat!" crowed Mr. Starling, still sitting on his stool with a vial in his claws. "You've caught me!"

"Starling!" gasped Miss Finch from where she had been sitting two rooms away. "How could you, ooh no!"

In a running leap, I pounced on the butler. He struggled as I pulled his claws behind his back.

"No!" he squawked. "I was so close! I could have made a fortune selling the voice juice! You can't stop me! My empire! My voice juice empire!"

"You're both daft!" I exclaimed, sitting on him to hold him down. "Like master, like servant!"

Daintily, the Janitor stepped over the mess and approached the vat. With a wave of their hand, the dentures floated out of the green goop, coming to a rest in their gloved palm.

"Is this your voice, Miss Finch?" they sang, holding it out to her.

Miss Finch came running at an astonishing speed, her skirts whirling. In one smooth motion, she snatched the dentures from the Janitor's outstretched hand, raised it up, and...

Gulp.

Swallowed it.

I stared. Mr. Starling wailed.

Miss Finch ruffled her feathers, puffing herself up. Opening her beak, she let out a few jubilant toots. To my surprise, she sounded much nicer now that her dentures... or rather, her "voice", was back.

"Oh, thank you, sweeties, thank you!" Miss Finch warbled, her feathered head bobbing. "Now I can attend the concert tonight! I must make singing stars there, ooh yes. I can make my singing stars again! Ohhh, lots of singing stars I must make."

Sitting atop a now sullen Mr. Starling, I grinned as I watched her dance around the parlor. Her cotton skirts whirled as she pranced, bursting into jolly, upbeat song.

"Singing stars, singing stars, glittery sweetie treat!" she raised her head, her throat swelling as her voice rose higher and higher into a piercing soprano. It swelled wider than her beak, than her cheeks, then past her shoulders. "Singing stars, singing stars, taste——— the——— me——— mo———

"-RIES———!" As she reached the highest note, Miss Finch swelled up further, her voice trembling even higher, until...

Pop!

Miss Finch's head exploded in a shower of confetti. Her singing abruptly stopped, cut short by a wet gurgle. Her body stood motionless. It swayed on neat buckled shoes, before tilting, toppling, then falling with a thump onto the carpet.

The Janitor bent over to survey the fallen body of the bird-headed woman, their legs remaining perfectly straight. With one gloved finger, they prodded the bloodied stump.

"Ahh, pardon me," said the Janitor in a nonchalant sing-song. "It appears I've made a mistake in my sleuthing." They straightened back up and spun around, their arms lifted high in jubilation. "You see, Chuff, there was a twist!"

"A twist?" I gaped in awe. "What twist?"

"Turns out, Miss Finch wasn't the true owner of the voice after all!" they sang. "The real owner was Mr. Starling!" they waved me off the butler, helping the disgruntled bird-head to his feet. "Congratulations, Mr. Starling, for retrieving your voice!"

"Ohhhh, I see," I giggled into my hands. "It was the singing stars, wasn't it? That was the critical clue. The singing sta—"

"No."

The sharpness in the Janitor's voice cut me off mid-sentence. Their spray nozzle head turned to me. I stiffened.

A tense silence filled the room for one moment. Two.

"Well, anyway," sang the Janitor brightly, and the world went back to normal again. "Supper, my dear Chuff?"

Bidding goodbye to Mr. Starling, the new lord of the house and owner of the lost voice, we headed home. By now, it was nearly dusk. The grinning sun had come to nestle amongst crooked roof tiles and chimney pots. Its wires slack, its little eyes squinting, its toothy grin stretched wider into a yawn. The aftershocks of its yawn sent the shingles tinkling like little bells. Huge masses of cotton candy streamed out from its toothy maw, giggling as they tinted the sky a deep pink.

Entering the house, I took the Janitor's hat from them, hanging it on the rack next to the door. Stepping in after me, the Janitor tickled the door again. It hiccupped, and was replaced by the plaster once more.

That was the rule in the Janitor's house. The front door should only be summoned during the day and dismissed at dusk. No entries or exits from twilight till dawn.

Of the secrets the Janitor kept, this was one that had buggered me the most when I was younger. Back then, the windows, much like the front door, disappeared for the night. It had seemed like some mysterious, forbidden thing, at the time. Something sinister that lay prowling in New Penumbra at night, that I was not allowed to see.

The Janitor had many mysteries. Like, why did they have a spray nozzle head when I didn't? Or why I was never told about the past. Or what that word on my arm, "electus", meant.

Of all the mysteries, this was one of the first that I'd started with. I'd badgered the Janitor with questions. Yet like trying to hold on to a fish with soapy hands, they'd always slipped out of my grasp before I could get a proper answer. Sometimes it was a change in topic, other times it was an interruption. Once, when I'd racked up the courage to pester them properly, it had started raining cats and dogs.

"Oh dear, a storm," the Janitor had said, just as a purring Siamese landed heavily in the center of their hat, thoroughly ruining it. "Sorry, Chuff. I'm afraid we'll have to discuss that over dinner."

Dinner came and went, and only after I'd settled happily into bed, stuffed full with meatloaf, that I realized the Janitor had not, in fact, discussed the issue over dinner.

Naturally, when asking didn't work, the next course of action was to break things. I'd made it my mission to figure out how the Janitor prodded the wall to open it up. Many a sleepless night had been spent crouched in the dead-end hallway, knocking at the plaster in my attempts to get the front door to reappear.

The Janitor had been sharp. During that period, they'd sporadically appear in the front hall, fully dressed in their shirt and slacks. They'd tell me things like "this isn't the way to your bedroom", or "silly, Chuff, it's not morning yet", before ushering me firmly back to bed. Then I learned to hide. Then they learned to find me. Upon which I'd learn to hide even better.

It had been the 3rd week of this back and forth when finally, the Janitor, having caught me for the 30th time in the hallway at midnight, sighed.

"I'm tired of this, Chuff," the Janitor smoothed the slightly rumpled front of their dress shirt. Their voice didn't carry the sing-song and whimsy that it usually did. Instead, it was dull and weary, with the consistency of radio static. "Why do you want to go outside so badly?"

"Why do you want to keep me inside at night so badly?"

"There's nothing interesting out there at this hour."

"Show me then," I'd retorted. By then, I'd been certain that something was outside. Some important secret, so terrible and life-changing that simply knowing would put even the Janitor, as powerful as they were, in deep trouble. "If it really is nothing, why are you trying so hard to hide it?"

I'd rehearsed a dozen lines, prepared a response to every scenario. Except for the one that happened.

With a deep sigh, the Janitor had turned to the blank wall. They'd run their fingers over the odd bumps, summoning the front door. The door didn't laugh like it usually did. It just quietly emerged from the wall like a piece of driftwood surfacing from the ocean and lay there, watching.

"There you go," the Janitor had stepped aside, motioning for me to come forward. "See for yourself."

I'd stepped forward in trepidation, my nerves giddy as excitement coursed through my veins. The door had opened smoothly, swinging outwards without a sound. And yet, the Janitor had been telling the truth all along. There was nothing outside.

Outside, where during the day had been busy streets and green skies, cotton candy and dancing houses, was now a black void. Boundless. Bottomless. It was as if sometime after the door shut for the night, the house had been picked up and deposited in a pitch black abyss. A few other structures were hanging suspended in the void, but nothing as large as our house. A door here and there, a smattering of windows looking out on somewhere foreign, a piece of someone's lawn... The void was almost as silent as New Penumbra was rowdy during the day.

Almost, because there was still a sound in the void. A small sound, as quiet as a whisper, that could only be heard because of how silent the void itself was.

That was when I first saw the singing stars.

They were small and chubby, with a shape much like folded paper stars. Each one was the size of my hand, glowing pink and purple with sparkling stardust. In clusters of five, they travelled through the unending darkness like voyagers at sea, twinkling, glowing.

Yet most enchanting was the singing, the quiet tune amidst the silence. Their song was gentle, the notes delicately tinkling out much like the sound of a music box. A light and happy song, but somehow mournful at the same time. Like the last bloom before harsh winter, like the overgrown ruins of a fallen empire. Like deep snow over an abandoned grave, like fields of wild wheat with no one left to harvest them.

The tinny melody accompanied the dance of the singing stars, the only sign of life amidst the still, unending darkness.

"See?" the Janitor had come to stand behind me in the doorway. "There's nothing special here."

"I think it's lovely," I had said, entranced.

"Do you?" the Janitor had replied.

We spent the night standing there, silently gazing out at the bottomless abyss and the singing stars. When the dawn came, New Penumbra was once more situated at our doorstep, and the Janitor and I once more returned to our daily routines. But since that day, while the front door still disappeared from dusk till dawn, my window stayed, looking out onto the city during the day and the singing stars at night.

Even now, countless years in the future, as I tucked myself back into bed at the end of the long day, I could hear the faint, faraway tune of the stars singing in the void behind the glass.

That was what I'd been trying to express after the Miss Finch case.

The Adventures of Chuff and the Janitor

The stars were always there. Regardless of whether she had her voice, they would sing every night anyway. The thought had seemed to upset the Janitor, though. I supposed they still didn't like the singing stars.

I lifted my arm up against the window. In the dim light of the shining stars, tattooed in black ink, was my birthmark.

E-L-E-C-T-U-S.

That was the second secret I'd tried to pry out of the Janitor's pockets. Yet the outcome had not been as fruitful as the first. All I was able to glean was that, firstly, "electus" was not my name. And secondly, it was a word that didn't exist in New Penumbra.

The Janitor had never warned me to stop snooping. But I could see it in their gestures, their eyeless gaze, the way their voice lost that sing-song every time something bothered them. They hoped that I would follow along, as their trusty assistant Chuff, and go on adventures together happily day after day.

But truthfully, they'd picked the wrong occupation. Even if I were just a detective's assistant, mysteries called to me. The truth called to me. After all, special was memorable, and once something special stuck to your mind, it would eat away at you until you either threw it away, or dug up whatever was hiding underneath it.

We were special, the two of us. We were unlike anyone else in New Penumbra. The two most special people in the world… playing house on the surface, while passing a revolver with a single bullet underneath the table.

The Janitor was like my parent. They meant the most to me in this city I called home. Which was exactly why the truth mattered. I needed to know.

Underneath all their secrets and lying words, did they truly love me as their child?

Or was I just a stand-in? Was I merely filling in the shoes of the genius detective's assistant, and it didn't matter just who was standing in those shoes?

Just like how it had never mattered whether the voice's owner was Miss Finch or Mr. Starling.

VOICES LIKE THESE
ACT 2
In Which a Rogue Map is Sentenced

The next day, I rolled out of bed to the sound of the Janitor's morning call. Hustling over to the window, I lifted my leg to dodge the snap of the fourth floorboard and opened the blinds. The sun tried to beam in again but a punch to the teeth dissuaded it. I then headed to the bathroom to wash up, complimenting my reflection on its incredibly clear skin. In the kitchen, breakfast was served, a set of crunchy fish fingers with the nails removed, paired with a flaming hot dipping sauce. Across the table, the Janitor continued to read their favorite 20th November news.

Our task of the day brought us to the mapmaker's abode south of New Penumbra. The mapmaker himself, a rotund little quill-head, greeted us at the door.

"The name's Inker. Pleasure to meet you at last, Janitor," said the mapmaker. "See, I was tidying up the old shop here, when one of my maps went missing."

"Ah, a common issue," the Janitor said sympathetically.

"Pesky little bugger bolted when my back was turned. I was thinking about smoking it out, see, but realized I don't have a light."

"Seems easy enough," I remarked. "We can finish up early."

"If you would do the honors, Janitor," Inker gestured towards the unlit fireplace in the corner. "I'm certain that with you here, it'll bolt out in no time."

The Janitor headed towards the fireplace, their steps light and graceful. The mantle was much lower than their head, needing them to bend to see into the firebox. I watched from the side as the Janitor rummaged around.

"Just needs a spark, aye?" said Inker. "A tiny little one. Right on the logs."

The Janitor hummed, then paused.

"Well, what do we have here?" they mused. "Chuff, come here, won't you?"

I plodded over to the fireplace, kneeling on the hearth to look inside. The Janitor pointed at the far corner.

"You see that, Chuff?"

I squinted. Then my eyes widened. There was a flash of fluttering white, hidden amidst the heavy logs. Reaching into the firebox, I dug through the pile. Something was moving under there, trying its best to avoid my grip. I braced my knees against the pilaster and reached further in.

My fingers closed around some squirming, coarse, cylindrical object. I pulled. The force of my pull sent me tumbling onto my back, my prize clamped tightly in my hand.

A squealing, struggling piece of rolled up parchment was clenched in my closed fist. Its tiny legs, knobby and yarn-like, kicked weakly at my fingers.

"A rogue map," observed the Janitor. Before I could react, their slender, gloved fingers had plucked it from my grip. "Was this what you were looking for, Inker?"

"Oh... hehe, why yes," Inker laughed, a hint of sheepishness in his voice. "Aye... so you found it after all."

"What do you mean?" I asked.

"Down in the dumps, aye, down in the dumps!" the map squealed. "Hup, hup, left, right, right, right, ho! Repeat six, 3R, 104, straight ahead, aye aye, captain!"

"Rogue maps... nasty little things. Always charting about where they're not supposed to," Inker's feather waved about as he shook his head. "Bad karma for a mapmaker. Aye, very bad, indeed. Ruins business. Should be destroyed immediately. But only the Janitor's flames can destroy a rogue map. I was hoping to get rid of it discreetly, see? Pressed it under the logs and hoped you'd set it ablaze unknowingly. Alas... You're better detectives than I thought."

"Only the best in New Penumbra," sang the Janitor. "Don't worry, Inker. I'll take care of it. No harm will come to your business."

"Aye, thank you kindly, Janitor."

The Janitor bade the quill head goodbye and stepped out the door.

Following along behind them at a trot, I did my best to be subtle. I hadn't reacted fast enough to even glimpse what was inside the rogue map before it was taken away. I arched my neck and strained on my tiptoes, trying to catch a peek from the corner of my eye.

"Curious, are we?" remarked the Janitor, raising their arm, and the map, out of eyeshot. The map flicked tantalizingly with the movement.

"Yeah, it's been ages since we've seen a rogue map." Having been caught, I began hopping up and down alongside them. My fingers managed to lightly graze the grainy surface at the peak of each stretch, only to fall just short of gripping it.

"Weren't you the one who caught it?"

"You took it away too fast!" I pouted. "I didn't get to see anything!"

"Never understood the allure these maps hold over you," the Janitor tutted. "Compared to everything else I've shown you, they're not quite as interesting."

I shrugged. I didn't really know either.

The Janitor sighed, "Very well, then."

Lowering their arm, they unrolled the parchment, tilting the marked surface in my direction.

"To satisfy your thirst."

I eagerly hustled over, only for my excitement to fade as my eyes skimmed over the squirming map. Turned out it was just a regular map of New Penumbra. The only thing mysterious or forbidden it seemed to contain was the detailed cross-section of the Janitor's home. Which, all things considered, wasn't very mysterious at all.

"Boring," I booed, pushing the map back towards the Janitor.

They scoffed and pinched the corner between their fingers. In a flash of light, it started to burn. The rogue map screamed. Orange tongues of flame licked up the edges of the curling parchment, the paper blackening and crumbling wherever they touched. The Janitor shook the soot off their hand. The wind carried the ash away, glowing cinders fading into cotton candy.

Each day continued much like the last. I'd wake up, wash up, and head downstairs for breakfast with the Janitor. The Janitor would put on their hat and coat, and together we'd set off to handle the case of the day. Two, if the first one didn't take too long. Then back home for dinner and an early bedtime.

Yet anomalies would occasionally pop up. A raving lunatic here, a quiver in the cracks there. Disruptions in our routine, little life in the big city of New Penumbra. The Janitor pretended nothing was out of the ordinary, and I did the same. But cracks were premonitions for something bigger. And bigger things presented opportunities.

I just had to wait and be ready.

One day, we were on our way home when we were stopped by a fellow running down the road. A hulking gorilla dressed in a tweed suit came barreling into us, huffing and puffing as he went.

"Janitor! You must come to the square at once!" the gorilla belted out, the tiny bowler hat atop his head slipping from his nervousness. "There's a... two lunatics on the loose!"

"Lunatics?" I asked.

"Now that won't do," sang the Janitor, throwing their arm outwards. "Lead the way, my dear gentleman!"

The streets were abuzz with activity when we finally arrived. Various citizens of New Penumbra gathered around the entrance to an alleyway, whispering to themselves. The gorilla-head we were following shoved them aside, shouting, "Move, move, the Janitor is here!"

As the sea of heads parted, I could finally catch a glimpse of what was inside.

New Penumbra was odd, but this alley had somehow become even odder. Like a rift in reality, the world beyond the entrance had become something bizarre. No cotton candy drifted there. The chalked lines of the hopscotch tiles dissolved into rubbery, pebbled surfacing at the boundary between dark and light. What rose on all sides of the alley was not the fidgeting, living bricks of the buildings, but some sort of padded wall. There was no green sky to be seen above the liminal space. Instead, there was an endlessly stretching assortment of giant, metal pipes. A lone, flickering lamp cast a beam of harsh, white light down from amongst the pipes, where they stood.

A pair of children, holding hands inside the circle of light cast by the lamp. Hairless apes. Just like me, yet not at the same time. They looked much younger, their cheeks still rounded, so short that the top of their heads barely reached my waist. The spot atop their skulls where they would've had hair had been chopped short into an uneven buzz, while loose, ragged nightgowns draped around their sallow frames. They stood there, bits of rubber caught between their bare toes, staring out at New Penumbra through the narrow opening in the alleyway.

The smaller one was crying.

"Wake up, wake up!" cried the bigger one. Their eyes were glazed over and unfocused, staring unseeingly into the crowd as they repeated themselves over and over again. "Singing stars! Chop chop!"

"Singing stars," wailed the smaller one in an oddly grown-up voice. "We won't make the cut on Sunday! You have to make singing stars! Or the boss will have our shins!"

"Our shins!" exclaimed the bigger one. "Our life and our shins! Scraped off, squished and moulded!"

"Stuffed into a jar and shipped off to France! To sing lullabies to the toffs!"

The Janitor had just arrived behind me when everything got worse.

The children's dull eyes lit up.

"You! Please!" the bigger child wailed. They ran forwards, only to stumble and fall. They landed heavily on their hands and knees with a thud. From there, they crawled eagerly to the Janitor's feet. One bony hand reached out and gripped their ankle tightly. The child looked up with forlorn eyes.

"You're special! You can make them. Please, nobody can do it right! Poor quality! Poor quality stars that cry all the time. But you can make them right! You're the only one that can! You—"

The Janitor made no move. Their spray bottle head tilted down silently, expressionlessly.

"Please!" wailed the child. "Please! We won't make the cut! Singing stars, singing stars!"

Slowly, the Janitor raised their gloved hand.

"We'll die! We'll all die!"

Snap.

The child exploded in a shower of confetti. Bright paper scraps rained down on the empty spot where they once knelt. The Janitor was passive, their body language giving away nothing of what they might be feeling.

The second child stared at the Janitor, their eyes blank and unseeing. They opened their mouth.

"ELECTUS!" they screamed.

E-L-E-C-T-U-S, spelled the word on my arm.

I reacted with a jolt. The child turned and ran into the liminal space of padded walls and rubber tiles. One pale foot after another, till their pattering steps were swallowed up by the darkness.

Before I could react, I took one step forward. Then another. Then another. The world seemed to move in slow motion as I began to run. The boundary between New Penumbra and the space rippled as the tip of my shoe crossed the border.

The Janitor slowly turned their head, their faceless spray bottle nozzle looking at me. Through me, to somewhere deep inside that even I couldn't see into.

I ran after the child.

Behind me, the world disappeared like a curtain was drawn. I was running hard, as hard as I could. Far in front of me, I could see the ghostly silhouette of the child running into the dark.

Then the rubber tiles below me crumbled.

And I fell into the abyss.

ACT 3
Penumbra, Electus, and the Singing Stars

The world crumbled into a dark void as I fell. The padded walls, the rubbery floor, the curtain of light beyond which the Janitor and the city stood. All of it crumbled and was blown away like soot in the wind. There was just me, the darkness, and the abyss's collectables. A door here, a window there, a piece of a lawn. Just like the void outside the Janitor's front door at night, the abyss I was sinking in was littered with the empty echoes of someone's life.

As I looked up, I couldn't see any sign of where I had begun falling. Instead, the singing stars circled overhead. Dancing, twirling... Singing that same mournful little tune over and over again.

I fell further, and even the structures disappeared. Surrounded by nothing but darkness, I fell for what felt like eternity.

Down.
Down.
Down.
. . .

And then I landed with a bump.

The ground beneath my hands didn't feel like anything. No texture, no temperature. It was as nothing as the void I'd been falling in, except I was lying on it instead of falling through it.

I couldn't hear the stars. What replaced their voices was a deafening silence.

I blinked and patted myself over. I was intact. Despite the distance I had fallen, I was just as fine as I'd been this morning. There wasn't even the soreness of falling flat on my back. Pushing myself up into a sitting position, I looked down. My shadow stretched in front of me, long and spindly, basked in a cold, white light.

I turned.

Behind me was a building. One that I'd never seen before. Unlike the houses in New Penumbra that were three stories high and had tiled roofs, this building towered much higher, a square block of white. No seams, no roof, no traces of where plaster might have peeled off with age. It was as if the entire structure were made from one solid piece of flat, white stone.

There were windows embedded in the side of the building. Big windows, with massive panes of glass sitting in them. The inside was dark. The glass reflected white light in a chilly halo.

Near the top of the building was a series of glowing letter blocks. They looked solid, but somehow, their surfaces radiated a harsh light unlike any rock I'd ever known. The light screeched down over the stone walls and the dark windows, a blinding, white glare that illuminated the surrounding ten miles of the abyss.

PENUMBRA INC, screamed the sign in uniform block letters.

Slowly, I stood up and walked towards the building. There were a pair of doors in the base and more of those large windows. I peered through them, but all I could see was my reflection peering back in the glass. Unlike in New Penumbra, this reflection didn't talk. It simply watched, mirroring my every move.

The place felt wrong. It cast an uneasy chill up my spine, putting me on edge. But stronger than the chill was an itch. An itch of a notion that told me to enter the building.

Opportunity. This was the opportunity for the answers I'd been looking for. After all, what better place to hide something than the bottom of a yawning abyss?

I walked up to the entrance. The metal doors felt cold as ice under my palm. The doors glided open without a sound. Inside was a long corridor made of the same white, seamless stone as the exterior of the building, illuminated by lamps as harsh and cold as the sign outside. A series of doors lined the hallway at equal intervals. Unlike the ones at the entrance, these were all painted white as the walls.

My footsteps echoed hollowly across the smooth tiles. It was so quiet that even my strides sounded loud. I felt out of place, in my colorful clothing and clackety shoes. It was as if my presence itself were disturbing the sanctity of this cold, white place.

The itch grew stronger, pulsating into a tugging pull. It drew me to one of the indistinguishable doors. I pushed that open, and found another hallway, the same as the one I'd just left.

I was about to enter, when suddenly, I found a hand on my shoulder.

"Hey."

I turned.

The Janitor was standing behind me. Their blue dress shirt and black slacks were as neatly pressed as always. Their shoes still shone with cotton candy.

The nozzle of their spray bottle head faced me directly, gaping and hollow.

"Chuff," said the Janitor. "You shouldn't be here."

I looked back down the hallway. The pull was insistent. It tugged at my feet, tugged at my mind, begging me to walk through another door, to follow it deeper.

"Where are we?" I asked them.

"You shouldn't be here," the Janitor didn't answer my question. "You're lost. Follow me back."

"Is there something here?"

The Janitor's hand was firm on my shoulder, their fingers gripping into my flesh like claws.

"Chuff," the Janitor's tone was flat. "Let's go home."

I looked at the Janitor. I looked back down the hallway. I hesitated.

Am I really your favorite child, or just a stand in?

I bolted. Their fingers loosened as I shrugged them off, seeming to jolt in surprise as they lost their grip.

The Janitor was shouting, but the blood pounding in my ears deafened me to what they were saying. I followed the pull to another door and slammed it behind me, shutting their cries out.

The pull was stronger here. It was taking me somewhere. I followed it faithfully, step by step. As I reached the next hallway, the door behind me slammed open with a bang.

"Come back—" a monstrous wail resonated from behind. It ground like gravel and reverberated like crystal refractions. It pitched high and low at unpredictable intervals, sometimes deep, sometimes shrill.

I didn't look back. Gripping hold of that pull inside me, I ran.

Hallway after hallway, door after door. The pull guided me as I went, taking me swerving and ducking through the labyrinth of white corridors and identical doors. I didn't know where I was going. But the pull was insistent, demanding. It demanded that I follow. So I did.

Behind me, the Janitor's wails could be heard as they crashed through the rooms after me. Every so often, as I turned a corner or entered a new door, I'd catch a glimpse of the shadow their figure cast against the wall. It was spindly, crooked, with multiple gangly limbs that moved in intricate patterns, bracing against the ceiling and the walls like a spider. I never looked back. I just lowered my head and kept running.

The further I ran, the stronger the pull became. The corridors became more distinct, gaining furniture and noticeboards. The doors gained labels and name cards. Suddenly, I realized what this was. My strides grew longer, stepping in tandem to the pull as I took initiative over where I was going.

Hup, hup, left, right, right, right, ho! Repeat six, 3R, 104, straight ahead, aye aye, captain!

"Chuff!" the Janitor howled. Their call echoed down the narrow hallways, no longer sounding like themself. "You'll regret this!"

I didn't know how long I had been running. The stretches of hallways and doors felt endless. All I could do was recite the directions that the rogue map had sung as I barreled through door after door. The Janitor was gaining on me. I could hear the rumbling crash growing louder and louder, their shadow that had once been just a glimpse of a limb now encasing half the corridor in darkness.

But I was close. I could feel it. The pull that had guided me this far was near irresistible now. Adrenaline pumped through my veins. I felt more alive than ever.

I crashed shoulder-first through a door with the letters "104" printed on the doorframe, the momentum sending me tumbling into a new corridor.

The Adventures of Chuff and the Janitor

It was different from the rest. There were no identical doors lining the walls here. Just a long hallway made of stone. Strobing, red lights lined the ceiling, casting long blades of scarlet in flashing patterns along the walls and the floor. At the end of the hallway, bathed in red, was a rolling metal shutter.

Straight ahead, aye aye, captain.

This was it.

Blood pounded in my ears to the beat of my drumming heart. I sprinted forwards, making the final dash towards the truth. As I did, the shutters seemed to groan. Then, they began to rise.

My joy was cut short by a thundering bang behind me. Through the flashing red lights, a hundred or so steps away from my goal, I finally looked back.

There was a monster behind me. It was tall, unnaturally tall, its spindly body as dark as the void itself and connected together in rod-like segments each the size of a metal pipe. It was so tall that it had to bend to fit in the corridor, its back arching into a question mark scraping against the ceiling as the rest of its segments dragged along the ground. Long, spider-like limbs protruded from the sides of its segments, each twice as long as the corridor was high. Emerging from the ends of the limbs was not a spider-foot, but a bony hand with long, slender fingers. These limbs bent heavily to brace against the walls, the ceiling, and the floor, pulling the creature through the tiny hallway at an alarming speed.

The only part of the creature that still resembled the Janitor was the head. But instead of that familiar pink spray bottle, it was as pitch black as the rest of its body. Where the Janitor had no eyes or mouth, the creature made up for it in plenty. Thousands and thousands of blinking, staring eyes lined every inch of their head, each a unique size and shape. Once the simple opening of a spray nozzle, it was now a gaping void filled with rows upon rows of razor-sharp teeth that glinted red in the light of the strobing alarms.

"Stoooppp–" the Janitor groaned, their voice simultaneously high and low, singular and countless all at once.

I dashed over to the metal shutter. It was rising slowly, too slowly, the opening barely higher than my ankles. I crouched and heaved upwards, bracing my palms against the bottom of the shutter. But it was no use. The

81

shutter retained that same, sluggish pace, no matter how hard I strained.

I looked back. The monstrosity that had once been my mentor was gaining speed as they raced towards me. Sweat beaded against my forehead. My head was light. So light that I felt dizzy. If I was truly just a stand-in, this was probably the last straw. The final strand of tolerance that the Janitor had for my antics. If they caught me, I would go pop. Just like the countless other extras in New Penumbra. A shower of confetti to commemorate my loss.

"Hey!" I screamed, banging on the metal shutter. "Open up!"

But the rise of the rolling gate remained agonizingly slow, creaking upwards one tiny centimeter at a time.

A giant hand slammed into the metal beside me with a loud clang. I dropped to my knees. The fingers desperately scrabbled at the spot above my head, nails screeching piercingly against the metal.

The Janitor was only short ways away, their once breakneck speed slowing as they dragged themselves in short bursts. Their thousand eyes looked down at me.

Five meters, four meters, three meters… one.

I took another glance at the slowly widening gap below the gate. The pull was inside, tugging me towards whatever lay beyond. The rise of the shutters was still too slow, the Janitor too close, but I couldn't give up. Not when I was almost there.

"Chuff…" the Janitor thundered. "Let's go home…"

The Janitor had reached me, their gaping maw staring straight down at me. They lifted their long, spindly arm, reaching for my head.

I dropped down onto my side and rolled under the shutter. The Janitor let out an anguished cry. A hand slammed down on the spot I once was, sending a tremor through the ground. I squeezed my eyes shut.

As I crossed under the boundary, the flashing blare of the red lights was replaced by darkness.

All of a sudden, everything went silent.

I sat up hurriedly to look back at the metal shutter. It had stopped moving. There was no sign of activity from the other side. No banging, no scraping, no wailing.

Just silence.

Somehow, it seemed like the Janitor had given up. Or maybe they simply couldn't follow me here.

I flopped back down, panting, blinking the sweat out of my eyes. My whole body was clammy with sweat. The rough floor was cold under my soaked shirt, the air chilly as it blasted down my airways in heaving gulps.

I took a few moments to catch my breath before taking in my surroundings.

I was in a large room, perhaps as large as the square in New Penumbra, with a tall ceiling much higher than that of the corridor outside. The walls were covered in some sort of padded squares, while rubbery surfacing paved the floors. With a jolt, I realized that this was the liminal space I'd stepped into right before I fell, the one where the two children had stood.

Pushing up against the rubbery floor, I got to my feet. The room was wide and spacious. The padded walls were littered with signs of age. Odd scratches here, some unnamed dirt and water stains there. A variety of toys lay spread out on the floor, long abandoned by their owners. Twenty or so different stuffed toys, a toy cooking station, model cars... There was even a large dollhouse sitting wide open, the dollies strewn haphazardly all over the room.

Lining the walls adjacent to me were smaller, subdivided rooms, separated from the main room by large panes of glass. Closer inspection revealed a homogenous layout. Each room had a cot and a dresser, with a heavy metal cell door barring the exit.

A nursery. I thought to myself. *A nursery... and prison complex?*

There was something uncannily serene about this place. Nobody was here and yet signs of life filled every corner. It was as if this place had lain dormant all these years, undisturbed by the passing changes of New Penumbra above.

There was another door on the far side of the room. I headed over to it, the rubber floor dampening the sound of my footsteps. The door looked more businesslike than the others – metal, and with a keypad on the side. The words "Staff only" were printed on the sign over the peephole.

I tentatively gave it a push. To my surprise, the door wasn't locked. I headed inside, one cautious step at a time.

Unlike the previous area, the walls of this next room resembled the hallways more closely, all smooth stone walls and tiled floors. It seemed to be a storeroom of sorts. Countless boxes littered the room, big cardboard ones, each as wide as my arm span. They were all stacked on top of one another in haphazard towers. Some of the towers were short, only about two boxes high. Others were so tall that they scraped the ceiling.

Treading lightly, I walked over to the nearest tower. The boxes hadn't been moved in a long time, their surfaces covered in a thin layer of dust. Wiping the dust off with my sleeve revealed a yellowing, rectangular label splotched with dried-up water stains.

C█73█
6-█2-19███
Qual█: Exc█e█t

There was an odd glow coming from the box. Some sort of pinkish-purple halo that seeped out through the walls of the cardboard, through the tape that sealed the edges. In fact, nearly all the boxes in this corner were glowing, a dim light that reflected off the tiles in a pool of syrup.

I looked around for the nearest glowing tower with a box that was low enough for me to reach. It took a bit of work to pull the tape off, but eventually, I was able to pry the cardboard flaps open. As I opened up the top, the room was flooded with purple light.

Inside the box were rows of jars. Large, glass jars with screwable lids, that resembled the ones the Janitor would sometimes use to store their fish fingers. The glow was coming from the jars. Or rather, what was inside the jars.

The jars were filled with glowing stars, chubby and sparkly, resembling folded paper stars. They looked like the singing stars that danced in the void, except smaller, each one about the size of a coin. They didn't sing, but instead made a light tinkling noise when you rattled them, the stars bouncing off the glass like translucent crystal pieces.

Turning the jar, I found another label. This one was much fancier than the labels on the cardboard boxes, complete with ornate, flowery borders and curling words calligraphed in gold ink.

Singing Stars Candy
Taste the memories!

One piece before bed
Hear the jingle and close your eyes
Dream your sweetest memory!

Since 1942
Penumbra Inc

Singing stars... huh.

I gently shuffled the jar back into its place and checked the other glowing boxes down the row. It seemed the towers had been arranged by year, with the same year's batch of boxes being stacked into a single tower. They were all filled with the same sort of singing star candy, all translucent and shiny and glowing pink and purple.

As I moved out of the glowing corner, the contents of the boxes began to change. Instead of "excellent", labels were starting to say "good", or "mediocre", with many of them even being labeled "failed". These "failed" products grew in number the further into the storeroom I went, their boxes no longer stacked into neat towers, but hastily thrown into a pile. Some of the boxes weren't even sealed, their lids simply held down by the boxes above them.

There were singing stars inside these boxes too, but they'd been simply tossed inside instead of being packaged neatly in individual jars. These stars were off. Instead of translucent pink and purple, these were sickly shades of brown and grey. They didn't glow, instead giving off an eerie, supernatural air. Some were disfigured, others flickered in and out of existence, and some had a staticky quality that gave me a headache the longer I looked at them. One of them was even singing a disjointed, uncanny little song that sounded oddly familiar.

It took a few moments, but then I realized that it was the mournful melody that the big singing stars in the void usually sang. Except missing a few notes here and there, off beat, and horribly out of tune.

VOICES LIKE THESE

I made my way through the piles of failed boxes. The storeroom got even more misshapen. Failed singing stars were starting to appear out of boxes and instead lay on the floor, glitching in bands of distorted color. There were singing stars on the floors, the walls. They formed heaps that rivalled the towers in height. There were singing stars that were more sphere than star. There were coin sized ones like the ones in the boxes, and larger ones as big as I was.

Walking past a small mountain of singing stars, I finally reached the end of the room. There, a long table had been placed against the wall, its surface shiny and metallic. On the table was a stack of old newspaper clippings, and one single, glowing singing star.

My eyes immediately gravitated towards the bold heading on the topmost clipping.

Chosen by Fate No More! Dr M. Finch Kickstarts the Electus Project!

I scrambled to grab the print. My knuckles turned white from how hard I was gripping the document, creases pressed into the ancient paper.

As the next generation hosting the new Electus approaches maturity, global discussions on the nature of Electi are at an all-time high. As the One Chosen by Fate, the Electus holds the devastating power of omnipotence. Electi have notoriously been known to be the cause for major turning points throughout the course of human history, from the London Massacre in 1732 to the creation and destruction of Paradise by the 27th and 28th Electus respectively in the 16th century. Despite being born human, the actions of the Electi have never been up to humanity to decide, until now.

Funded by the International Electus Security Convention (IESC), Dr Martha Finch, renowned scientist and the mother of electology, proposed a revolutionary Electus Project with the aim to shed light on the supernatural existence of the Electi. What causes a child to awaken as an Electus over another? What is the upper limit of an Electus' abilities? How can we nurture an Electus to develop into a savior of humanity instead of its destroyer?

"-during my research, [children] with a higher Electus Index (EI) are more likely to awaken into that generation's Electus at puberty. In the Electus Project, we aim to apply this knowledge to promote the awakening of an artificial Electus," said Dr Finch in an interview.

The Electus Project…

The print was filled with foreign words and concepts. The word electus had been mentioned more times in this single newspaper clipping than I had heard in my entire life. Humanity, International Electus Security Convention, Paradise, the London Massacre… what even was a London? My head spun. I didn't understand.

I picked up the next clipping. This one was newer and seemed to have been published a few years after.

Artificial Electus Predicted to Awaken Soon! A Warning From Skeptics

In a press conference on Friday, Dr Finch, head scientist of the Electus Project, reported that the Project has successfully nurtured a batch of Electus candidates. As the 6th batch since the start of the Project, the induced Electus Index of these candidates exceeds the natural EI value of past Electi by tenfold.

Dr Finch predicts that the Electus will awaken from their newest batch of candidates in the coming 2-3 years and is optimistic about the future development of electology.

The Electus Project is not without its skeptics, however. A spokesperson from Penumbra Inc, the number 1 sweets company in Britain, recently brought up ethical concerns regarding the Project.

VOICES LIKE THESE

"The Electus has historically only awakened in human children aged 5 to 14," said Mr. Arthur Starling at the annual CHS Convention. "Dr Finch and her team reported batches of candidates being cultivated to induce an Electus awakening, but the detailed method of cultivation has yet to be publicly revealed. Where is she getting these candidates? How did she bypass the unspoken rule that only children can be Electi? Or did she bypass it at all? As we all know, in the pursuit of knowledge, it is essential for scientists to retain their integrity and humanity…"

Faced with the accusations of child experimentation, Dr Finch has refused to comment.

I read through the newspaper clippings in silence. Headlines jumped out at me, each bolder and more shocking than the last.

The Electus Project: Should We Stop Before It's Too Late?

New Evidence Against the Electus Project: The Public Calls for Transparency

Children's Remains Found Downstream Of Electus Project Facility. Dr Finch Denies Connection

Where is the Electus? Dr Finch Remains Silent.

Penumbra Chairman Hears Screams During A Visit To the Electus Facility: It's Worse Than We Thought

IESC Withdraws Support! What Will Dr Finch Do Now?

The Legitimacy of the Electus Project Questioned: 10 Years With No Results

Finally, I reached the bottom of the stack. The last clipping was significantly more bedraggled than the rest, crumpled wrinkles littering the page. What looked like a shoe print had been planted over the photo at the top of the clipping, right on top of the face of a smiling old man.

Dr Finch Steps Down. Electus Project Under New Management

Controversial figure, Dr Martha Finch, has officially announced this Friday that she is stepping down from her position as the head scientist of the Electus Project. After years of empty promises and alleged child experimentation, the scientist has finally yielded to the calls for her abdication.

Penumbra Inc, the company at the forefront of the crackdown on Dr Finch's shady practices, was the one to purchase the rights to the Electus Project. The chairman of Penumbra, Mr. Arthur Starling, promises to reform the project into one that services the people.

"Here at Penumbra, we value transparency, integrity, and efficiency. I am honored to have been entrusted with the task of overseeing the Project. As the spokesperson for Penumbra, I pledge to build on the efforts of our predecessors, and set the Electus Project back on the path that was promised to the public 10 years ago," said Mr. Starling at a press conference.

New management will be in place this coming Monday. Dr Finch has refused all requests for an interview.

I dropped the stack of newspaper clippings back onto the table. They landed with a thump on the metal surface, kicking up a cloud of dust.

The room was quiet. My breaths rang loud. I turned to the other object of interest on the table.

A singing star. It was one of the excellent quality ones, all sparkly and translucent and glowing pink and purple. It looked out of place here at the back of the storeroom, surrounded by the mountains of failed, distorted stars piled up on the floor. It was currently acting as a paperweight for some sort of card-like paper. I lifted the singing star off the card. It was light, delicate, and fragile in my hands, as if it were made from actual crystal. With my other hand, I picked up the card.

"Eat me for the truth," read the card in a wild, unruly scribble.

I turned the card over. On the back was a torn-out part of a product insert for the singing stars.

"Candy for ages three and up, no preservatives or sweeteners. Upon consumption, the candy will act on your brain, allowing you to relive ~~your best~~ memory," here, "your best" had been scribbled out. "For instant effect, chew thoroughly for 10 seconds and swallow. For the dream experience-"

The torn-off edge of the insert stopped me from knowing what to do for the dream experience.

Unknown instructions telling me to eat food of unknown origin, found in a secret facility at the bottom of the world. It was suspicious. But after reading all those clippings, I found, somehow, that I didn't care. The promise of the truth didn't have the pull that it did just a few minutes ago. I felt hollow, heavy, as if a weight had been tied to my mind and was dragging me down. But other than the heaviness, I didn't feel anything.

Apathetically, I supposed that I was in shock.

I turned the card back to the front.

"Eat me."

Tipping my head back, I popped the star into my mouth.

It was crunchy, the texture like chewing on ice cubes. A sweet syrup oozed out from the brittle candy shell, filling my mouth with the taste of sickeningly sweet strawberries. It wasn't bad, but the Janitor gave me better sweets for breakfast every day.

I counted 10 seconds, then swallowed. And waited.

After 10 seconds, nothing happened. After 30 seconds, I started to hear the singing stars' tune in my head. After 50 seconds, the memory came creeping in.

It wasn't instantaneous like the insert promised. Instead, the memory crept in slowly, like a low fog, slowly encompassing my senses until I'd become a different person. Not Chuff, the Janitor's apprentice in the city of New Penumbra. Someone else. A child of 6 years old who wore a ragged nightgown, whose hair was cropped short into a buzz cut.

The Adventures of Chuff and the Janitor

I was an orphan, then a test subject, then a candidate. A lady took me away from the orphanage and brought me to the facility. There were others like me there, other candidates, and we all lived together in the nursery.

I had a name, but I also had a number. Every kid had a number. Mine was F19. The grown-ups called us by number when it was time for the tests. There were shots, many shots. They were sharp, and the grown-ups would poke them into my arm. They used to hurt so bad I could still feel it the next day, but I got used to it after. Some days, I was brought into a room to be strapped to a beeping machine. I'd sit there in the machine, and the grown-ups would stand in front of a big screen and nod their heads. The grown-ups changed sometimes, but there was always this old lady present. The grown-ups called her Doctor. She told us to call her Miss Finch.

Miss Finch was a strange grown-up. She had many faces. When talking to us, she wore her smiley face, which was warm and friendly. With the other grown-ups, her face would go serious and flat. But the face I saw most was her droopy face. She liked making it when she was looking at us, but only when we weren't looking back at her. If she caught us looking, she'd put on her smiley face again.

For some reason, the big kids didn't like Miss Finch. They called her a rat some days, and a cow on others. I really liked her, though. She called us sweeties and would always give us milk after our shots. She also said funny things a lot, like "ooh" and "thank goodness" and "special is memorable".

She said "special is memorable" an extra lot of times when it turned out I was something called the Electus. I didn't know what being the Electus meant, but I knew it was a title, like how the other grown-ups called her Doctor. It must have been an important title, because after that, none of the grown-ups called me F19 anymore. They all called me Electus. They stopped giving me shots and started sitting me in more machines so they could look at the big screen. They also stamped "ELECTUS" on my arm with a really hot stamper. I didn't like the stamp at first. It was ugly and hurt a lot right after, but then Miss Finch said her favorite words – that special was memorable. How would people remember who I was if they didn't know I was special?

And I thought about it and decided that she was right. So I just sat sipping at the warm milk Miss Finch gave me and waited for the stamp to stop hurting. Then I showed it to all the other kids. They were super impressed. The big kids were especially impressed. They looked at the stamp and their eyes went huge, and then they started talking to me all nice the same way they talked to the grown-ups.

Apparently the Electus was special because they could do magic. And because I was the Electus, I could also do magic. The tests went from being machines to being things where the grown-ups sat in a circle and told me to do magic tricks for them. I wasn't very good at magic. Nothing happened most of the time. I set one of the big kids on fire once, though. He called Miss Finch a rat again, and I got mad and pointed at him. And then a fire appeared, and he was jumping and squealing like a pig, and all the grown-ups were running around, and it was so funny that I wasn't mad anymore. After that, Miss Finch took me to another room to talk about how I wasn't supposed to set anyone on fire, and then we went back into the nursery and pretended nothing happened. I didn't see the big kid anymore after that. I guessed he got kicked out for calling Miss Finch a rat.

I liked being special. Everyone treated me nice, from the grown-ups to the other kids. They didn't have to take shots anymore because the shots were supposed to help find the Electus. And since I was the Electus, the grown-ups said everyone else didn't have to take shots anymore and would go to new homes. Some of them went away. Some of them, like Annie, Emily, Casey, and Francis, stayed here and played with me every day. Because I was special, they said I could be the leader.

But then everything started to change. The grown-ups began leaving. Sometimes, new grown-ups would come in and look around, and when they left, they'd always take some of our grown-ups with them. Miss Finch started making her droopy face even when she wasn't looking at us.

More grown-ups left, until it was just Miss Finch. Then, one day, even Miss Finch stopped coming.

New grown-ups came in. They started changing things and moving stuff around. They put these glass rooms in the nursery, and everyone had to stay in their own room unless a grown-up came to fetch them.

Because I was the leader, I told them that this wasn't how Miss Finch did things. The grown-ups laughed. I showed them my stamp and said I was the Electus. They laughed even harder. Then they told me that Miss Finch was gone. Mr. Starling was in charge now. And this was how Mr. Starling did things.

Mr. Starling wanted to see what kind of magic I could do. So I showed him a fire. He waved his hand and told me to do something else. I made his clipboard sing the alphabet. He didn't seem very impressed. Then I turned a pencil into another Mr. Starling that said oink over and over again. He just laughed nastily.

After that, I was taken to a room and left there. When they came back, they brought some other kids and left them there with me. They told me that from now on, I was going to make candy. I was going to make gummies that gave you a happy dream when you ate them. And when I was done, the other kids were in charge of packing them in jars and then packing the jars in boxes and sticking tape on them.

My first few gummies were terrible. They were all brown and nasty and bigger than what gummies should be. I also didn't know how to put happy dreams in them. So I told the grown-ups I couldn't do it. They told me it didn't matter. I was going to keep making gummies until I got it right, and if I didn't, none of us would get any supper.

I kept trying and trying. They were all either too nasty or too lopsided or too big. Then just as I finally managed to make one, the grown-ups changed their minds. This time, they wanted it to be a hard candy. Then they wanted it to be a hard candy with filling in it. Then they wanted it to be star shaped. And to sing. And to be addictive. And then they wanted it to let you relive your best memories instead of giving happy dreams.

The "singing star" was the final version of the candy they wanted me to make. It was going to sell all around the world and make a lot of money for Mr. Starling, enough to match the amount he'd paid to buy us and then some. Mr. Starling had invested a lot into this operation, the adults said. He'd dreamed of this plan since he was a child. He'd spent billions of money, and nearly 10 years of time playing good cop to the media.

All for me. The Electus, the most special person in the world, that only showed up once every 50 years. The only person who could use magic to make something from nothing. The most cost-efficient factory for Mr. Starling's one-of-a-kind sweets.

I had to give it to him. Mr. Starling was better at getting results than Miss Finch had been. He was sharper, shrewder, more willing to get his hands dirty. He saw the Electus as a business opportunity and wanted to use it to become the richest person in the world.

I wanted to refuse, but I couldn't. The first time I did, he pulled out a pen knife and stabbed it into Annie's arm. She was screaming. I wanted to help her, but fear filled my head, and I could do nothing but watch as she screamed and cried and screamed some more.

"Get back to work," said Mr. Starling. "Unless you want someone to get hurt."

He stayed there watching me shakily make singing star after singing star. Every time I got it wrong, he'd twist the knife, and Annie would scream again. She kept screaming until her voice grew hoarse and she couldn't scream anymore. Still, Mr. Starling kept going.

It was only after I'd filled the jar to the brim that he finally pulled out the knife. He smiled. Patted my head.

"See, I knew you could do it," he said. "Now keep going, little fella. Time's a ticking."

I never saw Mr. Starling again after that. It was just his goons, who'd been given instructions to follow his example if production slowed.

Day after day, I sat on the floor of the locked room, making singing stars. None of the other children spoke anymore. They just sat there doing their assigned tasks. When there was nothing to do, they'd sit and stare at the floor. Mr. Starling's men stood behind us, watching us work. If progress was too slow, they'd enact punishment. Some of the kids couldn't take it and died. The guards just dumped their bodies in the corner, right where I could see them.

I kept making singing stars. I was getting good at it. By now, I could make excellent quality singing stars in my sleep. Mr. Starling was probably pleased. Then eventually, the guards stopped hovering over us, instead standing watch outside the door.

"Are we still friends?" I once broke the silence to ask the other kids in front of me. They'd grown a lot since the day we were first shut in here. Casey was as tall as the guards now. The room was too small to store all the singing stars, so some of them would be escorted out every now and then to help transport the boxes to another storeroom. Only I wasn't allowed out.

The ones who remained, three of them, looked at each other with hollow eyes. They were quiet.

"Are we still friends?" I tried again.

Finally, someone spoke.

"Can't you do something, Linden?" Casey asked. "You're the Electus. Aren't you all powerful?"

"Aye," said Francis. "Like bust down the door. Kill all those numpties outside."

I looked over their shoulders at the rotting corpses of my friends lying in the corner. My hands shook.

"I can't."

"Why not?"

"I... I..." my voice shook. "I don't know, I just... just can't."

"What are you even good for then?" Casey scowled. "You're useless, Linden."

And then we went back to being quiet.

Yeah. I thought miserably to myself as I made another singing star and popped it into the jar. I was useless. I was supposed to be special. The world's most powerful being. I should be able to rescue my friends. I should be able to put everything right. But I couldn't. I was too scared. My magic refused to turn against the guards, against Mr. Starling, against the prison I was trapped in. I was nothing more than a human factory that made singing stars.

Another few years passed. One day, Casey didn't come back. Apparently, he'd been found dead in the old experimentation room left over from Miss Finch's days. The one with the machine that measured your Electus Index. Wedged his head in between the gears and turned it on with a remote.

The others were envious of him. They talked more in that one day than they had for the past 5 years.

"Takes a lot of courage to do that," said Emily admirably.

"Aye, at least one of us was brave," said Francis. "Unlike Linden."

I said nothing.

We were still stuck, and still slaving away for Mr. Starling, but somehow, Casey's escape had put the others in high spirits. That entire week, they stopped working whenever they could, whispering together far away from me. They kept going out of the room to "use the loo", only to come back half an hour later.

I warned them to be more discreet. If they kept this up, Mr. Starling was going to find out. They didn't care, though.

"And what's he going to do?" Emily rolled her eyes, slipping a screwdriver into her shoe. "Kill me?"

Then she went out and came back two hours later.

It was the second week of this when they finally came up to me. The two looked happier than they had in years, their sallow faces grinning with the sort of childish mischief I hadn't seen in a long time.

Proudly, they dragged me out of the room to the girls' bathroom. The guards were gone, somehow. Lunch break, Emily told me. They'd been leaving us unguarded during lunch for a whole year now. Yet I'd never noticed.

"Where are we going?" I asked as they ushered me into the farthest stall and closed the door.

"We're going to escape," said Francis giddily. He put the toilet lid down and stood on it. I watched, entranced as he pulled away one of the bricks and tossed it down to Emily, who laid it down silently on the floor.

"Get up here," he pulled me up to stand on the toilet lid next to him. "See, this stall here is right below the gas stove in the pantry."

Peering through the hole left by the brick, I spotted a thick pipe. It looked worn out, littered with little puncture holes.

"They're going in for lunch right now, so the gas will be flowing," Francis continued. "We need you to light a spark so we can blow up the wall."

"Boom," supplied Emily. She pulled out a plastic water bottle from under her shirt and poured it over her head. "And then we'll be out of here."

I watched as the bottle was passed to Francis, who did the same. Shaking the clear liquid out of his eyes, he tossed the empty bottle onto the floor.

"This is what you've been doing this whole time?" I asked.

"Aye. Planning, prepping, everything," said Francis, sopping wet, but his smile was more radiant than ever. "This is the last step. See, we need you to help us. You can make a spark, aye? A tiny little one. Right on the pipe."

"It's not going to work," I said glumly. "Mr. Starling's going to find out."

"Don't be a downer," Francis grabbed my face. His fingers were slimy. "By the time he notices, we'll be long gone."

"But everyone else—"

"They're all at lunch," Emily interrupted. "They're convinced we're brainwashed. They won't expect us to try anything. Not so soon after Casey died."

"Linden," said Francis firmly. "Trust us. We worked a whole two weeks for this one moment. We're your friends, remember? Just make that spark and it'll all work out, see?"

Something was wrong. Something that wasn't the risk of getting caught. But I couldn't tell what. It was all happening so quickly. I could do nothing but be swept along by the flow.

"I—"

Francis lifted my hand and brought it up to press against the pipe. I could feel a light gust blowing out from the tiny holes in the metal. The wind of freedom.

"Trust us, Linden. We're friends. We wouldn't lie to you."

I took a deep breath. I called upon the magic. The magic that for five long years, had been used for nothing but making singing stars.

A spark bloomed at the tip of my finger. It was bright, shining with a gleaming light. More vibrant and vivid than anything I'd seen.

I turned to smile at my friends. I'd done it. We were going to be f—

The room exploded.

I couldn't register what happened in those few moments. By the time I came back to my senses, the bathroom was a wreck. Fire was everywhere, burning orange and yellow. My ears were ringing. My head hurt. Something trickled down my brow and pooled in my eye, painting my vision red.

Everything hurt.

I looked down. Francis. His arm poked out from a pile of rubble. The rest of him was buried, crushed by the wall when it came down.

Emily had been blown a few steps away. She was burning. Like a living torch, like the older kid that I'd set on fire when I was 10 years old. I stumbled over the rubble, collapsing to my knees by her side.

"Thank..." Emily's voice was raw. Her hair was gone, her skin blackening and smoldering. "Free... no..."

She trailed off. The fire burned.

There was an alarm ringing. People were shouting, running about outside the bathroom. But it all felt far away. I knelt there amongst the blazing inferno, my friends dead around me. The smoke clogged my lungs.

I couldn't breathe.

I couldn't see.

Belatedly, I realized what had been wrong.

97

The liquid they'd poured on their heads. The holes in the gas pipe. Francis' oily fingers. They'd wanted this. They'd wanted to die. They just needed a spark.

A spark. I gave them a spark. I lit the fire. I blew it up.
I killed them. With my own two hands.

I killed them.
It was me.

You're useless, Linden.

I threw my head back and screamed.

The world *screamed with me.*
I painted the world. It painted me.
Pink, blue, shiny green.
Just the way I wanted it to be.
Cleaned up the rot, cleaned up the stench
Cleaned up the buildings and cleaned up the men.

Confetti for the dead, objects for heads.
The houses sing, the rooftops clap.
As a shiny new me, I sat down for tea.
Looking out over my very own city.

Special.
Just like how I was always meant to be.

ACT 4
The Janitor

I didn't know how long I spent in the memory. One moment, I was still Linden, and the next, I was Chuff again. It felt like a bad dream, the lingering anguish from the memory already fading into an odd sort of calm.

Yet even as the emotions faded, the feeling of magic still lingered on my fingers. I rolled up my shirt sleeve. The word "ELECTUS' was printed there on my skin, similar to the one that Linden had had.

I looked at it.

I rolled my sleeve back down.

There was nothing else to be found here, so I headed back the way I came. Back through the storeroom, back through the nursery. The metal shutter that had given me such grief was fully open, looking out onto the long hallway I had run through.

The Janitor was gone.

I headed back down the hallway at a much more leisurely pace than I had gone through it the first time. Having reached the door, I paused. The way back was so long, with those endless looping hallways and identical doors. Truth be told, I didn't think I knew how to get back. Especially with how I couldn't fall up the abyss the same way I fell down it.

I rubbed my fingers together, still tingling with Linden's magic. Wasn't I an Electus too, though?

I put my hand on the doorknob. I closed my eyes, focusing on recalling that feeling.

I twisted the knob.

The door opened onto the kitchen of the Janitor's house, who knows how far up above where I was supposed to be. The aroma of breakfast drifted in through the opening. Flapjacks, drowned in oil and covered in rainbow sprinkles.

I pushed the door open further and walked in.

The Janitor themself was sitting at their usual spot at the table, looking the same as always. Blue shirt, black slacks, pink spray bottle head. They were sitting back leisurely in their seat, reading the November 20th newspaper.

"Hello, Chuff," the Janitor sang, setting the paper down. "Welcome home."

I slid into the seat opposite to them. My flapjacks were served on the table in front of me, steaming hot and honey-sweet. They didn't flap, though. They just lay there quietly on my plate, completely still.

"Are you still mad?" I asked hesitantly.

"I was never mad," the Janitor replied. "This day would come eventually."

"You sounded mad down there."

"Really?" They laced their fingers together nervously. "I suppose I got a little agitated and lashed out at you. That place has that effect on people, you see. I apologize."

"It's okay," I replied.

There was a moment of awkward silence. I picked up my fork and poked at my flapjacks.

"So…" I decided to ask. "Linden. Is that you?"

The Janitor tilted their head. "Was me, yes. Once. Linden is dead now, however. Died long ago. All that's left is your friendly neighborhood Janitor."

"And New Penumbra?"

"Is a little place I made to settle down in. While the days away. Electi are emotional creatures, you see. Everything tends to distort when they go cuckoo. Places, animals, people. But the people can't take that sort of metamorphosis. Too sentient, it blows their minds. When I came to my senses, I was the only one left."

"But there are citizens here," I said.

"Just dolls I made to keep myself company," the Janitor sighed. "I can make as many of them as I like. They don't match up to the real thing, though. Too dull."

"Am I a doll?" I rested my head on my arms as I listened.

"Oh no," the Janitor shook their head. "You're an Electus. The one that comes after me. They appear every 50 years. Many years ago, the humans outside dropped you off right at the edge of my little sanctuary. A little babe of 5 years old. They hoped we'd finish each other off, I presume."

"Oh," I said. "Then why didn't you?"

"Why should I? You're the only company I've had in decades," the Janitor sang, spreading their arms out. "It wouldn't have worked even if I wanted to anyway. We Electi may be all-powerful, but we can't use magic on one another, you see. It just bounces off. Found that out when you climbed out the window when you were six and I couldn't just levitate you back." They tapped the side of their nozzle. "Luckily, you fell at night. Plenty of time to personally drop down and bring you back."

I snorted at the thought. The Janitor hummed. The tension broke as I lowered my head and tucked into my flapjacks. Sweet and light. I decided that I preferred these to the taste of the singing stars.

"So, what did you think?" the Janitor asked as I finished.

"About what?" I wiped off the excess butter on my napkin.

"The truth. You've been looking for it for a long time. Does it meet your expectations?"

"I don't know what I expected..." I admitted. "But you... you were the one who put those things there, weren't you? The newspaper clippings and the singing star?"

"Yes."

"Why?"

The Janitor tilted their head.

"Because, Chuff, I won't be around forever," said the Janitor. "We all die eventually. That includes me, having squandered all my life in this twisted sandbox. And wouldn't you be lost, then? Not knowing the whats and hows and whys. That wouldn't be very responsible of me now, would it?

"I knew there'd come a day when you'd grow tired of this place. When you'd want to venture out, make your own decisions, discover who you are... And a day when I no longer prowl this ruin, this most special place on Earth.

"And don't you know? Special is memorable," the Janitor said fondly. "But there still has to be someone who will remember. Otherwise, special doesn't mean anything."

"You want me to remember you after you're gone."

"Precisely. I knew you'd have to know the truth someday," the Janitor said, their tone turning mournful. "I'd planned to tell you when you turned 12. But I couldn't bring myself to, so I set it back to 15. Then 18... I kept putting it off, until I thought that maybe it wouldn't be so bad if you only found out after I passed away. Then, we could keep how we are just a little longer. You and I, the best detective duo in town, going on happy little adventures every day..."

The Janitor fell silent. We sat quietly, the Janitor with their newspaper, and me with the empty plate in front of me.

"So, what now?" I asked.

"What now?"

"What do I do… now that I know all this?"

"Anything you like. You could go out, explore. Conquer humanity or save it. You could make new friends, go on brand new adventures in the whole wide world. You're an Electus. The one chosen by fate and magic. Nobody could stop you if you put your mind to it."

"If I leave and do all that," I said slowly. "Would you still be here when I come back?"

"…I don't know. That depends on how much time I've got left. Truth be told, I don't really know how old I am. I never counted."

I raised my head. Light streamed in through the window and pooled atop the table in a puddle of honey. The kitchen cupboards rattled quietly, the kettle whistling as it boiled water. The aroma of my breakfast lingered in the air, warm and sweet in just the right way.

The Janitor sat across the table from me. Their slender fingers were laced together, gloved hands resting on the table surface. Their favorite newspaper was folded neatly to the side. Their features no longer resembled the human that they were 50 years ago. And yet this was more familiar, more comforting. More parental than any human I had and would likely ever know.

They looked at me kindly, as kindly as a pink spray bottle could look.

"So, Chuff," the Janitor said gently. "What do you want to do?"

ACT 5
Another New Day

"Good moooorning, New Penumbra!"

I rolled out of bed and skipped over the snapping floorboard. Throwing open the window, the sun tried to beam in. A slap sent it flying back out into space. In the bathroom, I washed up, joking with my reflection about needing to reflect on my image.

Heading down to the kitchen, breakfast was ready. A sponge cake, freshly plucked from the river. Across from me, the Janitor read the paper. November 20th, the same as they did every day.

Having finished up breakfast, I hustled over to the entrance hall. The Janitor was already there, in their top hat and white coat.

"Are you ready for another day of sleuthing, Chuff?" the Janitor sang, their voice pitching high and low at unpredictable intervals.

"Aye, aye, Janitor," I replied cheerfully.

The Janitor opened the door, and we were off.

As we walked down the street, I had a sudden thought.

"Say," I said. "What's so interesting about the November 20th news?"

"Oh, that," the Janitor chuckled. Reaching up, they pulled the paper from the air. The newspaper opened with a flap. November 20th, 2001. The bold headlines screamed, one after another.

The Electus Project: Survivors Recount A Chilling Tale

From Darling to Demon: Arthur Starling Stoned to Death Outside Mansion

Chuffed! Suspected Electus Child Bites The Prime Minister And Laughs

"Just a lot of good news."

ANESTHESIA

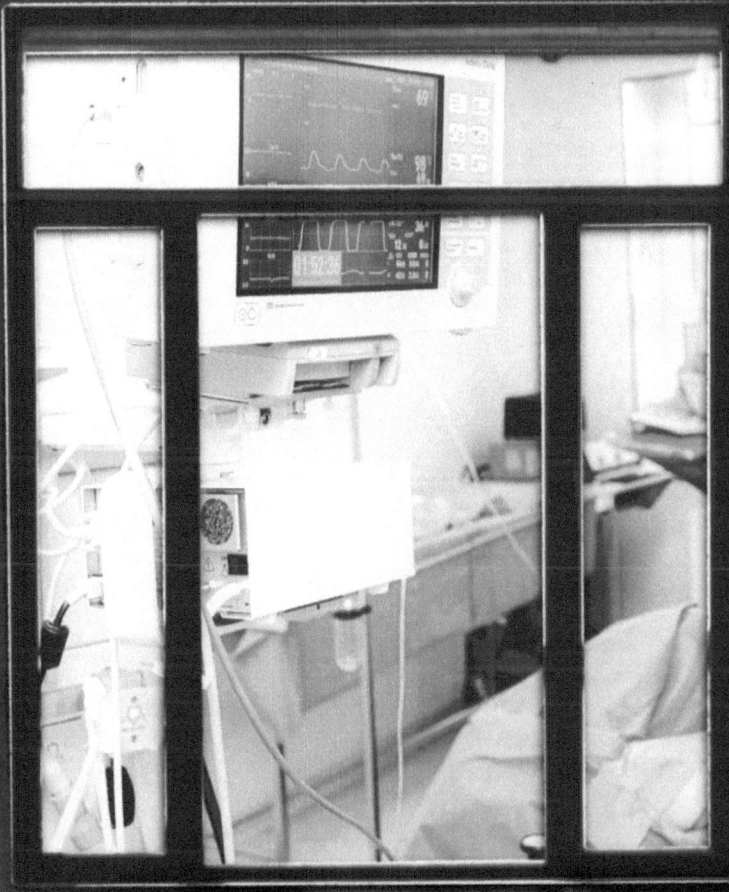

A SHORT STORY BY
ALEX CLAPPER

CONTENT WARNINGS

This story contains themes that may be distressing to some readers, including:

Blood/Surgery

Anesthesia

I've only gone under anesthesia twice—when I had my wisdom teeth out and when I had my tits off. Both times, I marveled at how quickly it took me under, and how, when I woke up, it felt like no time had passed.

The rooms all look the same in a hospital, so when I fought to open my eyes after top surgery, I asked the nurse if we were about to move down to the OR. She said, "Sweetie, you're already done." I wanted to respond with, "I just (apparently) had my tits cut off, do I look like a 'sweetie' to you?" But she gave me saltines and water, so I didn't.

When my partner was allowed to see me, they asked how I was doing.

I said, "My chest is sore."

They said, "No shit."

I said, "Can we go home?"

They said, "Oh my God, please, five hours in the waiting room of The Price is Right at full volume is five hours too many."

I said, "Five hours?!"

Then, like an obstinate toddler, I attempted to dress myself while lacking any of the motor coordination to do so. You don't really realize how hard it is to put your shirt on until your chest is bound in gauze and you can't lift your arms above navel height. Luckily, flannels were easy to get on, and I'm gay, so I own a lot of them.

§

I texted everyone on the way home that I'd survived. My mom was the first to respond, of course, a paragraph about how she hoped I was feeling alright and wondering how soon her daughter— sorry—kid—would be able to see her— sorry—their new body. She was bad at this, but she was trying. She'd get it eventually, or she wouldn't, but I love her anyway.

My dad said, "Hey kiddo, I hope you're feeling okay." Classic Dad. I love him too.

When we got home and I'd answered the first round of texts, I handed my phone to my partner, "You're my secretary now. Feel free to ignore everyone." Then I fell asleep on the couch for four hours.

The following two days passed slowly and sucked. My chest hurt, my partner had to help me empty drains because I dislike blood, even my own, and I wasn't allowed to sleep on my side, which meant I slept like shit.

§

Then my follow-up appointment. The nurses unwrapped my bandages for the first time. I was gross and sticky, the gauze glued to my flesh by sweat, blood, lymph fluid, and iodine. I hadn't showered in two days, because I wasn't allowed to. Stitches were still in, drains were still in, and I smelled like decade-old period underwear. When I tell you I was gross, I mean it. But, when I looked in the mirror, disheveled and unwashed though I was, the eyes that met mine were no longer those of a well-known stranger.

The nurse said, "What do you think?"

And I said, "That's me."

Anesthesia

THE OBITUARY
OF A PLANET

A SHORT STORY BY
J.R. MERRICK

CONTENT WARNINGS

This story contains themes that may be distressing to some readers, including:

Apocalyptic themes

To my wife, Reshma, and my daughter, Avia,
who make up my whole world.

The Obituary of a Planet

```
> Earth is dead.
```

The text flashed upon the screen in an unassuming monospace font as if it were declaring a syntax error in some poorly-written code. Red stared at it in a sort of disbelief that defied anything any human, by virtue of the singular uniqueness of such an event, had ever exhibited in the history of mankind. The message held an almost matter-of-fact finality and simplicity that belied its devastating implications.

Red glanced at the chronometer. The lower display indicated the ship's local time—they'd been traveling for nearly five years now, a long time for any space voyage, to be sure. The other display gave an accurate account of how much time had passed on Earth since their departure. Over seventy-five years. Accelerating at one gravity for nigh on five years had allowed the ship to outpace the Earth fifteenfold. Relativity: gotta love it. He was fine with the time dilation; he'd long since come to terms with the fact that everyone he'd ever known who wasn't aboard this ship would be long dead by the time they reached their destination. It was a sacrifice demanded of his entire crew.

He hadn't accounted for any reality that included an extinction-level event. Who would, or could, consider such a possibility? Sure, the Earth wasn't exactly a paradise when they'd left; it was the main reason he was undergoing this one-way voyage into the vast emptiness of interstellar space. But for it to just be... gone? It seemed impossible.

Red turned his attention back to the Q-Com. Nothing had changed. Those three, pernicious words glared back at him remorselessly. The message's digital signature indicated that it came from an off-world base in the asteroid belt. When they'd left, such prospects were but nebulous plans for future development within the local star system. As it was, the base was only about 25 Earth local years old. They frequently got updates about how far humanity managed to advance while he and the crew drifted along through the cosmos.

After a minute or two, Red shook off his stupor and placed his hands on the terminal's keyboard. He didn't often respond to the updates from

Earth or any of humanity's outposts, but this seemed too momentous to ignore.

> What happened? Did anyone make it out? How many of us are left?

It seemed pertinent to know just how endangered a species he was now a member of.

Almost immediately, several messages appeared on the terminal at once. The Quantum Communicator was an ingenious and useful device for communicating over long distances. Red didn't know the technical details of how the hardware worked, but some part of the coms on either end was connected by quantum entanglement. When something changed on one end, the same change took place on the other, amounting to instant communication across light-years of space without worrying about the insurmountable decades-long lag and unreliability of sending radio signals. As a former software engineer in the United People's Militia Corps, he knew how to perform some basic programming of the thing and had done so on multiple occasions. The designers of the device had at least made the human-to-machine interface easy to understand, so it was only a matter of understanding some basic networking and performing a bit of low-level bit-wise arithmetic—*or is it qubit-wise arithmetic?* he thought with a touch of gallows humor.

The only problem with this method of communication was the difference in relativity between the two ends. Yes, messages arrived instantly thanks to the Q-Com's quantum link. Still, because the ship was traveling so much faster than any Earth-based communicator, any reply would seem to arrive after a long delay. A moment of deliberation to form a response on his end could amount to apparent days of lag time for them. Several days, possibly weeks, would have passed for his current response to reach them. The upshot of this was that the ship usually received responses in a matter of milliseconds.

> Self-imposed. The details don't matter much now, do they? It's too late.

> A handful of terrestrials escaped the carnage, mostly the trillionaires with the resources to build their own rockets. Not enough, obviously.

> We estimate between 50 and 100 thousand of us remain, not including the Trinity generation ships we sent out 42 years ago. And yourselves, of course.

> We aren't optimistic about our own survival here in the Asterion outposts. Without Earth's resources, we'll be hard-pressed to produce enough food with the 'ponics farms. We might eke out another generation or two before we starve to death, but it'll be a meager living if we can't figure something out.

> Your mission just became 1000% more critical. You'd damn-well better find humanity a new home for all those poor souls aboard the arcs, or mankind's legacy will be gone in a matter of decades.

> Godspeed, Prometheus. You're all we have left.

Red perused the handful of messages several times. Compared to the original message, this was quite the outpouring of information. Where the first gave the sense of shell-shocked admittance, the follow-ups felt increasingly bitter and hopeless. Whoever was at the other end of these coms had been given many days to process the events and had come to very unhappy conclusions indeed.

There was a lot to unpack. Self-imposed? That could mean anything. Planet-wide war, climate-related devastation, a scientific experiment gone wrong. Whatever it was had to be bad to completely wipe everything away. Historically, life on Earth had proven to be extraordinarily resilient, surviving everything from super volcanoes to meteor strikes to global ice ages. What did they do, ignite the atmosphere?

He paused for a moment on the word "terrestrials." It felt strangely alien, as if the message writer was attempting to attach a strangeness to what, until very recently in the grand scheme of things, had been the only form of existence for every human ever. Red was unfamiliar with the intricacies of the politics between Earth and the outposts, but it sounded as if they had already begun separating themselves from those who were Earth-bound.

Fifty to a hundred thousand humans left. It wasn't nothing, at least, but it was a far cry from the twelve billion it had been only moments before—moments relative to the crew of the Prometheus, that is. That was fewer people than a moderately populated city. And even those would be lost if the outposts didn't innovate the hell out of things over there. Or, more accurately, innovate their way out of hell. They could do it; Red was sure. It might be touch and go for a few decades, but… *Ha!* He'd almost thought, *people have been through worse.* That was, categorically, incorrect.

So, humanity wasn't quite doomed… yet. There were those surviving among the asteroids, not to mention the seeders. If his memory proved accurate, each of the three Trinity ships were packed with ten thousand passengers and several million frozen fertilized embryos awaiting the artificial womb. They were the real hope for humanity's longevity. Of course, their fates were dependent upon himself and the rest of the crew of the Prometheus. If their mission to find a habitable planet for humanity went, as they said in the Corps, to utter shit, then the human species was that much closer to extinction. The fate of the world, quite literally, rested upon his shoulders.

A new message appeared on the screen a few moments after the previous several, meaning days must have passed.

> Some of the best scientists we have remaining managed to pull together an RCA. We're sending the binary to you now. For the record.

Red actually gave a short bark of manic laughter upon reading that. There was no humor in it; he was merely reacting to the irony of it. Performing a root-cause analysis on the destruction of the Earth felt incredibly clinical, as if they were diagnosing a crashed server. What a joke! It was exactly the kind of thing he would expect from intellectual purists.

Red turned his attention briefly to another console. The words "Receiving fat-line file transmission…" blinked back at him. It took a few moments before the words changed to, "File received." It had taken many hours on their side to send just one file. The Q-Coms excelled at sending bare text, but it was in no way optimized for sending anything of even moderate complexity. Red tapped a few keys on his keyboard and saved the file to the ship's computer. He'd look it over later. He didn't have the emotional energy to read about the causes of the destruction of his home planet just yet. He bent over the Q-Com's keys and typed out a final reply.

```
> 10-4. File received.
```

With that, he fell back in his chair and squeezed the bridge of his nose with thumb and forefinger. What a nightmare! Everything he'd once known, every person he could potentially call kin, had winked out of existence. He was now one of the very few remaining of his species. Not to mention every other unique species of the Earth that had suddenly become extinct. They could be recreated from the exabytes of genetic data stored within the onboard servers, but it would never be the same as it had once been on Earth. Red had always considered this voyage to be more of a fact-finding, exploratory mission to find new planets to potentially colonize, not a "last hope for humanity" type of mission. What was he going to tell the crew?

The crew. They would be devastated by the news. And, if they were anything like him, the notion of upgrading their mission to one of critical importance would only cause undue stress. They had just over a year of acceleration to go, and that would only mark the halfway point of their journey; they still had to decelerate for another six years until they finally reached their destination. Seven more years of travel aboard this vessel. And he was about to deliver news that would turn that time into a seven-year prison sentence on death row. No, it was worse than that. At least people on death row knew what awaited them at the end of their sentence. And the burden of an entire species didn't rest on their shoulders.

Red stared for a moment at the com logs. The obituary of a planet. This knowledge could destroy the crew, cause infighting, erode morale. Just knowing that the Earth was a pile of rubble could spell disaster for their mission and result in the true extinction of humanity. He couldn't let that happen.

Heart racing, Red leaned over the keyboard again. He hesitated a moment. Did he really have the right to withhold the truth from the rest of the crew? His brows furrowed. To hell with it. What good was the truth if it resulted in all their deaths—and, quite possibly, the death of their species? With practiced fingers, he opened a command terminal and saved the com logs and the RCA to his personal, encrypted file share—for future posterity. He took a deep breath. This was for the future of mankind. He'd tell them once the mission had been completed successfully. He felt sick. His fingers moved over the keys almost of their own volition. He hit enter.

```
> purge logs --system q-com --previous 10
```

```
Do you wish to delete logs? This action cannot be
undone. Confirm (Y/N):
```

```
> y
```

```
Purging logs
...
...
...
Logs deleted
```

The Obituary of a Planet

CHRIST'S BLOOD

A SHORT STORY BY
ANA GUARDIA

CONTENT WARNINGS

This story contains themes that may be distressing to some readers, including:

Violence

Blood

Fire injuries

Ritualistic cannibalism

Christ's Blood

"**H**ere we are, miss."

The cart creaked and swayed under the driver's weight. He gave you a toothless smile, his pustule-ridden nose breathing the stench that killed prostitutes and decent men alike.

You lifted your face. The man swallowed his words. He glanced for a second at the woods surrounding the mountain path, at the monastery building silhouetted against the cloudless sky at the top of the cliff. Black goats were hopping between the rocks. Then he looked back at you with that expression somewhere between disgust, curiosity, and pity.

You opened your mouth to distract from his horror when you realized you couldn't remember his name. He was there after hearing about a fire, a family, and a letter from the monastery to a disfigured orphan.

You touched the tips of your hair, light brown against the earth beneath your nails. You caressed your neck, the burning red marks over the blue veins filled with sweat. You lowered your eyes to your skirt, not long enough to cover the bandage already browned by hours of travel. The sun was at its zenith, but the hairs on your arms were standing on end.

"Do you need help getting out?" He cleared his throat with the compulsion of politeness. "I still have one more trip to make, miss..."

"Reyhan. Novice Reyhan. And no, I'm fine, thank you very much for bringing me here."

You shook your head, not wanting to waste another minute of his time. Despite the weight of your luggage and the weakness in your left leg, you jumped to the ground. You weren't yet used to judging distance with just one eye, so you reached the ground sooner than expected.

You bent your knee in agony and stumbled forward a few meters, the wound on your face throbbing with shame. Only the grating stopped you from falling to the ground, the groaning of the metal echoing the birdsong, the cows' mooing, and the faint murmur of the midday mass chants.

In your periphery, a red spark hid the sun for a moment. You raised your eyes to the stained-glass windows, as tall and magnificent as the cloister building itself. You searched for red in the angels' image until your pupils ached. Nor was there any sign of the color in the building itself. The surface was gray rock, black wood in crude decorations of fleurs-de-lis and crosses.

Behind you, you heard a whistle. Then a "hey," followed by a "miss," in an annoyed and monotonous tone.

"Yes?" You replied, tilting the good side of your face toward the driver. Your courtesy earned him a smile full of puffy gums. The donkeys swatted the flies away with their tails.

"There's a shepherd's village to the south, a two-hour walk away." He nodded toward the cliffs. He spat beside the wheels as he took the reins. His parting words reached you on the breeze, too chilly for the approaching summer. "God is not here..."

"Thank you," you said without waiting for an answer, the shapes of the car and men soon disappearing behind a cloud of dust.

Alone again, you kept your grip on your bag as you walked the last few meters to your new home. You gasped for air with that final breath, but your lungs swelled with the scent of sulfur and burning flesh instead of fresh air. You swallowed, the image of your parents and siblings silhouetted against the fire racing your heart. Arms of melted flesh stretched between the fallen beams.

Behind you, a bleat tore you from your memories and drew your attention back to the road. You stifled a yelp. Standing on its hind legs, a Billy goat the size of two men watched you. A spark of mockery lingered in the gold of its irises. It took a step forward, the crash of its kicks like the roof crack giving way in the fire.

The monastery gate trembled beneath your hands as you closed it with a force you didn't think you were capable of. Behind you, the footsteps didn't slow down, patient and measured. You ignored the constant pain in your knee from falling up the stairs. By the time you reached the large wooden double doors, your throat was dry.

You opened it as the bars creaked slowly.

Inside, darkness greeted you with its scent of burning candles and incense. You encountered the confusion of the sisters' faces, baskets, and books in their arms. Some let out cries of surprise or horror at your features. You sank at the feet of a figure, the mountains and rivers on its face almost as terrifying as the monster outside.

"Miss Reyhan, we've been waiting for you." You kept your gaze lowered, sitting on your heels, your hands in the chasteness of your skirt. Without anyone offering a hand to lift you, you shook out your skirts. You curtsied.

"I saw something terrible, sister... A monster with the face of a goat and the shape of a man."

The Great Mother sighed, making a motion to disperse the crowd. She folded her hands across her belly as they were left alone. She looked at you fearlessly, blue stones as icy as winter.

"Silence. The Devil enters our hearts at the mention of it." She gave no room for your subsequent questions, her gestures impatient while guiding you. "You're late. I hope you'll be more responsible from now on. The nuns take care of the bread, the monks the garden. Everyone takes care of the chickens and the cows. You only have to worry about the two meals at the right time."

You pushed the ghosts from your mind and focused on keeping up without stumbling. You passed the entrance to the garden, crossed the orchard, and then the building with the rooms. Duty devoured fear as Mother Cecilia's instructions rained down relentlessly on your travel-weary soul.

The letter for that job arrived while you were still in bed, bandages covering the swelling on your features. The Vatican's ink seal was enough to quell doubts and misunderstandings, and enough money to cover travel, clothing, and food expenses. Your father knew some great people.

Now you are in your new home.

"This is..."

The ceilings were high for a basement, the skylights were grease-stained, spectral in their yellow color. Strings of garlic, cured meats, and dried meat hung from various slats. Barrels filled with wine lined one wall. Fresh fruit from the garden filled the woven baskets on the shelves, from large tomatoes to long, orange carrots. Next to the hearth of the room, rags covered the baskets with a still-warm, fresh peace. At the back, next to the tiny cell of a bunk and table, the cupboard door held cheeses, hams, and jars of sauces.

You blinked, your face multiplied by tens of thousands on every knife, pot, and pan, as clean as the first day they arrived. Again and again, you saw the milky eye wrapped in a circle of pustular skin like the rest of its body; half its head was missing hair, half its mouth drooping like a dog.

Mother Cecilia awaited your attention, as still as the statues on the columns.

"We eat two main meals. Wine, bread, soup, and a main course. Breakfast at dawn, dinner at dusk. At midday, just a light plate of fruit, wine, and cheese. The week's menu will be written on the back of the cupboard door." Her figure glided through the room, her robes resembling the waves of the sea. "The meat in the cold storage is exclusive for the Father, the special guests, and me. All the ingredients will come to you, even the fish for Holy Week and Christmas. As for the brothers in seclusion, you must bring only water, bread, and grapes. Twice a day."

You frowned in confusion at the mention of fresh pieces of meat. How could they consume it daily without salting it? The walls and ceilings of the abbey were clean, preserved by the work of several generations of monks, but the passage of time was visible in the splinters of the furniture, the cracked stone floor in the garden, and the rusty details of the lanterns. If you strained your ears, the whistling of the wind accompanied the murmur of prayers. Even the uniforms, still deep and unstained, were stiff. This was no monastery with a chest full of gold to waste on fresh meat.

You lowered your head.

"I understand, sister. Thank you for the opportunity."

The old woman nodded, her expression soft now that she wasn't facing the other sisters. She clasped her hands together.

"The brothers have heard of your situation and want to offer you our prayers." Sister Cecilia moved the beads of her rosary. Then, she tapped her fingers on one of the shelves. "Now, on earthly matters, on your cot you will find three pairs of novice robes, a pair of pajamas, and the rest of the money your father left. During your breaks, you may use the library and participate in prayer activities to prepare for your exams."

You smiled.

"I will always be grateful for the support."

The Sister nodded, wiping the dust off her face with a rag before disappearing upstairs.

"Okay, now unpack and get to work. Father Ignacio gets in a terrible mood when dinner is late."

As you unpacked, you changed into one of your new habits and protected your clothes with an apron. That evening, you would eat a stew of seasonal vegetables, stuffed hen, and wine. Separately, you had to cook the meat for Father Ignario and Sister Cecilia.

Christ's Blood

Once you found everything you needed for the dishes, the work was as easy as it had been in your previous life. Silently, you worked the pieces, chopped carrots and potatoes, found firewood, and lit the fire to boil the water. Soon, the kitchen smelled of a hearty dinner, and the smoke rising from the skylights drew the brothers into the dining room once they'd finished their daily tasks.

You served the trays and lifted them with the pulley lift in pairs. Your burned shoulder ached, the kitchen fumes made you cough, but being useful again was priceless. You served the rest of the food in several small bowls alongside the portion of the penitent brothers. The day was warm, so the evening in the garden offered a good place to dine.

You went up to the main level, turned left into the library, and went down a staircase shrouded in torchlight. The whisper of prayers reached you before the smell of sweat, feces, dampness, and the grease of tinder.

The cells occupied a long corridor, three on each side.

Silently, you collected the trays filled with morning crumbs and left the new ones within easy reach. The whispers continued.

However, the darkness wasn't total. In the distance, on the stone wall, a white lightning bolt-shaped line reminded you of the storms where you would hide in your parents' bed.

Curiosity led you to push the stone without letting go of your tray until an invisible mechanism opened enough space for an adult. For a second, the light blinded you.

"Oh, hello, miss."

A child's voice was the last thing you thought you'd hear in that gray, airless space. In the damp chamber, a figure chained by arms and legs stared at you with a toothy grin.

The child was very blond, his curls the same shade of gold. His eyes were as large as his eyelashes, the green of grass bathed in dew. His cheeks were round, heavy, and full of color. His lips and nose were like spring blossoms. On his back, two pairs of white wings sprouted. His beauty still retained the sweetness of divine perfection.

Yet, when you looked down at the rest of his body, the horrors of humanity were tattoos on his skin. The wounds on his wrists and ankles were raw, the blood on the floor darkened by days, months, or years. On his neck, a knife mark crossed like a smile from side to side. His thighs were stained black, the white of his bones easily discernible in the indentations.

You trembled, tears blinding your one eye. You struggled not to drop the tray. You placed it near the boy before releasing his restraints for him to eat. You waited for him to swallow the soup, lick the remains from the bottom, and suck the pulp from the bones.

"Who did this to you...?"

"The lords say I'm God, so they have me here to protect them from Evil." He took the bread. He handed you one of the pieces. His voice was like chimes in the wind. "What happened to your face?"

"There was a... Accident at my house and I ended up like this…" You sighed, covering your profile."... Do I look too ugly?"

"In my eyes, kindness is the only face, and you are beautiful."

"Reyhan. Miss Reyhan, if you like," You shook the small, warm hand. "Nice to meet you. What's your name?"

"I'm Melek. I saw it in a book and I liked it." He laughed softly, warmth shifting from your hand to your pockmarked cheek. "I saw this in a book, too."

The fire from his fingers consumed your vision. You didn't feel the pain or the agony of the burning, only a feeling of lightness that covered your lips, cheeks, and eyes like a veil. Conversations replaced memories of the accident with your parents, harvest fairs, and winter dances.

As soon as you came to, Melek's face was staring back at you. From that distance, his skin was a constellation of freckles, his eyes contained the universe. You blinked, and the world once again filled with every imperfection. You brought a hand to your face, the craters of your skin buried beneath new skin. In your once-healthy eye, the room was much smaller. You jumped to your feet. You took a couple of steps back.

"Reyhan... Aren't you going to take the tray?"

You managed to grab it before leaving the room, Melek's voice calling you as you closed the door. The whispers of prayers continued as you retraced your steps to the kitchen, took the priest's tray with his supper, and headed to the top of the spiral staircase leading to the offices.

Despite the distance, you were still drowning in the aroma of the basement. The hallway was a wolf's mouth. The light of the torches reflected on the fat of the meat and the surface of the soup and wine. You climbed the spiral staircase in silence, barely breathing audibly in the dimness. You concentrated on not tripping, images of Melek suddenly assaulting you.

Still, the cart driver's warnings echoed in the walls of your brain, and every new step made you question your future within those walls. The goats' presence, the boy who called himself God, and even the weight of darkness in every corner of those hallways were warnings difficult to ignore behind the excuse of paranoia. The church was dark inside, windows and candles unable to dispel the shadows filled with something that ate and breathed.

"God really isn't here."

You swallowed, cold sweat trickling down your chin and sliding onto your shivering skin. The tray trembled in your grip. The walls around you were narrow, cold, and damp like the icebox's. You avoided looking at your now healthy, whole arm. You paused at the top of the staircase.

The hallway leading to the tower's living quarters was lined with large windows, but neither fresh air nor sunlight reached the building. Terror rose in your stomach instead of hunger, your muscles tensing with something far from exhaustion.

You lowered your head without slowing down. You knocked on the large wooden gate twice without waiting for a response. You had to leave the tray on one of the hallway tables to push the door open and enter.

You sighed, the darkness inside the office even more palpable than that of the stairwell. You didn't lock your door behind you, your instinct warning you to leave a way out. You held your breath, the interior of the room conjured straight from your nightmares.

The place was littered with objects. Candles in skulls, chandeliers and candle holders illuminated the shapes of the library. Books crammed in haphazardly. A pair of armchairs, shelves full of animals and strange figures floating in liquids complete the place. In the background, under a stained-glass window depicting Saint Lucy with her eyes in a tray just like yours, sits a huge pine desk. Only a quill and ink are on top, waiting for their next letter.

You placed the food carefully. You blinked, your fingers sore and swollen from the force of your grip. You clenched and unclenched your hands, your eyes wandering over the shapes of the objects as you regained feeling.

You touched the leather trim of the armchairs, stroked the edges of the desk. Then, you approached the bookshelves. Despite the thick layer of dust on most of the containers, you marveled at the two-headed corpses, with large eyes as black as the void. You were examining a dog fetus when you noticed a carafe on the lower shelf.

The cleanliness of the glass indicated use. The cork was so new it gleamed in the dim light and gave way easily to a tug.

You made sure the door didn't close before leaning in and sniffing. Instead of wine's strong, acidic aroma, you were enveloped in a cloud of rust and familiarity. A feeling of heresy washed over you. You stood still for a few seconds until you realized the source of that liquid. Pigs. It was pig's blood.

Without knowing why, something made you turn to the plate on the desk. The meat that, when cooked, reminded you more of the texture of pork than beef. The same meat that was raw was the same size as the wounds on the angel.

Did not God give his flesh and blood for human consumption?

A wave of nausea made you jerk away from the furniture and the barely lit candles. The place was no longer the sanctuary of a saint, but of someone much more dangerous. In the darkness, something saw you running away and kicked the fallen cork on the carpet.

You reached the safety of the kitchen before you knew it. You were surprised to see no one following you, your heart pounding. You took a few steps toward the dirty dinner dishes, but the energy that pulled you into the office guided you to the fresh food area.

You pushed aside the jars of spring onions, olives, and other preserves. The vinegar stained your fingers, nose, and eyes, dripping with chili, garlic, and black pepper. You left everything on the floor, careful as you slid the slit open. At the bottom of the tiny stone cave, the remains of a piece of meat were barely larger than a woman's hand. You looked up at the sausages hanging from the ceiling.

That was the scent. People and pigs smelled the same when cut with a single stroke across the neck.

You covered your lips, vomit seeping through your fingers as you tried to contain the disgust, fear, and confusion growing in your body. You hesitated, your legs barely holding you against the wall, your knees on the verge of giving way. Several minutes passed, where the weight of your life, of the decisions you'd made up to this point, pressed your soul into very dark places.

You didn't know where you got the energy from, but when you were aware of your surroundings again, more than half the plates were clean, the food scraps had been set aside for the animals, and your body was tense with fatigue. Dinner was out of the question, so you washed with the clean water from the bucket, changed into your convent pajamas, and lay down on the cot without thinking about anything else.

You avoided looking at yourself on the surface of the pans, your face complete again.

At the darkest hour of the night, you were awakened by noises in the kitchen. A plate being moved, feet walking, and even the distinct sound of a mouth chewing. You remained still, straining your ears and calming the panic that threatened to swallow you up. You sat up, searching for your shoes, careful not to make a sound. The cold penetrated your light clothes, so you pulled on your still-dusty travel cloak.

You were tempted to light a candle, but you were afraid of what you would find in the light, so you peeked from the safety of your room into the kitchen.

Your soul returned to your body at the sight of the white wings, the figure of the little boy enveloped in a white aura so intense you could define the shape of every object. The feathers shuddered with each bite he took from the leftovers bucket.

"Melek?"

The boy swallowed just enough to turn his face in your direction.

"Reyhan... Are you the guardian of the food?"

You let out a laugh, approaching much more animatedly. You took off your cloak to carry the tiny body, much lighter than it looked. Melek's warmth was pleasant, tender, like her brother's when he was little.

"Not for long..."

You left Melek on your bed while you spoke in whispers. You quickly prepared everything you needed for a trip, moving here and there as you prepared bundles of cheese and fruit, and grabbed as much bread as possible for the following days. "It's not a good place. Do you want to come with me? We can work on a farm..."

"Sounds good..."

You smiled despite yourself when you found him in the same place you left him, his fat legs hanging off the edge of the bed.

"I assume you got away because of me. But that's okay. You may be God, but you are still just a child."

Melek didn't speak, expressing his agreement by letting you strap him to your back so you could have your hands free with the luggage. The warmth of the fire returned, but now it seeped from the surface to your legs, and every part of you burned. His breathing soon evened out, sleep finally bringing relief from his wounds.

Your heart was heavy, of course. It wasn't a bad job for a person in his position. However, something infectious lingered in the air, and you didn't want to catch the virus.

You slipped up the stairs in complete silence, the darkness fleeing behind you both. The infant's glow protected you like a shield against the ghosts of your past. Your limp disappeared completely before you reached the main hall. The candles still lay warm in the sconces despite the solitude of the hallways.

Still, your senses picked up on the changes in the air.

The front door gave way under your push, and the moonlit landscape welcomed you into its icy embrace. Your muscles were tense, filled with blood and adrenaline. The goats were calling to you.

Your courage faltered as you caught sight of the goat with the pentagram on its forehead standing in the middle of the road. Soon, the screams of the priests and the fire of the Abyss would welcome the dawn.

You clutched the knot of your luggage.

"Don't look back, don't look back…"

With prayer giving you courage, you crossed the gate for the last time. You left it open for the billy goat, who brushed against your shoulder as he entered the monastery.

Christ's Blood

SAVING DAISY

A SHORT STORY BY
AURORA LYNN MORTENSEN

CONTENT WARNINGS

This story contains themes that may be distressing to some readers, including:

Animal death (mentioned)

Saving Daisy

Jessa should have picked a different bus stop. This one was too close to her house, and the bus was taking longer to show up than she'd thought. A neighbor returning home from dropping a kid off at school might see her. She hadn't had time to change into her ninja clothes. If she snuck off behind a bush to change, she might miss the bus and be stuck waiting longer in that risky place. She could get up and move to a different bus stop, but a delay like that would be unbearable now. She felt sick to her stomach and wanted to be done with Phase 1 as soon as possible.

So, she hunched over, with her face behind her backpack, which she was wearing in front of her instead of back, and hoped no one who knew her well enough to recognize her by her hair would pass by.

Daisy wriggled in the backpack. Jessa unzipped the pack just enough to peer inside at her, a petite, sable ferret with gray eyes. "It's okay, girl," Jessa cooed. She would know she wasn't alone if she heard Jessa's voice. "I'm here, girl." But the ferret kept squirming and scratching. Jessa thought the ninja clothes inside would make a good bed, but Daisy wouldn't stop trying to claw her way out. Jessa hoped she would settle down soon.

She heard scratchy voices from behind and subtly turned her head. Two women, older than her mother but a little younger than her grandmother, were approaching, deep in conversation. One of the women had a walker. She couldn't tell what the conversation was about, but she was pretty sure she heard the word *shit*. She squeezed her backpack tighter and hoped the bus would come soon.

A minute passed. The women's conversation ebbed. One woman sighed. Another minute passed, and Jessa smelled smoke. She couldn't help but lift her head and stare in righteous indignation. Good guys did not swear, and more importantly, good guys did not smoke. It could make other people sick. These were bad guys. Jessa could tell.

The woman with the cigarette caught her eye. "Ah, shit," she said, puffing. "I didn't know you were a kid. Ain't you supposed to be in school?"

"Today's a holiday," Jessa murmured. It wasn't a lie. Technically, every day was a holiday because every day was somebody's birthday. But even though it wasn't a lie, she felt a little guilty for saying it.

"That's so? Where you headed, kid? The movie theater? I know kids your age always like to go to the movie theater on a holiday."

Jessa wasn't sure what to say to that. She never went to the movie theater on holidays, but maybe other kids did. The other woman rescued her, butting in, "You're scaring her. She knows not to talk to strangers. Don't you, little girl? Don't talk to strangers."

"I'm not scared," Jessa said.

The woman with the cigarette dropped it on the ground and crushed it with her foot. "I'm just trying to be friendly. I'll leave you alone. You have a fun holiday." Jessa thought the woman might litter, but she picked up the cigarette and threw it away in the little bus stop bin, and Jessa thought maybe these women weren't really bad guys. Maybe they just didn't know that swearing and smoking were bad. She tried to think of whether she should say anything to the women, to make sure they understood she wasn't scared of them and didn't think they were bad guys, but soon the bus appeared at the bottom of the hill, and Jessa's heart started beating so hard she couldn't think. Focus on the plan, she reminded herself. If you were a ninja, you'd just do it!

The bus screeched and exhaled as it came to a stop. The women stood with what looked like great effort, hoisting themselves up. A ramp came down with a mechanical winding sound. Every sound suddenly seemed louder, and the ramp seemed so much higher. The bus driver looked right at her, and she wondered if he recognized her and was going to ask her why she wasn't in school. She wanted to chicken out. But Daisy squirmed in the backpack, reminding her why she had to be brave.

One step at a time, she boarded the bus. The old women behind her were talking - "Hey, sweetie, you left your bike here!" She looked out at the seats and the people in the seats, and Daisy let out a little muffled snore.

Before she could stop herself, she pulled out her tablet from her backpack's front pocket, dropped it onto the floor, and barreled down the ramp. She made sure to dodge the ladies climbing up, but they let out little yelps of surprise and called after her. Then she hopped onto her bike, kicked the kickstand up, and dashed far away.

Phase 1 was complete.

Saving Daisy

§

She felt better once she was on the bike trail, though she could hear the sounds of the road running parallel to it, she felt protected from the eyes of every driver in the neighborhood by the hills of overgrown dead grass and backyard fences. Daisy seemed to have settled down, but Jessa felt thrilled. They were finally on their way to San Francisco—to freedom.

Unlike the rest of California, ferrets were not illegal in San Francisco; that's what her neighbor Karen said. She'd be able to take Daisy out of the backpack once they were safe in the city and go for a real walk on the leash. Except she was blind now. She wouldn't be able to see anything. She could sniff, but maybe she wouldn't want to. She wasn't used to being blind. Daisy was scared. She didn't like to come out of her cage and sniff things very anymore, and when she did, she would just run around in circles frantically until Jessa picked her up. Then she'd try to hide in Jessa's hair.

Sorrow curdled in Jessa's stomach. She loved Daisy and always would, but she missed the way Daisy used to be. She remembered when she first met Daisy, when she was six, and when Dad's job said he couldn't work from home every day anymore, and they first moved to Brentwood from Washington, and met their new neighbor Karen was the first friend Jessa's mom made in California, and her ferrets, Daisy and Checkers, were the first friends Jessa made. Before she started school and met Lexi, they were her *only* friends. Jessa's mom would go over to Karen's house, and Jessa would tag along, and she'd play with Daisy and Checkers.

She'd loved them from the minute they met. Ferrets were kind of like ninjas. They could climb anything, they could jump, they were so fast and so sneaky, exactly like Jessa wished she could be. But they were friendly, too. Especially Daisy. Daisy used to climb up Jessa and sit on her shoulder. She'd liked being able to see from up high.

When Karen went on vacation, she hired Jessa to babysit the ferrets. She got ten dollars a day, which, after two weeks, was more money than she'd ever had in her life. She'd spent the money on a trip to the trampoline park with Lexi, the first human friend she met in first grade. They played ninjas all weekend, and Jessa bought them nachos to share. And that was before Lexi made friends with Payzlee Miller and started being mean. Before Checkers died. Before Harman was born.

Everything was better back then.

The *only* good thing about now was that Daisy was now Jessa's, not Karen's, and she got to see her every single day. A few weeks after Checkers died, Karen came to her and said, "I talked to your mom... Daisy has been all alone, and I can't play with her as much as she would probably like. I know you took great care of her, and I think she'd be happier with you."

But still, Jessa wished that it could have happened without Checkers dying. She knew Daisy still missed her.

§

When they got to Darby Park, Jessa locked her bike to a tree and went into the bathroom to change. Eight rolls of toilet paper were stacked on top of an empty toilet paper dispenser. Sink clogged with sand. A mom in the handicap stall, talking to a toddler in Spanish. Jessa took the smaller stall and carefully hung her backpack on the hook. She'd hoped she could let Daisy out for a second; Daisy wouldn't go far. But she couldn't risk it if the other stall was occupied. The mom or the toddler might step on her if Daisy went under the stall. They might think she was a rat. Payzlee Miller said Daisy looked like a rat. Or maybe they'd know Daisy was a ferret and call the cops on them for being an illegal animal.

"Sorry, girl," Jessa whispered to Daisy as she gently retrieved her ninja hoodie, which Daisy had been sleeping on.

Daisy lifted her head and sniffed the air as Jessa slipped it on. Next, she took off her tennis shoes. Gross - water from the wet floor seeped through her socks. Hopefully, it was just water. She tried to avoid letting her khakis touch the floor as she pulled them off, but the ankles were wet when she pulled them up. At least Daisy wouldn't mind. She loved stinky, gross things. She was always trying to climb into the trash bag when Jessa emptied the litter box.

She stepped on her shoes to avoid touching the gross floor with her bare feet as she put her black leggings on, but she lost her balance several times. If she were a ninja, she could've just pulled off all her clothes in one swipe, and her ninja uniform would have been on underneath it; that's how they changed their disguises in Ninja Friends. Last, she pulled her distinctive long hair into a bun - not the nice kind that her mom could make, but functional - and pulled the ski mask over her face. She gave Daisy another kiss on the nose before sitting on the toilet to put her shoes on, zipping up the backpack, and stepping out to look at herself in the mirror. There was basically nothing recognizable about her now. They'd never know it was her.

And now, finally, she was a ninja. Jessa had always wanted to be a ninja. She liked every TV show about ninjas: Ninjago, Naruto, and even American Ninja Warrior. But her favorite was Ninja Friends. Because it was about ninjas and friendship. Unlike Naruto and Ninjago, the characters never died, and it never got too sad.

§

It was starting to get hot. Even though it was still morning, or should be - she didn't have a watch, but she hadn't been biking that long. But when they got to San Francisco it would be chilly. San Francisco was always chilly.

The bike trail looked more or less the same for miles and miles, dead grass and dead grass, but now, there were shops instead of houses on the other side of the trail. She knew the shopping center she had to go by before she turned, it was the one with the Bed, Bath and Beyond, Target, Barnes and Noble, and A Street Beauty. She and Mom used to go there to get their nails painted once a month and then get lunch after, they called it a daughter-mom date.

And every report card, if Jessa got good comments from the teacher, her mom would let her pick out a book at Barnes and Noble. And then, when Mom got pregnant with Harman, they used to go to Bed, Bath and Beyond after their daughter-mom   dates to pick out stuff to go in his room. That was kind of boring, but Mom let Jessa pick out some books to buy for Harman at Barnes and Noble, picture books she'd liked when she was a kid, so she could be the one to introduce them to Harman, and that was kind of fun. But then, after Harman was born, Mom needed to recover so that they couldn't do a   date, and now she was recovered, but she was busy all the time and never got enough sleep, and they hadn't done a daughter-mom date in *forever*.

Jessa also noticed a lot of homeless people camping around this part of the bike trail. Tents lined the canal, and parts of bikes were strewn about all over the place. Someone had a bunch of clothes strung up on a clothesline. One man seemed to be cooking something by a fire, but Jessa had no sooner noticed him than she noticed a police car drive *onto the trail* in front of her and tell him over the megaphone to put the fire out because there was a no-burn order. Jessa felt bad for him, then she realized she should feel bad for herself. *She* was homeless now, too. She knew she was probably safe in her ninja outfit, but she kept her head low as she biked past the police car, just in case.

She was pretty sure she knew the way to the BART station. She and her mom had biked there to visit her dad last summer, back when everything was better, when Lexi and her were still best friends and Checkers was alive and Mom hadn't even been pregnant with Harman. The Ninja Friends movie had just come out in theaters, and she and Lexi had already gone to see it at the midnight premiere, and they'd gotten the souvenir popcorn bin, which she now kept her throwing stars in, and they'd refilled it with popcorn over and over. (That was also before Lexi started saying Jessa was fat and shouldn't eat carbs.) Jessa and her mom had ridden the bikes all the way to the BART station, locked their bikes there, and taken BART to Jessa's dad's office in San Francisco. They saw his office and met his coworkers. Then he took the rest of the day off and said they were going to go to a history museum.

They stopped at Pier 39 to see the sea lions, got clam chowder for lunch, then took the cable car to the history museum. But it turned out, the history museum had a special exhibit all about ninjas! Her parents knew that, but didn't tell her, because it was a surprise. There was even a little class where Jessa got to learn all about the weapons ninjas used, and how to use them. And at the gift shop, she got to buy her very own throwing stars. She'd had to leave them at home, though.

She only had room in her backpack for Daisy, her ninja costume, and her wallet with her clipper card and birthday money. And of course, she'd sacrificed her tablet to complete Phase 1 of the plan. She felt a little pang in her heart when she thought about that, but she had to do it. Because when people ran away, they always tried to track their phones, and Jessa's tablet was kind of like a phone, even though she could only call her parents and 9-1-1 on it, and she needed them to look for her in the wrong direction. For Daisy. Because…if they found them…

Stopping at a crossroads, she unzipped the pack just a bit. Daisy wasn't completely asleep in there; her cloudy eyes were open. She looked at nothing, sad and confused. It was probably scary for Daisy to be so far from home when she couldn't even see. That's why she had to talk to her, she reminded herself. So, Daisy knew her buddy was there, and she wouldn't be so scared. "I'm sorry, Daisy," she said. "I had to do it. Mom and Dad were going to kill you."

She'd heard them whispering through the bedroom walls two nights ago. *"Think it might be time..."* *"How do we explain to Jessa...?"* *"She has no quality of life anymore. She can't run and play..."* *"We should tell Karen, too. She might want to be there."*

She'd needed a night to plan and another night to prepare. But she couldn't risk waiting any longer than that.

"They said they had to do it so you wouldn't suffer anymore," Jessa said. "But you can't kill someone just for being blind! ...I'm sorry I didn't tell you before. I didn't want to scare you." She knew Daisy couldn't actually understand what she was saying, but she still felt like she had to say it, just in case. "But I'll never let them do that to you, Daisy. I promise..."

§

The sun continued to rise, and Jessa felt hotter and hotter in her ninja uniform. She thought of the episode of Ninja Friends when the ninja squad had to find a bad guy who built a secret hideout in the desert, and they kept their ninja outfits on the entire episode. She didn't know how they managed that. Daisy stretched out to the best of her ability in the backpack. Jessa felt worried. Ferrets had to stay cool. It would be cool in San Francisco, and probably on the BART train, but they still had a ways to go before that.

Maybe it would be good to stop for a break?

At the next break in the trail, Jessa exited and turned into the shopping center nearby. She recognized this shopping center, but they didn't go to it often. Hopefully, that meant no one would recognize her. There was a Wendy's, a Burger King, and a McDonald's; Jessa chose McDonald's. She ordered a cheeseburger with a Barbie toy. The Barbie toy was for Daisy. Checkers used to LOVE the little Barbie toys; Karen had a bunch of them in her garage for her grandkids, and Checkers was always dragging them around by the hair and stashing them under the couch. Maybe it would remind Daisy of Checkers and make her happy. As she waited for her food, she filled her cup with suicide mix, which was usually a bad thing to talk about, but this time it only meant all the sodas mixed together, then she filled a little ketchup cup with water for Daisy.

The food costs $8.29. She'd brought $80.50 with her birthday money that she'd been saving up to buy a Nintendo Switch, which had the Ninja Friends: Return of the Oni game she always wanted. She looked wistfully at the money she had left, but reminded herself that this was for Daisy. And she'd make more money.

People in San Francisco made money by using their talents. There were dancers and musicians who just started dancing or playing music on the streets, and people who liked the show gave them money. Jessa couldn't dance, and she'd had to leave her drums behind since it was too hard to carry them and her backpack, but she could sing. She'd split her days between singing and practicing her ninja skills in the park, and when she became a better ninja, people would give her money to see her do parkour, too. It should be enough to buy a little food every day, and cat food for Daisy when the food she'd stuffed into the front backpack pocket runs out.

She knew it was against the rules, but she took her food into the play place to eat. She needed to let Daisy out, just for a minute. A few little kids were in the play area but were towards the bottom with their moms. Jessa climbed past them up to the orb that let you look back over where the parents were eating, pressed her back to it, and opened her backpack.

Daisy didn't want to wake up. She was completely passed out. Karen used to say that the ferrets were dead when they slept like that, but then, when Checkers died, it wasn't cute anymore. Jessa held Daisy in her arms and rubbed her finger up and down her soft nose, but Daisy didn't respond. Finally, she pulled out some Ferret-Vite and put it on her finger in front of Daisy's nose. Daisy's nose began to wiggle, then she yawned, stretched, and started licking.

Ferret-Vite was Daisy's favorite treat, and it was also healthy for them, like vitamins. Jessa made sure to bring the tube along so she could feed Daisy lots and lots so she would feel better soon.

When Daisy finally stopped licking Jessa's finger, she put some cat food in a pile next to her and put Daisy down next to it. Daisy sniffed but wasn't hungry. She began looking around with those blank eyes, then started running around in circles, stumbling and slipping on the plastic floor.

"I'm right here, Daisy," Jessa said. "Don't worry. You're right - it doesn't smell like home, does it?"

Daisy walked backwards a few steps and then pooped. She'd have to go back for a napkin. Jessa put the ketchup cup of water in front of her face, and she sniffed it and began lapping it up.

Daisy would need more water than that, though, she realized. She hadn't brought any with her. The suicide mix wouldn't be good for Daisy. After eating, she decided she would back down and fill her cup with water.

Daisy ran in circles for a few more minutes, finally laying back on the plastic and falling asleep on her side. Jessa savored her food and her drink. I have to go now, she told herself. I have to clean up Daisy's poop and refill my cup with water and get out of here. But it was so hot, and they were so tired, and maybe it would be better to stay hidden in the day and ride in the cover of night? When it was nice and cool and blended in?

She hadn't decided about staying when the echoes of clumsy but quick footfalls echoed through the tunnel and a little girl, older than Harman but still little, poked her head into the orb. "What's that?" she asked, looking right at Daisy. Jessa scooped her up and put her into the backpack, Daisy barely lifting her head.

Jessa tried to think of something quick. Lying was bad, but little kids were dumb, and people constantly lied to them.

"It's a rat!" the little girl declared.

She didn't sound upset about it, just excited. But it still made Jessa indignant enough to snap back, "No, she's not!"

Before the little girl could respond again, the whole room suddenly echoed with the sound of vibrating phones. Jessa and the little girl both looked around, and when Jessa looked out through the plastic window, she could see the moms sitting down at the table, also looking around and pulling out their phones to check.

Dread crawled up Jessa's spine. She knew that sound! It had happened before, everyone's phones going off at once, and Mom had told her it was because a little girl had been kidnapped and everyone was supposed to look for the kidnapper's car. What if this was because everyone was supposed to look for her? She quickly cleaned up Daisy's poop using the wrapper of her burger, refilled her cup with ice water, and bolted out the door.

§

It wasn't long before she had to stop again. The ice water melted fast, and she was sweating like crazy in her ninja costume. It stuck to her skin like the juice from a fruit cup. At a 7/11, she'd bought ice cream for herself and packages of frozen mangoes. She'd put one package under her hoodie and one in the backpack to keep Daisy cool. When they lost their coolness, she could eat them. Hopefully, by then, they'd be safely in San Francisco.

The bike trails were weirdly empty. Whenever they passed by a park, she noticed that it would be mostly empty, too. Only a few homeless people were there, sleeping in shady areas. And she could see the heat waves rising off the ground before her.

The ride was longer than she remembered. She didn't recognize where she was anymore. But she was pretty sure she remembered the way, back from that day she rode with her mom; they'd just gone straight until they passed by the shopping center. Most of the shopping center was hidden by hills, and the trail was behind it, but she remembered noticing the Bed, Bath, and Beyond, because it was tall and had a sign on the back. When they saw it, they crossed the street and turned left. She hadn't passed the Bed, Bath, and Beyond yet, so she was supposed to still keep going straight.

But as she went on and on, she wondered more and more if she was lost. The trail now ran   along a busy street, no more parks or shopping centers or hills. And she wasn't feeling good. The heat was getting to her. She felt like she could barely breathe, and the air was heavy. She hoped Daisy was okay in the backpack. She peeked inside at her - she was still asleep. Maybe it would be better if she left the backpack open, so she could feel some breeze?

When she stopped to unzip the backpack, a wave of blackness washed over her eyes. She really wasn't feeling good. She stumbled a few feet over to a signpost and the measly shade it provided and knelt down on the ground below it with her head between her knees. She peeked in at Daisy after a few seconds - still asleep. Jessa was glad she gave her the mango packet.

She just was going to rest a few minutes, she told herself. Then she'd have to keep going.

But footsteps approached, and she looked up to see a man walking towards her. She lifted her eyes just enough to make sure he didn't steal her bike, which was standing up in front of her. But when his shadow fell over her and he just went still, she lifted her head.

"You okay, little girl?"

He wasn't supposed to know she was a young girl; that's what the ninja costume was for. But she didn't ask him how he could tell. Instead, she just said, "I'm fine. Do you know where Bed Bath and Beyond is?"

"Bed, Bath, and Beyond?" He paused. "Didn't it go out of business?"

Jessa couldn't help it; she burst into tears. She'd never find it now.

"Hey-hey-hey now," said the man in a voice that was probably supposed to sound nice but just sounded baffled. "Are you all alone out here?"

"No," said Jessa, but didn't explain she was with Daisy. When she finally got a hold of herself, she sobbed, "Do you know how to get to BART?"

"Well-yes-yes..." the man said and pointed. "You cross over there and go left, then straight, and you'll see it... But... are you okay out here? Do you need me to call anyone for you? There's a heat advisory; I just got a text to seek shelter. It's gonna be a hundred and eight."

She almost wanted to say yes. She didn't want to cross over there and keep biking for who knew how long; she just wanted to go home and drink water and watch Ninja Friends - but how could she? How could she go on without Daisy? How could she explain any of this to Mom and Dad?

So, she just said, "No. Thanks." Stood up, ignored the wave of dizziness that washed over her. And got back on her bike.

§

There was no bike trail on this side of the road, only street and sidewalk. She was allowed to ride on the sidewalk because she was a kid. But she didn't want anyone to know she was a kid. So, she rode in the bike line and tried not to be scared as the cars whizzed by. It was uphill and took all her effort to stay on the bike. At least the cars made a nice breeze, she thought, and she unzipped the backpack just a little bit so Daisy could feel the breeze too.

She wasn't worried when the cop car slowed down next to her, but she nearly jumped off her bike when they spoke to her on the loudspeaker. "Hey, excuse me, can we talk to you for a second?"

No, no, no, Jessa thought. She didn't slow down; the cop car matched her pace. "What?" she asked.

"We got a report about a little girl all alone, is everything okay?"

"Yes!" she called out and kept peddling.

The car pulled out in front of her, blocking her path. She squeezed her brakes and put her feet on the ground. The cop opened the door and poked her head out. "Where you headed?"

"BART," said Jessa.

"What for?"

"To visit my dad at his job," she said, "and go to the museum. And see the sea lions."

"That so?" The cop stepped out. "You know, we heard about a little girl who never showed up at school today, and she had a Ninja Friends backpack like yours. Are you Jessa Singh?"

"No," she said, "My name is Daisy! I hope you find the missing girl!" She jumped onto her backpack and swerved onto the sidewalk, going the opposite way, down the hill, with the cars now going towards her. The cops put on their lights and made a U-turn to chase her. She had to go. Back to the bike trail, somewhere that they wouldn't be able to chase her; if they caught her, they'd put her in handcuffs and then they'd find -

"Daisy!" Jessa shrieked as the ferret went tumbling out of the backpack. She couldn't catch her or break fast enough, and Daisy was on the ground. Jessa jumped off her bike, letting it fall on its side, and ran back. The cops would see her. And Daisy couldn't see Jessa, the road, or the cars she was heading right for.

Or the car that was heading straight for her.

"No!" the shriek erupted from her, and she drove onto the street like a football player, landing on her face on top of Daisy, shielding her with her body. The car slammed on its brakes and stopped just in time.

A horn. A scream. The sirens. The cops shouting stuff through the loudspeaker. And Daisy, wriggling in her hands.

"Don't scare me like that again, Daisy," Jessa said. And then she burst into sobs.

Still squirming, Daisy found Jessa's chin and licked it. *I'm still here,* she seemed to be saying. *Your best friend is still here. You saved me!*

And for a moment, just a moment, Jessa felt like a true ninja.

Did you know that ferrets are ONLY illegal in California due to being mistakenly placed on a list of wild animals that cannot be brought into the state?

Ferrets have ACTUALLY been domesticated for thousands of years.

*If you'd like to know more about the fight for ferret legalization,
go to legalizeferrets.org.*

And to support an organization that goes above and beyond to help the ferrets that are already here (including transporting seized ferrets out of state so they won't be euthanized) you can donate to West Coast Ferrets.

I AM A
BUTTON

A SHORT STORY BY
BENJAMEENA KING

CONTENT WARNINGS

This story contains themes that may be distressing to some readers, including:

Gender dysphoria

Bigotry

This is for my partner,
whom this story would not exist without.

I Am A Button

I am a button.

A big, round, red button sitting atop a slim white pedestal. What do I do? Well, I help people be happy with themselves... usually.

Though my surface is shiny and free of smudges, I haven't been pressed since yesterday because the mall was closed. But now...

Lights begin to flicker on the stores surrounding me. The doors of the one next to my alcove slide open, allowing quiet rock music to filter out. The windows are filled with mannequins wearing a variety of punky clothes. They're mostly black, studded with metal spikes, but there are also streaks of color here and there. Neon pink, green, dark red...

After a few minutes, a broadly built security guard in a drab grey uniform wanders by. He stares straight ahead with unfocused, tired eyes. He's not the same one who was here yesterday, but I've seen him before. And he always looks unhappy. Maybe if he pressed me, he wouldn't be so glum.

I am a button.

In the distance, I can see the shapes of people starting to meander around the mall. Finally! I'm so ready to be pressed!

A man strides past my alcove, not even glancing at me. Darn. But look! A woman is walking right toward me, and I recognize her! She's slim with short brown hair, wearing tan cargo pants and a somewhat baggy tank top. Her eyes are glued to the phone screen in her hands until she stops before me. She looks up and slips the phone into one of her pockets.

"Hmm..." She hums in thought, observing the hollow inside of the shiny white device that fills most of my alcove. "What do I feel like today...?"

It's large enough for any size or shape of person to stand inside. The interior surface is dark grey metal. Seams run along the human-shaped curves, broken up by recessed round pads. The look of it is almost reminiscent of an iron maiden, sans the spikes, of course. It's my counterpart in our grand purpose. Neither of us could function without the other.

163

The woman pulls out a plastic card before swiping it over the small patch of dark glass on my podium. Electricity surges into me, igniting the light deep in my internals to make me glow bright red. What an exhilarating feeling! But it's nothing compared to what comes next.

She raises her hand to lay atop me. The warm, softness of her palm is like an old friend. Then she pushes me down with practiced firmness.

Bing!

Power vibrates through the device in my alcove. The round pads on the inside light up a soft blue. Without hesitation, the woman steps into the device and turns around. It closes shut around her, encasing her entirely. Mechanical whirs and buzzes sound from within, slightly muffled.

It goes on like this for almost a minute. With every passing second, my anticipation mounts. My light extinguishes as the vibrations of the device cease. There's a low hiss as it slowly reopens. Steam billows out, briefly obscuring the inside.

The woman steps out, only she's not a woman any longer. He's taller, more muscular, and his facial features are more chiseled. His clothes are more form-fitting, stretched slightly over his build. The man smiles as he reaches up to rub the little bit of stubble that's grown on his chin.

"Perfect." He says to himself before striding off confidently.

Ohhhh, that's the stuff. That moment when they come out gives me such hope, I must almost feel as alive as they do.

I am a button.

More people filter by, most of them just going about their business. Mornings at the mall are usually quiet, so my eagerness rises whenever someone nears. It's hard to wait, but eventually my patience pays off, and two new people come close.

One is a young woman with long purple hair hanging past her shoulders. She wears a white t-shirt with a band logo and tight high-waist jeans. The other person is... possibly a man? I can't tell exactly. His features are somewhat broad, thicker than the woman's, but his face is smooth shaven and his blond hair hangs past his chin, longer than I see most men wear. As a button, I have no need for fashion. Still, from what I have observed, the person's outfit, an orange skirt over white leggings and a tight-fitting tie-dye tank top, makes me believe that there's more to their identity.

"Y-You sure you're okay with this, Sarah?" They ask, the trepidation obvious in their voice.

"Hon, it doesn't matter what I want for your body." She says and loops an arm around their waist. "Will this still make you happy?"

"I... I think so."

"Then go for it." Sarah smiles wide at them. "If you're happy, then I'm happy."

She stands on her toes to press a quick peck to his cheek.

"You've got this, Alex. I believe in you."

"Yeah, you're right." They smile, seeming more assured now, and gaze at me. "Wish me luck..."

"Good luck!" She cheers, even clapping a little as they move up to me and pull out a card.

Ooooooh here we go! Swipe me! Press me!

With a pass of their card over my reader, I light up, readier than ever. They bop me enthusiastically, opening the device. Stepping inside, Sarah gives them a double thumbs up as it closes.

Thrumming with energy and light, the device does its work before splitting in half and belching steam. When they emerge, my suspicions are confirmed. The strong features of their body are not gone but seemingly smoothed over. A feminine delicateness to their face is merged with the handsomeness of their previous self.

They run their hands down their sides, a grin slowly spreading over their lips.

"AHHH!" Sarah shrieks happily before throwing her arms around their neck. "You look adorable!"

"Y-Yeah?" Alex says nervously, "Do I look like a girl?"

"Not quite!"

"Do I look like a guy?"

"Noooope!"

"Haha!" They laugh without restraint, beaming as they grab Sarah around the waist and twirl her around. Leaning close, Alex and Sarah kiss passionately. "Thank you, love."

"For what?"

They clasp hands before wandering off.

"For encouraging me to be... well, *me.*"

Maybe it's the residual charge of electricity in my metal and plastic body, but I feel so... warm.

I am a button.

"Grandma, look!"

A small child wearing overalls with short, scruffy blond hair runs up. His wide blue eyes practically sparkle as he looks to the chamber and then at me. He reaches up, his small hand splayed wide.

"Jeffery, no!"

An older woman in a drab brown blouse and long off-pink skirt grabs his arm. Her thick glasses magnify the deep wrinkles around her narrowed eyes.

"You stay away from that monstrous machine!" She snarls before dragging him away.

Monstrous…?

"But grandma!" He whines sadly, still looking right at me as they leave. "I wanna be a girl…"

"Feh!" The woman spits, "Only degenerates would do such a thing! God made you exactly how you are."

"But why-"

"Quiet! No more talking or you're gonna get it!"

The fearful whimper the child makes off in the distance is heartbreaking, even to someone like me who has no heart. None of the humans who witnessed the scene said anything. They merely watch the grandmother and granddaughter for a moment before going about their business.

How… how could she say such things? And to a child?

People always leave my alcove in such good spirits, as if they've discovered a well of joy that was hidden deep within them. I don't know anything about God. It's always been something about humans I've never understood. But if their God did make them, why was their being happy not part of such a creation? And how could such dissonance really be worth threatening a curious child?

It just didn't make any sense.

I am a button.

The blinding brilliance of the sun steadily makes its way down from the heights of the blue sky, visible through the glass roof of the mall. Shadows cast by couches and stands placed in the middle of the walkways shrink and expand with their movement. It's been a slow day. I can only hope the afternoon will pick up. Being stuck here, ignored, is an agonizing experience at best.

I Am A Button

A couple slows as they pass me. They appear middle-aged for humans, holding each other's hands comfortably. The woman tugs the man to a stop, her curious gaze on me.

"Something the matter?" He asks.

"I didn't know the mall had this."

"Mm?" The man finally looks at me and nods. "Ah, yes. It's good they have it here for people with gender dysphoria. Very progressive."

"It must be nice... Greg?" She looks at him keenly. "Would you still love me if I were a man?"

Greg's eyes go wide, his brow furrowing. He opens his mouth, then quickly closes it. Her eyes narrow. Letting go of his hand, she folds her arms over her chest and cocks her hip.

"I asked if you would still love me. I'm waiting."

"W-Well, I... uh..."

"Seriously?" She scoffs in disgust. "You can't even give me an answer. Fine."

Turning on her heel, the woman stalks off.

"Gloria, wait!" He pleads and runs after her. "I can explain!"

Huh. That was a new one. Human relationships sure are strange. Not like me and my counterpart. It's always there for me, stalwart and faithful. I treasure it, even though we can't talk... or hold each other... or...

I am a button.

"I'm going to press it."

A young teenage boy wearing all black, chain-draped clothes with a mohawk, strides up to me. An older woman in casual jeans and a flowy blouse catches him by the shoulder before he can touch me.

"Rowan, wait! Maybe you should think about this some more."

"Mom, please." He says, shrugging her off. "I've been thinking about this for years. You said I could change when I got a job and made my own money."

Rowan pulled a card out of his pocket.

"Now I do, and I'm not wasting another day of my life in this body."

His mother looks frantically back and forth between him and me.

"But... how can you be so sure this is what you want?"

"Because I feel wrong!" He growls in frustration. "Every day I wake up and see myself in the mirror, I wish I were a girl. I shower with my eyes closed because one look at my body hurts deep in my chest!"

"Are… are you really that unhappy with our life together?" She asks, tears gathering in her eyes. Sighing, Rowan shakes her head.

"It's not about our life. This is my life. Why don't you try it? Maybe then you'll understand how I feel."

"Me?" Her mother looks taken aback, blinking multiple times before turning toward my alcove. "I don't know…"

"Why not? You can always change back. Hell, I'll even pay for it."

"No!" She blurts out, "No. I won't let you do that."

Digging around in her purse, her mother takes out her own card. I light up when she swipes it over my reader.

"If I can't talk you out of this, it's my job to make sure it's safe."

"Heh, then be my guest…"

"How does it work?"

"Just imagine yourself as a guy when you get in. The machine does the rest."

"If you say so…"

Delight fills me as she presses me and gets inside the device. This is incredible! I hardly ever get two people at once wanting to use me.

When she exits, the mother looks at her new body with uncertainty.

"This is… strange." She says with a deeper voice. Rowan smirks knowingly.

"Great. Now, while you're wrestling with this existential new experience, I'm getting in. Shoo."

"Yeah…"

As her daughter begins the process, the mother has only eyes for herself. She runs her fingers down her thicker arms. She cups her chin, feeling the wider bones and beginnings of a beard. The whole time, her eyes express a fresh, unknown wonder at her new existence.

Exiting the device, Rowan whoops with excitement as she too beholds herself.

"Well, mom?" She says and strikes a flamboyant pose. "How do I look?"

Startled from her reverie, her mother gives her a small smile.

"Honestly, you look really cute."

"Yes!" She squeals, dancing on her feet. "God, that feels good to hear. So… ready to change back now?"

"Um, actually…" Her mother averts her gaze, twiddling her fingers. "I thought I might try it out a bit longer."

Rowan gapes at her.

"Wait... really?"

"Yes. I haven't quite figured out how I feel about it yet. Come on, let's go home. I have to get started on dinner."

Rowan's surprised expression quickly morphs into one of amusement.

"Alright. Dad's face when he sees you is gonna be priceless."

I watch them go. This one is going to stick with me for a good long while. If only more people were brave enough to be themselves and try new things, maybe humans would be happier.

I am a button.

"Hey, look at that!"

A group of teenage girls in track uniforms approach.

"Isn't this one of those gender changers?"

"What? Ew." A girl says as she makes a disgusted face. "Why would you do something so unnatural?"

"Michelle, you should try it." One girl pushes another forward with a derisive giggle. "You already look like a man, why not go all the way?"

"Shut up, Claire!" Michelle snarls and pushes her back. "You don't have to be such a bitch all the time!

"Hey, watch the names!" Snaps Claire. "I was only joking, you know that."

"Whatever."

"C'mon everybody, let's get something to eat."

My mood sinks when they all turn to walk away. However, one girl stops and looks back at me. She was the only girl who'd said nothing the entire time they were here. No makeup adorns her face. Her black hair is cut short and spiky.

Her light blue eyes are crinkled around the edges, her eyebrows sinking low. She stares with such focus, like she can't avert her gaze.

I might not have a heart or soul like humans believe they have, but even I can tell she's in pain. Every little detail of her tightly wound body language wails without a voice to express her innermost feelings. The sheer, desperate need in her facial expression says everything she does not. Or... cannot.

"Dana, we're leaving!"

She spins on her heel before running after the other girls. As she moves, something tiny and glimmering falls from her eye. It shines with the sun's light all the way to the dirty tiled floor. No audible sound is made when it splatters.

How... sad.

I am a button.

The number of people in the mall thins as the deep orange light shining through the roof windows turns purple before dying in darkness.

Someone shuffles up to me. They wear a pink hoodie that is faded and tattered by age. Their simple grey leggings are worn down at the knees. Reaching up, they pull the hood back off their head. His features are masculine, though he only has the barest hint of stubble on his chin. Shoulder-length ginger hair hangs around his face, seeming slightly greasy from not having been washed.

Dark green eyes focus on me, and his mouth presses together in a thin line. He releases an unsteady breath before reaching into his hoodie pocket.

"Here we go..." He says, pulling out a card. His hand is shaking. "C'mon, you can do this."

When the card swipes over my reader, I burst with light. His wide hand presses me down gentler than anyone else has today. The device opens, and he steps up to it. Closing his eyes, he draws in a long breath before getting in.

The doors snap shut before the process begins yet again. Once it's finished, it opens, allowing him to exit in the cloud of steam.

This time, he's just a little shorter, slenderer beneath his ratty clothes. He reaches up to touch the slight bumps on his chest. He sucks in a sharp breath, his eyes widening as they shimmer at the corners. Next, he touches his face, caressing the smooth lines and hairless chin.

A sob escapes her as she squeezes her eyes shut. Tears fall down her cheeks. She wraps her arms around her chest, quaking on her feet.

"F-Finally..." She says beneath her breath with a higher-pitched voice. A broad grin stretches across her plump lips. When her eyes open again, there's a confidence in their sharp gaze that wasn't there before. "Now... I'm ready."

Clenching her fists at her sides, the woman walks away with a determined purpose.

...

I Am A Button

I am a button.

There are no clocks where I can see them, but it's been a bit since I've seen anyone. Unfortunately, that can only mean one thing. Closing time.

Lights within the stores begin to flicker off one by one. A woman in a black and green punk outfit briefly comes to the front of her store to pull down the gate over the entrance. The lock snapping onto the floor joins the chorus of others as employees close up for the day.

I'm going to miss the people terribly. Being here all alone for so long is torture for one such as myself. I can neither move nor speak. Such is my lot.

The squeaks of unoiled wheels reach me before I see someone coming. A wrinkly old man in a grey-blue jumpsuit drags a large cart packed with cleaning supplies. He stops in front of me.

"Okay now..." He mutters before getting a rag and a white spray bottle from the cart.

The cold, foamy liquid sprays over me, blurring my surroundings. Then the soft rag wipes it away beneath his firm fingers. When he pulls it away, I'm shining and clean of smudges like the day I was installed. It's refreshing, if a temporary measure.

The janitor replaces the bottle and rag before walking off, tugging his cart along behind him. A broken, jaunty whistle carries from him as he leaves, bouncing off the high walls of the mall.

Quiet settles over everything I know. It's almost suffocating as it closes in around me, louder than the crowds on a Saturday afternoon. My limitations scream like unhappy children being dragged out of the toy store.

What I wouldn't give to experience the vibrance of the humans' existence. The joy, the sadness, the struggle... All of which is beyond my understanding. If only I could step into the device and change into something that could bring me such euphoria.

But I am just a button.

End

SHADOWS OF THE MOUNTAIN

A SHORT STORY BY
GLEN WEATHERHEAD

CONTENT WARNINGS

This story contains themes that may be distressing to some readers, including:

Intense and graphic fantasy violence

Horror elements

Child abduction

Grief and loss

Death

Emotional and psychological distress

For my son.

Shadows of the Mountain

"Look out!"

The blade from a scythe flew through the air. Ko-Rel raised his forearm, blocking the flying blade. It bounced off his arm and fell to the ground with a thud. A bead of blood formed where the blade had struck him.

"Ko-Rel, are you alright?" a voice shouted nearby.

Inspecting his arm, Ko-Rel replied, "I am. Barely a scratch."

One of the villagers pushed his way through the tall crops towards him, eyes wide.

"I thought I would have killed you," he said.

Ko-Rel tore a piece off his tunic and wrapped it around his forearm, covering the small cut.

"Had that been another person, it could have done great damage. You should see about securing your blade better before continuing again."

Still somewhat shocked, the villager nodded silently and returned his broken tool to the village.

Even after all this time, the people here still had moments of shock at what seemed unnatural. Between the toughness of his skin and his raw physical strength, Ko-Rel stood out in contrast to the locals here.

He took the chains from a nearby cart laden down with the harvest and pulled it behind him, following after the villager. The cart's wooden wheels bounced over the path's uneven dirt as he hauled it along.

It had been four years since he moved here with his family. At the time, it seemed like a good idea to venture towards one of the outer towns closer to the ocean port. But on their way, Ko-Rel's wife came down with a debilitating sickness.

Why didn't we stay in the city? Maybe she wouldn't have died in some foreign village, Ko-Rel thought.

He gripped the chain tighter, hearing it creak under his grip and felt the metal pushing into his palms. One foot in front of the other, Ko-Rel dragged the cart back to the village.

As he approached, he saw a group of villagers securing their belongings to carts and preparing to leave. Word was, a large fleet of ships was departing for another land across the ocean. At one time, Ko-Rel would have considered joining them, but with his young son being his only surviving family member, he couldn't risk it. Even though he still got the occasional odd glance, thanks to his large size and strength, Ko-Rel had found a semblance of peace here.

The villagers need me. Who knows when they'll be able to afford another horse or mule since the last ones went missing?

Ko-Rel told himself that he might consider moving on once the village replaced their beasts of burden, but he found it nice to be of some use to the villagers.

The people in the caravan said passing goodbyes as they began their journey. Ko-Rel watched them go. One by one, they slowly disappeared into the fields that lay to the northwest.

"Father, why don't we go with them?" A small voice sounded behind him.

Turning, Ko-Rel saw his young son, Dynaen, standing with his hands on his hips. Only six years of age, Ko-Rel could sense the determination in his son's eyes.

"Son, you and I have spoken on this many times."

"And why don't you do what I want? Most of the other children have gone with the caravans."

Ko-Rel stood silently and looked at where the caravan had gone, imagining what lay beyond.

"We are here for a time. When the light of the star pulls us on, we will follow its call. But for now, this is where we are."

"You don't think of what *I* need!" Dynaen shouted and ran towards their home.

Ko-Rel wanted to call out to him and apologize, but he found the words stuck in his throat. He reached his hand out for a moment, then lowered again to his side, standing in the quiet of the waning day.

"You best keep your eyes on that one," one of the villagers said from a nearby hut.

"That I do, as often as I can spare them."

"I pray that is enough. You know, not all of the children have gone to the ships, some are… taken."

A chill passed over Ko-Rel, "Be quiet, Ansel. You spread your *stories* to what gain?"

"You may be able to dismiss me for now and pray it does not strike your home and you see *them*."

The hair raised on his skin, but Ko-Rel tried to shake the feeling. It was true that people and animals had gone missing from the village. Most assumed they had left with one of the caravans.

"Go speak your empty words to someone else. I have real work to do."

"Aye, I'm moving on. But when you see their vacant eyes and hear their echoing screams, you'll wish you had listened to me."

Ko-Rel watched Ansel disappear around the side of the hut, slinking away. Shaking his head, Ko-Rel cleared the chilling thoughts and returned to his task.

After a few hours, Ko-Rel finished his task, and the last crops had been brought from the field. He pulled the cart to its resting place a short way from the village.

Walking along the path, Ko-Rel looked down in the dwindling light at his calloused hands and sighed. He didn't know how to talk to his son, ever since his wife had died. His son was too young to understand the loss. Ko-Rel felt like every time he went to speak, the words would get mixed in his head. Other times, he would overreact to some small thing his son had done.

Clenching his hands into fists, Ko-Rel resolved to speak plainly and apologize to his son. Maybe it was finally time for them to leave. The villagers would find a way to harvest without him.

A heavy weight grew in Ko-Rel's heart, feeling the darkening sky push in on him. The moment of clarity from making his decision to move on had passed, and in its place, he felt an icy grip close around his heart. His steps slowed autonomically, and he felt an urge to flee.

What is this feeling?

His body urged him to keep his eyes downcast, but he pushed past that feeling and looked up the path ahead. Nothing seemed out of the ordinary, yet his heart was pumping faster now than a moment ago. His eyes searched for a reason.

After a moment, he fixed his gaze on a darkness blacker than the night around it. Ko-Rel's body froze, his eyes open wide and breath held.

A few meters ahead at a bend in the path, he saw the shape of a dark, shadowy being. It was hunched over with a head twisted at an unnatural angle. But it was the thing's eyes that caused ice to pour over his insides. He felt the blood drain from his face.

179

Two small orbs on the being's face looked directly at him. Somehow they were darker than the night and yet shone with a glassy look. Pure black, no pupils.

A maw appeared on the creature's face as it twisted its head in a stuttered motion, opening its mouth towards Ko-Rel. It croaked and moaned a deep guttural vocalization, sounding like something was blocking its throat.

With a jolt, it stretched its arms outwards. The being jutted its head forward and let loose a terrible scream. Overlapping screams, sounding like several different voices, echoed out of the dark being. Its long, pointed fingers stretched to their full extent towards Ko-Rel.

He couldn't move. His mind screamed at him to run, but he found his feet weighed like boulders, holding him in place.

The being took a step towards Ko-Rel, its head twitching as it weaved its arms forward.

A scream in the distance snapped the beings head sideways.

That voice... I know it, Ko-Rel thought. He tried to shake off this frozen state.

Suddenly, his mind snapped to full awareness. That voice was his son's! A prickling sensation travelled the surface of his body as blood flowed back to his extremities.

The being before him snapped its gaze back to Ko-Rel, letting out another layered scream. It folded back onto all fours and sped off into the darkness.

Move... move... move!

Shaking with effort, Ko-Rel shifted his weight forward, breaking the icy trance. It felt like moving through a thick bog, and every few moments he heard that eerie shriek pierce the night.

A growing sense of anger rose in Ko-Rel as he used the heat to fight off the feeling of ice holding him still. Pushing, stepping, clawing his way through the black of the night. Ko-Rel growled, channeling his anger into each step to push past this invisible barrier that pressed in on him. His trudging turned to trotting, and the air around him didn't feel as heavy. The dark pressure he felt withdrew before him.

He knew this path well, a hundred steps to his home. Fifty. Twenty. At ten, he saw what he had feared this whole time. The door to his hut was open, and the lights were out. A slight breeze brought a chill over his mind. Ko-Rel forced himself forward once again, rushing into the small home. Pausing in the doorway, he took in the sight of disarray—Belongings strewn about, scratches on the floor, and drag marks along the ground out past the door... leading into the forest towards the mountain.

Another of the creature's screams pierced the night, but Ko-Rel's rage filled his senses and dulled the fear that threatened to overwhelm him.

With powerful strides he ran into the thick of the forest, ignoring the many branches that swatted at him as he raced forward. Ahead, he could hear sounds of a struggle. In the dim light of the moon, he saw a creature dragging his son, kicking and screaming.

"Dynaen!" Ko-Rel shouted.

The creature turned, and Ko-Rel realized this was not the same small creature as before. This one was much taller, and its eyes glowed an icy cold blue.

"Father!"

"I'm coming!"

Leaves rustled to his left and out burst the smaller creature. It slammed into Ko-Rel, catching him midstride. The force of the impact threw Ko-Rel crashing to the side, tumbling through a knot of branches. He flew through the darkness until he felt a sudden thunk, as his head connected with a large stone. The world faded, but those two icy blue eyes stayed with his dwindling consciousness. The creature turned away, dragging his son further into the darkness of the forest.

§

I can hear Dynaen...

He must be having another nightmare...

I'm here. You are safe, my son...

He shudders in my embrace...

I feel tears dripping from his eyes onto my forearm...

My son...

A pull, and I feel him draw away from me...

I tighten my grip, but his tears now form like rivers around his body and he is swept away...

Dynaen!..

I stumble forward, slow steps like walking through thick mud...

A scream echoes before me...

I know that sound...

Dark eyes peer at me from the end of the river…

The creature looms, pulling the river towards itself and speeding my son towards it…

No!..

My anger rises, but the harder I try, the slower I move…

Dynaen!..

The creature bends low and opens a black, toothy maw to swallow up my son…

Nooooo!...

Ko-Rel's eyes shot open, "Dynaen!"

A rush of pain brought his hand to his head. Feeling something wet, he pulled his hand away and saw blood. The sun was coming up now; the night was over.

"I must go after him," Ko-Rel said, but the fear of the sights and sounds lingered.

What if there were more? He thought as he remembered the force of the impact from the smaller creature. A pack of those creatures could do him damage.

I'll get the others. Together we can take them!

Ko-Rel pulled on a nearby tree branch and struggled to his feet. It took him a moment to catch his balance. Pain washed over him as he stumbled forward, shaking his head to clear the fog in his mind. He came into a clearing and walked unbalanced towards the village.

"Goodness, are you alright?" one of the villagers said.

They helped Ko-Rel sit on a bench and took a look at his head wound.

"Don't waste your time on me, there isn't time!" Ko-Rel said, swatting the villager's hand away.

"Ko-Rel, you're bleeding. I'm sure whatever it is can wait," the villager said, returning to cleaning the wound.

"Where is the village elder? I need to speak with him immediately," Ko-Rel said.

"It's your luck, he is passing this way now," the villager said, waving to the village elder while holding a bandage on Ko-Rel's head.

"What is all this then?" the village elder said as he approached.

"Elder, we need to gather a search party immediately," Ko-Rel said.

"Oh? What is the matter?"

"The creatures took my son!" Ko-Rel shouted.

He didn't mean to shout, but the nonchalant conversation irritated him. There wasn't any time to spare. He didn't even know if his son was still alive.

"Creatures? Oh, you have been talking with Ansel. That man cannot help himself from spreading these wild tales," the elder said, shaking his head.

"He speaks true! I saw them with my own eyes. Dark creatures, they were. Darker than the night, and their scream…" A chill ran over Ko-Rel as he heard the scream in his mind.

"Come now, I'm sure your son is nearby and playing with one of the other children. We will look for him."

"You don't understand, the creatures… They took him! I tried to stop them, but I was taken by surprise and got this," Ko-Rel said, hand to his head.

"I'm sure it may have seemed so, the night can play tricks on us. And there's this head injury of yours, who knows what images could have been scrambled within from such a blow," the elder said.

"There! Ansel is nearby. He can confirm what I saw is true."

"Ansel, come here and speak with us. Share your… stories and then let us search for Ko-Rel's son."

"Aye, elder. The shadows of the mountain took your son? I told you to keep both eyes on him."

Ko-Rel's fist clenched tight. He couldn't afford to fight with the man now; he needed the people to hear his case. A small group of villagers gathered around to listen.

"It began many hundreds of years ago. Men and elves. Dabbling in dark arts, they didn't understand. And in doing so, they brought about a deep darkness. It grows now," he said, pointing to the mountain, "in the peaks of this mountain. But it isn't strong enough yet, it needs more… body."

The crowd listened silently, eyes wide at the story.

"And how, Ansel, do you come to know these things?" the elder said, unfazed.

"I hear them, whispering in the dark. They cannot help but put forth their dark desires."

"And when you had 'foretold' of a coming storm not three moons ago, did it come to pass?"

"I said the time was unclear, but whispers have been growing in their veracity. The storm is coming!" Ansel said with a crazed look in his eye.

"Ansel, your stories are better suited around the campfire to scare children. Now is not the time for such foolishness," the elder said and shook his head.

One of the children snuck up behind Ansel and whispered, "There's going to be bread cakes in your near *fuuuuture.*"

The voice startled Ansel, whose eyes were transfixed on the dark clouds that ever floated above the nearby mountain. Laughter broke out, and the villagers joined the elder in shaking their heads.

"Come now, Ko-Rel, let us look for your son. And pay no mind to Ansel and his fanciful dark stories," the elder said, giving Ko-Rel a hand up.

After a few minutes of organizing, the elder sent out the search parties in different directions to search for Dynaen. Ko-Rel didn't join them. Instead, he returned to his home, where the door was still open wide and things strewn about. Rifling through a pile of belongings, he found what he was looking for. A wooden box, two meters in length, lay on the floorboards with a thin layer of dust on its surface.

Ko-Rel cracked the latch open and found it as he had left it, the sword of his fathers before him. Taking the blade by the hilt just above the flower pommel, he lifted it from its resting place and examined the blade. Even after all these years, it still shone bright with a sharp edge. He had no sheath to bear it, so he carried it in his hand. A normal man would require two hands to carry such a blade, but not Ko-Rel. His natural strength enabled him to do much more than his fellow villagers. This being so, he didn't know how to use it. It was an heirloom passed from his grandfather to his father, and Ko-Rel's father to him.

I may not know how to use this, but its blade isn't that different from the farming tools I have used in the field, Ko-Rel thought. *Better to be armed, for I don't know what I face.*

This thought lingered in his mind, standing at the entrance to the forest where he last saw his son being dragged away. Fear crept into his mind, and the terrifying scream cut its way to the forefront of his thoughts. With a tight fist on the hilt of his sword, Ko-Rel took a deep breath and strode forth into the trees.

As Ko-Rel walked, he listened to the sounds around him. Leaves and branches that lay across the path crunched under his feet. This path was less travelled than the others near their village. Dark clouds hovered above the mountains, leading most parties to take a wider approach to the village and beyond. Looking up, Ko-Rel watched as the sharp blue of the sky slowly changed to a muddy brown with the sun shifting behind the clouds. The world around him seemed to slowly change. Trees were more barren here, and where he had heard a scattering of birdsong, now it was eerily quiet.

Where have they taken you, my son... Ko-Rel thought, pressing on.

He continued to walk in the direction he had last seen his son, but the forest was vast, and there could be many places to hide or be unseen. The thought of the mountain and Ansel's story floated into his mind.

He was right about these creatures. I pray he is wrong about their purpose, but I have nowhere else to go.

Branches twisted out of misshapen trees, like small, clawed arms trying to reach Ko-Rel. He hacked off a tree limb blocking his path and pressed on towards the mountain. The smell of dirt, mud, and earth filled his senses with every step he took forward. Brown grass mixed with spattering of green covered patches of earth.

Words drifted into his thoughts, spoken from his father to him in the distant past. Ko-Rel focused his mind on the words to remember, distracting himself from the growing darkness around him and the lifeless earth.

It was a song, he remembered. Trying to bring out the words, Ko-Rel began a deep hum in his chest, matching the beat of his step. The words came clearer in his mind, spoken to him many years ago when he was a boy.

For the feet below me, press into earth.
Sky hidden from me, by the branches.
I remember the light that was.
I remember the light.
Nalstar, shine through.
With these words, I remember.

Warmth radiated out from his core, and he felt a soft tug on his heart. His focus shifted to the right. Unsure why, he followed this feeling. A break in the trees, and the full height of the mountain stretched before Ko-Rel. It was completely barren, dark rock mixed with dirt. He was still a kilometer away, by his reckoning. The sun retreated deeper behind the clouds, and darkness covered the area before him. A chill rippled through his skin, feeling a cold edge to the wind. It was at this moment, he heard it again. The agonized breathing and moaning he had heard from the day before. Straining his eyes, Ko-Rel readied his sword in a loose stance. He cursed. He should have trained more with this weapon, but how could he have known he would need it?

It took his eyes a moment to adjust to the lower light, but after a moment, he saw it. He saw *them*. Four dark creatures stood a hundred meters ahead of him along the old dirt path. They shuddered and ambled around aimlessly, staring off with their dark eyes in various directions. Ko-Rel growled and grit his teeth. His anger rose as heat filled his chest.

These are the creatures that took my son… they will pay with blood!

Ko-Rel took a step forward, stepping on a branch. It broke beneath his weight, letting out a loud *crack* across the clearing. The creatures snapped their heads towards his direction, limbs taut at strange angles. One of the creatures croaked, struggling to open its mouth. With a sudden *snap*, its mouth flew open and it let out a loud blood-curdling scream. Ko-Rel's limbs froze in place, eyes wide as he found himself unable to move. The creatures sprinted towards him, limbs flailing around them loosely.

Move! Ko-Rel shouted in his mind, but his body wouldn't listen.

The other creatures joined in the scream as they rushed towards him. Ko-Rel strained his neck and growled in a guttural struggle. With the creatures mere meters away, the sight of his son's face being dragged away flashed through his mind. Ko-Rel remembered the look of fear in his child's eyes. The tears glimmered in the moonlight.

With a heave of his chest, Ko-Rel bellowed, breaking through the force holding his limbs. He swung his blade with tremendous force and cut through two of the dark creatures, slicing them in half across their midsection. His burst of energy threw him off balance, and the blade rose high in the air, spraying black blood around. The remaining two creatures slammed into Ko-Rel's exposed side, tackling him to the ground. His sword flew through the air as they fell to the ground.

Stunned for a moment, Ko-Rel was struck by several clawed hands. They ripped and tore at his clothes and grabbed at his hair. The pain brought him back to his senses, and he wrapped his right arm around the neck of the creature on top of him. With his left arm, he pulled his right wrist and flexed hard. The creature squawked and gagged until, finally, a crunch, as its bones broke and crushed under the tremendous power of Ko-Rel's arms. Without a moment's pause, the remaining creature tore the limp corpse away and dove with its clawed hands for Ko-Rel's eyes. But Ko-Rel was no longer stunned from the fall. His hands shot up and grabbed the creature by its wrists, not a moment too soon. Its sharp fingers strained to claw at his eyes, only inches away.

Rage rose in Ko-Rel and he shouted, pulling the creature's arms out wide. The creature tried to jab its head forward and bite Ko-Rel, but Ko-Rel kept the creature just out of range. He continued to pull outwards until he met resistance. Fire burned in Ko-Rel's eyes, pushing past the fear that threatened to hold him. The creature frantically strained against the pressure until, after a moment of struggle, Ko-Rel ripped the creature apart, separating near its shoulder down to the middle of its chest. Dark fluid gushed out, spattering Ko-Rel. He rolled to the side and discarded the creature's corpse.

Ko-Rel stood, heaving at the rush of expended energy. A sliver of light cut through the clouds, and for a moment, he was able to see these creatures in a better light. Looking at them, their forms flickered like a flame and yet emanated no light. Bodies with shapes that resembled a human, but the edges were warped like shadows, making their true shape difficult to tell.

He looked down, and in the dim light, he saw his tattered clothes. There were several scratch marks on his chest and side, but nothing too deep. He thanked the light for his hardened skin. A normal man would have been shredded to pieces by their clawed hands.

Blinking several times to center himself, Ko-Rel looked around for his sword. In the rush of battle, he didn't see where it landed. The light disappeared behind the clouds, once again enshrouding the area in an unnatural darkness for the time of day.

No matter, I can take these creatures with my bare hands, Ko-Rel thought.

Blood pumping in his veins, Ko-Rel continued onwards. With every step he took, he felt the world around him growing darker and colder. His rage inside warmed his limbs and kept his feet pushing past the fear that pressed in on him. Reaching the base of the mountain, Ko-Rel strained his neck to look up. He took in the sight of the rocky terrain of the mountainside that stretched upwards before him.

Where have you gone, my son...

A few meters to his left, a rock slid down and bounced off a few boulders before coming to rest. Following the source of the rock, Ko-Rel looked up, and somehow the way ahead seemed even darker. He didn't know why, but somehow he knew that this was where they had taken his son. Gritting his teeth, Ko-Rel climbed over the sharp edges of the jagged boulders before him, making his way towards this deeper darkness.

The path upwards was steep. At times, Ko-Rel found himself flat against the side of the mountain, holding on by his fingertips. This was the way he somehow knew. And so, he continued on climbing inches at a time up the face of the mountain. After what seemed like an eternity of climbing, he reached a more level area. Hoisting himself up onto the ledge, he chanced a look down. It was a good distance down to the bottom, but in the dark it was hard to see. Through the gloom, he could barely see the break in the trees he had come through. A small pond near the foot of the mountain glinted in what little light found its way through the clouds.

Only taking a moment to catch his breath, Ko-Rel stood to his feet. He turned towards what felt like the darkest and coldest area of the mountain ahead. It was still an upwards climb, but more of a scramble than the previous steep slope of rocks and dirt.

As he climbed, the chill on his limbs grew, but not from the weather outside. It was like a force creeping into his skin and trying to freeze him from within. Ko-Rel pounded his chest with a fist to keep his heart warm and to pump up the flame he was holding onto—the image of his son. It wasn't long before he started to hear sounds ahead. Until now, the world around him had been painfully silent, beyond the crunch of dirt and rock under his boots. It was that same sound he had heard the night previous, and from the clearing below. There were dark, shadowy creatures ahead.

Trying to make his approach more silent, he slowed his pace and softened his footfalls. Ko-Rel reached another ledge with a large boulder tucked in along the face of the mountain. He strained his neck upwards and saw no way up. It was too steep and slanted outwards for a great distance above him. The moaning and croaking sounds increased in his ears, turning Ko-Rel's attention back down to the ledge. He noticed then that the ledge edged around the rock face he was up against. With slow and steady steps, he crept to the corner, fighting the urge to flee.

Fear washed over him as his eyes took in the sight around the corner. He could make out a thick mob of the creatures strewn about a large landing. The mob writhed and undulated, groaning and creaking while their limbs twitched and flexed. It was like a sea of twisted arms reaching out to their extent only to curl back in again, shivering. Through the murky air and limbs, he saw the tall creature. Its blue eyes pierced the darkness and bobbed as it plodded about, gathering stones. It placed them in a circular pattern on the ground, building into a small raised area. Twisting its head this way and that, it paced around the area like it was searching for something. A series of clicks and groans emanated from the large creature, and the mob before him croaked, seemingly in a form of a reply.

The large creature turned and scaled the wall behind it onto another ledge with deft ease. It then disappeared into the low light over the edge. Ko-Rel realized he was holding his breath but found it difficult to open his mouth or to force air into his lungs. The blue light from the creature's eyes burned into his mind. He had found them, but there was no sign of Dynaen. Was he even alive after all this time? Should he return with more of the villagers? He had proof the shadowy creatures existed, but no, he couldn't leave without finding out what happened to his son.

"Light, guide me," Ko-Rel managed to let escape from his mouth in a quiet prayer.

A wave of icy water washed over his mind as he realized he had made a noise. Ko-Rel held his breath again, eyes wide. The mob before him continued its aimless weave of twisted limbs, seeming not to have heard his utterance over the noise of their own groans and creaks.

Ko-Rel let his breath out slowly. A ray of light broke through the clouds, only for a brief moment. In that moment, he saw in the distance the outline of a small body that looked similar to Dynaen. It must be him!

The ice melted around Ko-Rel's heart, replaced by heat. Taking deep breaths, his nostrils flared. These monsters had stolen his son; they would pay for this. They would die for this. Fear slithered its way into his mind, but his anger rose up to push it back. Ko-Rel tensed his arms and legs, flexing to let the warm blood flow through him again, eyes lit like a fire. He saw a stone the size of his fist near his foot. Taking the stone in his hand, he stepped around the corner.

His mind screamed at him—*run, flee, save yourself!* But his rage could not be tamed; fire and blood were all Ko-Rel could see now. A shadow creature turned to see him stepping towards them. Its limbs shivered as it twisted its body towards Ko-Rel. Ice fought the fire in Ko-Rel's heart, but wave after wave, he resisted with gritted teeth. The creature alerted the mob with a sickening scream.

Expecting this, Ko-Rel let out a growl and shouted, "Beasts, you have stolen my son. Now you will die!"

With a long shout, he sprinted into the mob now turning to see him.

They twitched, groaned, and screamed-but even as the percussive waves of air hit Ko-Rel, he couldn't be slowed. His mass was set in a forward motion.

Pounding the dirt under heavy foot, Ko-Rel rushed the first creature. With a cry, he swung the rock in his fist into the creature's head, smashing it in. Ko-Rel felt the spray of its blood on his face but didn't pause. He pushed past its falling corpse and dove into the next two creatures behind it. The force of his sprint cracked bones as they fell under his weight into the hard rock underneath. Ko-Rel rolled from his dive and drove the heel of his foot into another creature's head, feeling its skull break and turn to pulp. He used the momentum of his stomp to launch himself up again and into another creature, grabbing it around the midsection.

They were no longer stunned but shrieked and clambered over each other to take on this wild human foe. He ignored the pain as they grabbed at his clothes and skin, clawing and raking at him. Twisting at the hips, Ko-Rel snapped the spine of the creature he was grappling with. They began to pile on top of him, and their collective weight forced him down flat onto the rock. He fought to bring his arms underneath him, feeling clawed hands pulling at his hair and ripping off part of his right ear. The pain gave him new energy as his palms found the cold stone beneath him, wet with his enemies' blood. Ko-Rel tensed his muscles and in a burst of energy shoved off from the ground with all his might. Creatures flew in every direction, screeching and flailing helplessly in the air. Several skidded and slid off the edge of the cliff nearby.

The cliff!

Ko-Rel stood to his feet, with a creature biting at his neck. He grabbed the creature's head in both hands and squeezed until he heard a sickening pop as its head caved in. Taking the limp body from his shoulders, he spun, holding the body by the neck. Ko-Rel knocked over several shadowy creatures with the corpse, then threw it into a clump of more creatures. The force blasted them off the side of the mountain, taking out several more.

Ko-Rel felt a wild energy racing through his body. He clawed through the blood on his face and let loose a crazed laugh. The fear couldn't match his anger. Creatures limped and flopped around him; many were now dead or broken. Their bodies twitched and writhed on the ground. Only a few remained standing between him and the body of the child he had seen. The light in Ko-Rel's eyes lit to blazing white hot as he felt a burning heat like the flame of the sun rise within him.

Ko-Rel sped across the mass of tangled bodies and rushed these final few. They stood their ground until the last moment, separating and allowing him to fall between them. Ko-Rel tripped and felt something strike him from the side of the head. Instinctively he covered his head with his hands as they bombarded him with many blows. In between the blows, Ko-Rel chanced a look ahead at the child who only lay a few meters away now. He knew those clothes. He knew that form. It was his son!

A war cry blasted out of him as Ko-Rel grabbed at the leg of the nearest creature. He bit down on it with full force, cutting deep into the creature's shin. His teeth broke through the meat of its leg, and its bone cracked under the force of his grip. With a twist of his head, he ripped a chunk from the monster's leg. It struck him in the head, blinking out his consciousness for a moment before he regained his flame. The creature hopped on its remaining leg. Taking a moment of respite from its blows, Ko-Rel kicked out, knocking the creature to the ground. He rolled over and wrapped his body around it, continuing to roll up to the edge of the cliff. Prying himself from the creature, he pushed it off to its death.

Two of the creatures pounced on him, but he was ready. His hands shot up and grabbed both by the neck. These ones had thicker necks than the others, but that mattered little to Ko-Rel. He yelled and tightened his grip, crushing their necks under his fists. Blood splashed over his face as the two wiggling bodies above him slowly went limp. He discarded them to his left and his right and slowly stood.

A few creatures remained standing scattered around this ledge, but they didn't risk moving closer. The wild rage that burned in his eyes kept them at a distance. Struggling, Ko-Rel walked towards the body of Dynaen. His adrenaline ebbed, and he began to feel pain from the many cuts and bruises about his body. His head ached and his balance was off, but he continued to stumble forwards.

Ko-Rel tripped on a stone, falling to his knees as he made his approach to the body. He crawled forward on his hands and knees and took up the boy's body into his arms. The body was cold. Tears welled up in Ko-Rel's eyes, brushing the hair out of the boy's face. It was Dynaen.

The boy's arms lay limp beside him as Ko-Rel whispered, "My son, I'm here."

But his son didn't open his eyes. Ko-Rel's vision blurred, and tears streamed out, "My son... I'm here now. You can wake up."

Dynaen didn't respond.

Ko-Rel screamed, straining his neck upwards at the darkened sky. Chest heaving, he lowered his gaze once again.

"My son…"

He continued to stroke his son's hair the way he used to when he had nightmares. The rage-fueled energy left Ko-Rel as he sat there holding the limp body of his son. He brought Dynaen up in an embrace and remembered the words his wife would say.

Voice breaking through tears, Ko-Rel whispered,

I remember the light…
Nalstar, shine through.

Silence filled the air. Even the creatures stopped their noises as Ko-Rel felt tears flow out of him, cradling his son. It was at this moment that Ko-Rel saw light through his eyelids. Blinking to clear the tears, he turned upwards and saw that a small break in the clouds had appeared. Out of this opening, a ray of golden light shone down on him, and he saw the gray skin of his son illuminated in the light. Ko-Rel felt a prickling sensation and a warmth returning to his son's body. The gray skin slowly shifted to a softer shade of tan. Dynaen's chest rose as a raspy breath was drawn in. His eyes fluttered open, struggling to see with the light in his face.

"Father?" he croaked.

"Dynaen!" Ko-Rel shouted, bringing his son into a tight embrace.

"Where are we…" Dynaen struggled to say.

"Don't speak, you're safe now. I'm here," Ko-Rel said.

They were anything but safe, with the monsters seeming to grow in their desire to come at him again.

Picking up his son in his arms, he whispered again, "I'm here now, close your eyes and this will all be over soon."

Ko-Rel took a deep breath, holding his son close to his chest in a firm grasp. Before he could take a step, he heard a sound behind him. Ko-Rel's eyes went wide. Turning slowly, Ko-Rel saw the taller creature standing at the top of the cliff, bright blue eyes piercing into him. A wave of ice covered his insides, fear freezing him in place.

"That boy… no longer… belongs to you… *Fulmenson*," the creature said, groaning and crackling with great effort.

Ko-Rel wanted to run, fight, or hide, but he couldn't move. He watched helplessly as the creature slid down the rockface to stand inches from him. Its breath was cold and stank of death. Long fingers stretched out towards Dynaen to take him again.

A word came to Ko-Rel's mind: *Remember.*

Like a lake of ice cracking in the spring, words burst out of Ko-Rel, "I remember... the light!"

A flash of light burst in the area, sending the large creature reeling. Ko-Rel somehow wasn't affected, and he watched as the creature drew back.

A single word burst into his mind, breaking his stunned state.

Run!

Ko-Rel didn't wait a moment longer; he twisted and launched himself back the way he had come. Lowering a shoulder, Ko-Rel plowed through a few of the creatures attempting to stop his retreat. They couldn't match his mass and energy and were thrown aside by the fleeing giant of a man.

With every pounding step Ko-Rel took, he felt pain shooting through his entire being. His arms ached, but he continued to run. He stumbled and rolled, tucking Dynaen in to protect him from the fall. The full force of the rocks crashed into his back. Ko-Rel felt something crunch, but he shook off the pain and continued running down the steep rock-covered slant.

His breath was becoming ragged now, and the weariness of much exertion was catching up to him. It was only his momentum that kept him rushing forward. His mind quickly awakened to remember that this path led to the steep climb he had made before. Skidding to a stop, his feet came to the cliff's edge. There was no way he could climb down carrying Dynaen. His son had drifted off—unconscious but still breathing.

Ko-Rel turned to look up the hill but regretted it. In the low light he could see a horde of dark creatures throwing themselves down the rocky hill towards them. They were only a few hundred meters away now, and their screams echoed down to him. Ko-Rel's eyes darted from side to side in the dark to see if there was another way down, but he couldn't see anything. Just when he felt like his hope was all but gone, there was a glint far below. *The pond!*

Taking another look behind him, he saw the creatures closing in. With a last glance down at Dynaen, he summoned his remaining energy and ran back towards the horde coming at him. Moments away from their outstretched grasp, he pivoted and ran towards the cliff's edge. The creatures were nearly on top of them. Pounding the rocks beneath him with every step, Ko-Rel raced towards the edge. With a shout, he leapt off into the darkness. Several of the creatures jumped after him, and others toppled over the edge, carried by their momentum.

Ko-Rel fell through the air. One of the creatures grabbed at him, clawing at his tattered clothes, trying to find a grip. Ko-Rel twisted and kicked at the creature, driving it downwards. Feeling the air rush past him, Ko-Rel twisted again, turning his back to the ground as he curled around Dynaen in a protective hug. He felt the claws of the other creature flailing below him, before moments later hearing several splashes. A great force punched into his back, landing with a loud splash in the water.

The sudden rush of water shocked his system, but after a moment it became somewhat peaceful. Lukewarm water encased Ko-Rel, but it was the silence that made him linger a moment. Thoughts of letting himself slowly drift off into the black and surrender to the depths played in his mind. He was so tired and weary, he thought of letting go so he could rest. Slowly, his eyes closed under the weight of dreariness...

Ko-Rel's eyes shot open. He remembered why he came, why he was here. In his arms, his son was still hugged tightly. Ko-Rel reoriented himself, feeling the water pull him down. With a series of kicks, he fluttered in the opposite direction. His lungs burned, what little air was left in them. It felt like his lungs would burst when he finally broke through the surface and let in a gasp of air.

Ko-Rel made for shore as quickly as he could while holding Dynaen in one of his arms. Once there, he laid his son down on the dirt shore and placed his hand on his son's chest. After a moment, Dynaen's eyes fluttered open again, and he sat up sputtering and coughing.

Ko-Rel hugged him in a tight embrace, "My son, I thought I lost you."

"Father, what are we doing here? I don't recognize it and can't see."

"Don't worry, you'll be home soon."

Their short moment of peace was broken by the sounds of rocks sliding down the side of the mountain. In the dim light, Ko-Rel saw creatures running after them, falling over one another down the mountainside.

"What are those?"

"I don't know, but we must go."

Ko-Rel picked up his son and began to trot back towards the Forest. It was difficult to see, but he seemed to remember the way. His feet felt heavy as he plodded along. Pain ached and stung throughout his body with the adrenaline wearing off. Every few steps he would stumble on the dirt, his feet catching on a twig or rock. After several times, he finally fell to his knees.

"Father!"

"I'm alright, I just need a moment to rest."

But Ko-Rel could hear the sounds off to the distance behind them. With few leaves on the branches, the creatures would likely see them.

Dynaen stood next to his father and put his father's heavy arm around his shoulder, "Come, let me help you a ways."

Ko-Rel wanted to refuse, but he had very little energy and couldn't speak. He accepted the help up and they struggled down the path with Ko-Rel guiding. The sounds were getting closer now, their wicked screams pulling at them.

"Here, come put me here for a moment."

"Father, we need to keep going."

"Yes, yes," Ko-Rel said, struggling to get up.

They continued in this way, stumbling and resting, until they made it to the clearing again, where he had fought the initial four creatures. It wasn't much further now. The noises in the forest behind them grew louder.

Ko-Rel turned to his son, "Dynaen, the villagers can't be much further. You can't carry me anymore, I'm too heavy. If you go ahead and get some of the others, they will be able to help."

"But Father…"

"Do not worry about me, I've faced them already and lived. I can hold them off till you return."

Dynaen waited for a moment, then nodded and ran off in the way Ko-Rel pointed. Ko-Rel watched his son leave, but he knew in his heart they wouldn't come in time. Just before his son disappeared into the trees, Ko-Rel said, "I love you, my son. Forgive me for not showing it."

Letting himself fall to rest by a nearby tree, Ko-Rel looked up to the sky. At this distance from the mountain, the clouds weren't as dark and he could faintly make out the blue sky beyond. It was still day, even though it felt like a long, dark night he had fought through. Resting his hand beside him, he felt cool metal and saw his family's sword lying next to him in the grass. It gave him some peace to know that he had found it again. Ko-Rel gripped the pommel and drew it close, but even this action felt monumental.

The peace was short-lived. Ko-Rel saw the tall blue-eyed creature burst out of the forest.

I am glad to die with this sword by my side.

It paused, looking around furiously before it locked on to the path that led out of the clearing. With great speed the creature sprinted towards the village.

No! It doesn't even see me, I stayed behind to halt its advance.

With the energy Ko-Rel didn't know he had, he staggered up and rushed at the tall creature, sword in hand. Moments before impact, he gave a shout and slashed with his sword. The creature skidded to a halt and sidestepped the swing. Ko-Rel's momentum carried him past the creature, and he felt a great blow strike him in the back. A loud crack emanated from his torso, and he felt bones break. Ko-Rel fell forwards, legs gone limp. A sharp pain filled his insides as it felt like many small blades cut him from within. Face down in the dirt and scattered grass, Ko-Rel felt the creature's presence looming over him. He then felt himself being lifted into the air by his neck. The grip turned him towards the creature, its bright blue eyes blazing with fury.

"Your son is mine…"

Ko-Rel's legs hung limp below him, suspended in the air. He coughed up blood and tried to ignore the pain.

"No, beast… He is not!"

Ko-Rel summoned the last of his energy and swung upwards with his sword, cutting into the monster's face. The creature reeled and dropped Ko-Rel on his back, sending another wave of pain through him. It shrieked as it held its face, flailing around wildly. After a moment of pain, it stilled itself and retook steps towards Ko-Rel.

Just as it regained its composure, a sound came from the forest behind them. Ko-Rel turned his head towards the village and could faintly make out torches in the distance, peeking through the trees. The tall creature hissed, turned, and sprinted off towards the mountain. Ko-Rel glanced at it and saw several other of the shadow creatures picking up their fallen before running off and leaving Ko-Rel alone in the dirt.

His breath was coming in ragged now, and blood seeped from his mouth. The pain was almost too much for him to bear. His eyelids grew heavy. Ko-Rel strained to open his eyes and clear his blurry vision. A small opening broke in the clouds, pouring light down on his face. In the midst of the blinding light, Ko-Rel thought he saw the face of a woman. His eyes fluttered, breath coming even harder now. He remembered Dynaen, and seeing the torches, telling himself he had been found.

"Rest now," a soft voice whispered.

Ko-Rel struggled to open his eyes but found his strength failing. A warm sensation filled his body, and for a moment, the pain subsided.

Shadows of the Mountain

"My son is safe..." Ko-Rel barely uttered, allowing his eyes to close. He let out a raspy breath and breathed his last, hearing the sound of feet rushing towards him.

§

Dynaen stood on the path where his father had died twelve years ago. He was a man now. Not as large as his Father, but his lean muscles grew taut, clenching his fist around the flowered pommel of his father's sword.

That night was burned into Dynaen's memory. When he arrived with the villagers, they had come too late and found Ko-Rel lying still and alone on the path, with sword in hand. Despite the many wounds on his body, Dynaen remembered the look of peace on his father's face, looking skyward.

Dynaen took a deep breath and looked up towards the mountain. The dark clouds remained even after all this time, and yet the villagers never truly believed Dynaen's stories. Only a few remained in the village, and it had been many years since anyone had been reported missing. But in the night, Dynaen could hear dark whispers in the wind.

He held up his father's sword with both hands, light glinting off the face of the blade. It was time. Over the last twelve years, Dynaen had tried to convince the people of what happened, but they didn't believe him. So, he began to train himself with his father's sword. Those shining blue eyes gave him motivation to train with every spare moment.

A faint shriek flitted across the wind, but Dynaen felt no fear. His heart was set, and he knew what needed to be done. The creature must be slain. Sword in hand, Dynaen stepped forth and began his march towards the mountain. As he strode forward, the words of his mother came to his mind, and he sang:

For the feet below me, press into earth.
Sky hidden from me...

I remember the light.

A FAIR PRICE

A SHORT STORY BY
M. O. MOALIN

A Fair Price

He sat on a cracked bench where the wind carried dust, and the streets gave nothing for free. Same coat, same scuffed shoes, same look in his eyes like he was waiting for something the sky had forgotten to deliver. No one knew his name. Some said he'd once had work. Others said he'd never tried, as he felt he was born better than the rest. His hands were big. His back was straight. His legs were long and strong. Just by looking, you could tell that nothing ached when he stood up. He had the kind of health people prayed for. And yet, he never moved much.

On that fateful day, people hauled carts through the dust, children ran barefoot past potholes, and the city was as fast and loud as always.

An old man who frequented that road with a limp came by, dragging a wooden cane. As usual, he smelt of dust and boiled onions. As habit reinforced, he stopped next to the young man.

"You're out early," the old man said, coughing once into his sleeve.

"I never left," the younger man replied with half-closed eyes.

The old man sat beside him with a groan. "The bakery's hiring. Just lifting crates in the back. Not hard work for a strong back."

"I won't break my back for crumbs," the young man said. "Not while others sit in silk without lifting a finger."

The old man blinked. "You mean the merchant with no arms?"

"Him. And the banker with no legs. And that blind man who owns half the street. You think that's fair?"

"They built something," the old man said gently. "Made deals. Paid wages. Paid taxes."

"With what? Inheritance? Luck? They were born into gold and got sympathy on top of it."

The old man leaned forward, elbows on knees. "You are so blind to what you have. You, young man, have a body that can build a home. That can plant trees, lift stone, carry—"

The young man scoffed. "I should've been born rich," he said bitterly. "I should've had a father who left me something. Instead, I get knees that bend and a stomach that stays empty."

The old man was quiet for a moment. Then: "You ever think you were the lucky one?"

"How?" The young man turned sharply. "You see my situation? My clothes? You think this is what luck looks like?"

"No," the old man said. "But I see a man with a full body and no chains on his arms. And I see him spit on what he has because he thinks the world owes him more."

The younger man's jaw tightened. He looked away from the old man to the streets.

"I think," the old man continued slowly, "that if you were missing something, you'd finally understand what you had."

Silence stretched between them. A child laughed in the distance. A hawker's cart creaked by.

The younger man spoke. "I think God plays favorites."

The old man had had enough. He stood up to leave, slow and stiff. "Maybe. Or maybe He's just waiting to see what you'll do with what He already gave you."

He limped away without another word.

The man sat alone again. The bench creaked under him. The city didn't slow. No one turned to look. The clouds moved on. He leaned back and closed his eyes.

§

He was still on the bench when the strange man appeared. A man with a pale robe that didn't match the dress code of the area. He didn't walk up, nor did he stumble into view. One blink, he stood just beyond the curb, as if the earth had let him rise out of the dust. Despite that, the dust didn't touch him. There wasn't a hint of dirt on his robe. His skin was smooth and golden, and his eyes were too light to be natural. They weren't green, grey, or any colour the young man could name. They were…off.

The young man straightened on the bench. The stranger in the robe had not looked away from him since his arrival. "Can I…help you?" he asked, sounding casual.

The stranger tilted his head. "You looked like you had something heavy on your chest."

The young man hesitated. "How can you tell? You watching me?"

"Only just now," the stranger said. His voice was soft and sluggish. He didn't sound real. He almost sounded like what a dream might sound like if it could speak. "You looked like someone waiting for an answer."

A Fair Price

The young man glanced around. Everything was still the same. Young boys chased each other in the distance. A woman folded laundry on a balcony. But here — just here — it felt as though time had stopped.

He swallowed. "There's nothing wrong with me."

The stranger smiled kindly. "Nothing at all? Are you sure about that?" Then he hummed and repeated, "Nothing... nothing nothing nothing. That's part of the problem, isn't it? Go on then," the stranger said. "Say what's on your mind."

The young man's bitterness surged like bile. "It's unfair. That's what's wrong. I've lived with nothing. I've watched limping people end up with more than I'll ever see. They were born with riches and success. While I sit here and rot with nothing."

Unlike the others, the young man would voice his sentiments to the stranger didn't judge him. However, he had to ask for good measure why the young man didn't work.

"I don't see how it's fair that I work," the young man replied. "Some lucky bastards out there don't even have to think about work. Why should I? I deserve as much and even more than them."

The stranger meditated on what the young man said. "So you want wealth beyond measure?" he asked at last.

The man laughed bitterly. "Of course I do."

He braced himself. This was the part where people ridiculed him and told him he was too big for his head. That he was delusional and maybe even pitiful. However, the stranger didn't echo any of that. What he asked made the young man sit upright.

"What would you give for that wealth you so desperately want?"

He looked the stranger over. Up and down and up and down, assessing him and looking for anything he might've missed. "Who are you?"

"You may call me the Collector," the stranger said, still smiling. "Most do."

"What do you collect?"

"Whatever people think they can live without. But I also give them what they think they deserve."

The young man leaned forward. "Really? So you help people for a price?"

"More or less. So think carefully before you let me help you."

The young man didn't hesitate. "You're saying you can make me rich? I agree."

They walked through alleys, past checkpoints and guards, up into parts of the city the young man had never seen before. Places with glass windows and cars that waited with engines still running.

He didn't understand how they got through the gates. How no one stopped them. No one even looked up or seemed to notice them. Armed men stood near the gate, but none raised a hand. One even stepped aside as if he knew the Collector by name. The young man stared in disbelief.

Inside, the house was quiet. No children were running through the halls. Any worker there seemed to have vanished. There was nothing but silence.

"Where are we?" the young man asked. "Is this your house?"

"Wait and see," the Collector said.

They found a blind man sitting near a wide window. A woman stood nearby and poured him tea.

The young man stood still and watched with wide eyes as the Collector approached without sound.

The blind man's head turned sharply. "Who's there?"

"Don't be afraid," the Collector said, gently. "You won't be harmed."

The woman seemed to finally take notice. She gasped. "How did you get in here?"

But the Collector raised a hand, and she seemed to forget her question. She blinked and stepped back. The young man watched speechless.

The blind man frowned. "How long have you been standing there? I didn't even hear you."

"You didn't see me either," the Collector said, kindly.

The blind man gave a bitter laugh. "That's the problem, isn't it? I see nothing. My body fools me at every turn. I can't even make it out of my own house without assistance."

The Collector stepped closer. "And what if I told you you could get your sight back? Here and now."

The blind man stiffened. "Is that even possible?"

"For a price," the Collector said. "Would you give up your wealth?"

There was no hesitation.

"Gladly," the blind man said. "What good is a palace I cannot see? What joy is a fortune I cannot share in the colour of my wife's eyes? I would give it all, just to see my children smile."

And just like that, the blind man gasped. He raised a trembling hand and touched his face. His eyes — once pale and clouded — were now bright and alive.

"I can see," he whispered. "I can see!"

He turned towards the window, laughing and crying. "God be praised! I can see!"

The young man, still by the door, was in shock. He could only stare at the scene before him with a dry mouth.

The Collector, as if nothing had happened, produced a sheet of paper and nodded at the once-blind man. The young man could not tell where he got the sheet. As if that was the most astonishing thing the Collector did.

"Sign here," the Collector said as he held the sheet to the blind man. "Your wealth is no longer yours."

The once-blind man reached forward and scribbled his name without reading a word.

"Who gets my wealth?" was the only thing he asked.

The Collector pointed to the young man standing still in the doorway. "He does. All of your current wealth goes to him."

The once-blind man didn't flinch.

The Collector turned and returned to the door where the young man stood with a pounding heart.

"Shall we go?" he said. "There's another who might be willing to trade."

The young man, speechless and shivering, followed.

Behind them, the man who could now see leaned against the window and gazed at the stars like they were something new.

§

They arrived at a large house hidden behind tall trees. At the front stood a big golden door. Its shiny edges caught the light. The young man stared at it, feeling nervous but excited.

Before opening it, the Collector paused and turned to him. "Ah, right," he said casually. "I must ask. You can stop here if you like. You already have the wealth of the blind man. That's more than most men see in a lifetime. If you're content, walk away now."

The young man looked at the signed deed in his hands. A full fortune. His life had changed so easily. Only someone without sense would stop here.

"I want more," he said.

The Collector gave him a kind smile. "Very well."

He pushed open the door, and again, there was no fuss. No one tried to stop them as they made their way inside.

They reached an armless man who sat in a grand room. He was dressed in silk robes. His sleeves hung empty by his sides. He looked up, startled by their sudden appearance.

The Collector stepped forward. "No need to fear. We mean you no harm."

The armless man relaxed slightly. "I didn't hear you come in. You can see, I, myself, am no threat to anyone. No hands. No way to stop anything. Most have tried to take advantage of that."

The Collector nodded. "It must be tough. But if you could have strong arms? Hands that feel, move, protect, and create…would you trade your wealth for that?"

The armless man didn't even think. "In a heartbeat," he said. "What use is all this gold if I can't even hold my children? If I can't embrace my wife properly or lift a glass to my lips?"

"If you give up all your wealth, you will be granted arms."

"Take it all," the armless man exclaimed.

The change was instant. Where empty sleeves once hung, flesh and fingers grew. The man cried out in joy, flexing his fingers, touching his face, and for the first time, wiping his own tears.

The Collector produced another paper. The young man did not question where he got it from this time.

The once-armless man signed the paper without hesitation. "The first thing I do with my hands." He laughed wholeheartedly.

The Collector handed the second deed to the young man, who stood silently, stunned by how easily everything was happening. Without another word, the two left the palace.

"Next one," the Collector said. And on they went.

§

They came to the last house, grand and ostentatious like the others.

This time, the young man didn't bother himself with how the Collector got them inside. He didn't care. His mind was already racing with his next fortune.

The Collector turned to him like last time. "I must ask again. Will you stop here? You have taken two fortunes."

The young man looked at the two sheets in his hands. "I," he said, and tightened his grip around his newly acquired wealth. "I thought I'd feel full by now. But the more I have, the more I want. I'm sure you understand."

The robed stranger smiled at him. "Very well," he said and opened the door.

The man with no legs sat in a high chair by the window. His eyes lit up when the Collector entered alongside the young man, as if he'd been waiting all his life for this visit. It seemed word had travelled fast.

The Collector spoke softly, almost like a friend. "I see you were expecting us."

"Yes," the man with no legs said. "My two dear friends have already told me about you. About the blessings they received. I humbly ask you to do the same for me."

"Are you not cross with them? They gave up everything they had."

"Cross!" the man with no legs exclaimed. "I am happy and proud of them."

The Collector smiled. "So you, too, are willing to give up everything you own so you could walk."

The legless man gave a small, breathless laugh. "Without a doubt," he said. "There's nowhere I wouldn't go."

The Collector nodded. Moments later, the man stood, shaking, moving around while tears ran down his cheeks. He didn't even look at the papers before signing them. He was too busy staring at his feet.

The Collector took the signed deed and handed it to the young man without a word. The young man smiled. He didn't look back as they walked away.

§

They returned to the bench where it had all begun. The moon hung low, casting long shadows across the quiet alley. The young man sat down, his face jubilant. He was practically glowing as he clutched the three deeds like treasures.

"I can't believe it," he said, almost to himself. "I'm rich. No, powerful!" He laughed and turned to the stranger. "Who are you, really? Some kind of angel?"

The Collector, who had smiled at every turn, was now quiet and motionless. His face was unreadable. The young man's grin faltered.

The Collector spoke. "It's time for my price."

"Oh, of course," the young man said, recovering quickly. He held out one of the deeds. "Here. You can have a third. That's only fair, right? This is why I asked for more, you know. To share it with you."

The Collector stared at the paper but didn't take it. "That's not fair," he said.

The young man blinked. "Alright… half, then. Half of everything. You've earned it."

The Collector didn't move. "Still not fair," he said again.

The young man's mouth twitched. "Two-thirds," he snapped. "Final offer."

The silence that followed was heavy and cold. The Collector tilted his head, his eyes almost glowing in the dark.

"That's still," he whispered, his voice hoarsened, "not fair."

The sound sent a shiver down the young man's spine. He stood up abruptly. "How much then? How much to make you satisfied?"

"Who said I want money?"

The young man gulped. "W-what do you want, then?"

The smile was back on the Collector's mouth. He was inches from the young man's face the next instant. He was closer than humanly possible. The air around them vanished. The young man could feel his lungs shrinking.

"You ask me what I want." In a voice that did not belong in this world, the Collector said, "I want your eyes, arms, and legs."

A Fair Price

We all want something.
But next time someone offers it to you,
maybe don't shake hands until you know what you're giving up.
Just a thought.

THE LIGHT THAT DRAWS THE EYE

A SHORT STORY BY
BRIANNA DINGELDEIN

CONTENT WARNINGS

This story contains themes that may be distressing to some readers, including:

Mentions of death

The Light that Draws the Eye

The cabin in the woods had been abandoned for as long as she could remember; perhaps for as long as anyone could remember. But one sleepless night, a candle burned in the darkness. *How can this be?* she thought. Surely no one would be within this cabin, where her feet had treaded the wooden planks to smoothness and the oils of her own hands had darkened the paneling. Surely there could be no one. It stood alone for miles around; it was so overgrown with moss, ivy, and Virginia creeper that she was most certain almost no one could find it.

She paid it almost no mind at first, determined to ignore the thing. Certainly, it was not a thing. Certainly, it was just an odd trick of the light. But as the hours passed by, she paced back and forth, watching it.

What can this possibly be? she thought. *The light is constant, yet wavers, sputters when a breeze blows by. The light draws the eye. I cannot look away. And why should I?*

Hours passed as she paced from left to right, the night wind tickling her arms each time the candle sputtered. Hours departed as she paced shorter and shorter lines, until at some point, eventually, she was simply turning back and forth, her long, thin hair briskly snapping into place behind her jaw, set hard against the night.

— SECOND NIGHT —

the temptation.

The candle had gone out during the day, perhaps. She couldn't really remember. But at some point, she was certain of this: after the sun had set beyond the trees, it had come again. She hadn't noticed at first. But all of a sudden it was there, this soft little beacon in the night. It seemed to whisper to her promises of sweet things, like wisteria and rhododendron and lilac, like perhaps a fresh-picked huckleberry pie such as her husband used to make, like the warm scent of vanilla. Like a billowy velvet blanket she used to crush against her bare skin on autumn nights like these. Could it be that the cabin in the woods held these long lost things of hers? *No. Of course not. That place holds only moss and vines.*

Her feet pitter-pattered softly. Pacing again. The night was starless dark. Was it cold? She couldn't tell. The soft swish of her linen nightgown held time with the subtle motion of that candle in the window. *An ill omen.* She knew this; didn't like it. *Someone is out there in my cabin!* She knew it; didn't like this. But how could she go out there when she was all alone here? When she was just a widowed lady, left with only damp and dust and dark. How long had it been now?

Oh, that light kept her up at night.

— THIRD NIGHT —
the memory.

She sat down, legs crossed beneath her linen skirts, and watched the candle glimmer in the distance like a lighthouse out at sea. The dark rolling lines of trees were the crests of midnight waves. The sound of the breeze blowing through leaves and needles was the salty crash of them. *Never more lonely was a man but alone on a ship out to sea.* Or so she imagined. She had never been out at sea.

Did the light burn all through the day? Or did it only light itself once the dark kissed the land? Perhaps the person inside her long-abandoned cabin was gone. A wanderer who'd stumbled upon it for one night and gone in the morn with the candle left burning.

Her mind was dragged slowly back, like a fish on a line, to a memory not long after her husband died. *How long ago was that now?* she wondered. Did she remember? Did anyone remember? And for that matter, how old was she? She looked at her hands. No arthritic knuckles, just soft wrinkles, dry skin. How long had she looked like this? Had she aged? Perhaps she was immortal. Time rolled like tides; drowning the shoreline, brining the memories, then rolling back to reveal them.

She remembered when she had lit a candle in the window one night. To keep vigil, she had said. Certainly, that was something that people did. She stood in her night shift and gazed at it, fidgeting, not certain it was doing its job. *Perhaps another.* She shuffled about, chattering more, she thought, than she had perhaps ever chattered before. She would turn to her left and say, *"My husband is here right now, I'm certain of it."* And then shuffle and chatter, turn to her right, and say *"This is the way to keep the spirits out, I'd say."*

She reeled in her line to the present, where the lone candle pulsed on. Perhaps it was keeping vigil, keeping the spirits at bay. No, no. She didn't like that and instead thought, *perhaps that's my husband out there with a pie and my velvet blanket.* She nodded. I'm certain of it.

— FOURTH NIGHT —
the hand.

When the trees purpled in the twilight and the tiny steely orange glow radiated from the window, she returned to keep her vigil. *The light draws the eye.* And her pale face drank the light, quaffed it like a withered bed of moss. She did not look away. Her gaze was a steady, ferocious thing.

She gasped. A frightened, desperate, rasping thing. A hand! *A hand on the candle holder! It moved, I saw it!* There was someone in the cabin still, she was certain of it. Oh, no, no, no, she shook her head. The pacing began. Why did she remain alone here when such evils were about? Perhaps she should go into town for help. But then again, perhaps she shouldn't. There was a nagging suspicion that maybe, just maybe, she couldn't. A trill ran up her, icy cold. Certainly, that could not be true; certainly, she had more important things to do.

Her feet slapped beneath her, and her neck tightened; cords taut, constricting itself from the rest of her body. *The light draws the eye. I must not look away. I must not look away. The hand!* Perhaps the hand was a hand alone, constricted from the arm, cut off, and was now wriggling its way through the brush to strangle her. She stopped the slapping of her feet. Stopped her ragged breathing, held it tight inside her lungs. She must listen now and wait.

The hand!

— FIFTH NIGHT —
the dream.

Did the candle extinguish during the daytime? She had failed in her vigil and still did not know. Where had she gone in the daytime, in fact? She could not remember sleeping, could not remember waking up. But there it was again, that light, and warm this night, not so metallic as it was. It spoke no evil things and threatened no vile hands upon her. With each shiver of the light wafted soft scents of leek and earthy mushrooms, the marrow of homemade chicken broth, the clean starch of fresh-cut potato. She blinked slowly, and began to hum to herself a long-lost lullaby. *Perhaps this is a dream,* she thought. The candlelight wrapped around her like a warm blanket, and she dreamed away, to her heart's content, in fact, of the soups her husband would make her on chilly autumn nights.

There is a soup brewing in my cabin when there cannot be, she thought. And she did not care. The lines around her eyes softened, her very cells expanded as thyme and pepper tickled her nose, and her hair seemed to float about her neck. Thick, rough hands cupped a wooden bowl before her, a wedding band glinting in the warm light. *Where am I now?* she wondered and realized that still, she did not care. Eventually, at some point, she would awaken, or then again, perhaps not. She was neither here nor there, but quite possibly, maybe everywhere. In a dream, or a memory, or her cabin, or the woods. *The light draws the eye.* And the eye was seeing soup and a long-dead husband and was filled with other visions of warm and sensuous things.

Perhaps I will be angry about this another day, scold these intruders for their wicked ways. But then again, she thought, the aroma of memory swirling thick in her mind's eye, *perhaps not.*

— SIXTH NIGHT —
the vigil.

There it was again, like a sun floating out in the darkness. When was it extinguished? When did it ignite? She had no recollection, had dreamed through all the night and it seemed, perhaps, through most of the day. Why could she not stay awake? Why could she not maintain her vigil? The candle sat there, taunting her, flickering out of rhythm, never letting her tear her gaze away. And yet, her gaze always faltered somehow, removed from focus in some mysterious way, lost somewhere within the day. *Perhaps I should take the candle away,* she thought. And then, *why should I?*

No, tonight she would watch, stay awake through night and day, and she would see the truth of its lighting and its snuffing. There would be no pitter-patters, no slap of hair against skin. Only silence, and the occasional scuffling of agitated hands against linen.

Will I see the hand? She wondered as she watched. *Is it that which has lit the candle?* She could no longer remember when she had first seen it lit.

The Light that Draws the Eye

Possibly it has been lit all along. The moon shone full and bright in the sky, a potent manifestation of the ebb and flow of life. Her teeth ground against teeth, her eyelids blinked dry against eyes. Her jaw clenched so tight it could crush, perhaps, a marble. *Perhaps the candle will not change while I watch it. Perhaps the hand will stay out of the moonlight, for it is hiding great secrets. They are hiding my soup and my pie, and my crushed velvet blanket.* Her hands formed stone fists around her nightdress; two pale, dense orbs, like the moon, manifest.

My husband is trapped there. I'm certain of it!

— SEVENTH NIGHT —
the truth.

Her vigil failed; her day was lost to sleep or dreams or the sea of memory. *Damn you!* she thought. And then, *I am already damned.* Her arms thrashed about, and she pulled at limp hair. There it was.

A warm yellow-orange suffused against those deep bluish blacks of shadows, leaves, and pines. So peaceful. How could she be brought to such anger by something so innocent and pure? In its light, she almost thought, that just maybe, perhaps, little purple buds were forming in the mess of ivy and vines.

Her cabin seemed a witch's cottage, a children's fairytale incarnate. Overgrown and alluring, it whispered of sweet and sensuous things, promised soft, lush blooms and sugar-dusted berries. Is this what she saw, or what they saw? The bearer of that wicked hand? Oh, she knew the truth. She knew behind that facade lurked nightmares and terrible visions to rattle the soul. And this is what it did to her. Enchant, entice, drive to rage. *A terrible witch has stolen my home. A terrible witch has imprisoned my husband.*

She began to quiver, to bubble with rage. And then, just beyond the orange haze of the light, she glimpsed a single, delicate, long-fingered hand. The witch's hand! But then a second, rougher hand cupped gently around the curve of a hip. *My husband's hand.* Fingertips wrapped daintily around the back of a neck. Skin traced skin down from collarbone to wrist. She put a finger to her own skin, felt nothing. Felt nothing! A deep sadness flowed through her like the swell of a tide. She felt herself to be a candle keeping vigil over memories that would crumble to ash. *A candle to keep the ghosts out, another to watch them dance.* She watched them dance in the candlelight. She watched the skin and the hands.

She sat down and let long-lost memories carry her out to sea somewhere. And drifting, she was lonely, but she was free. And she danced in the shadows those bodies cast in the candlelight, rode the swell of the waves, followed the will of the wind, and she kept her vigil.

— EIGHTH NIGHT —
the fury.

Again, she had failed. She had lost herself in dreams, in a rowboat out to sea, somewhere far, yes, very far away, where the waves were made of velvet and the candle pulsed like a lighthouse in the distance, slowly fading to black. But now she pitter-pattered, now her hair whipped about her neck, now she watched as shadows danced along her walls.

A fury swept through her, the wind carrying the candle's flame like a bellows, where it erupted like a bomb within her. She knew it now, was certain of it, there was nothing but terrible things in her cabin. *The candle has lulled me to passivity, stolen all my goodness from me, mocked it all away.* Was that laughter she heard? *I will not be lulled to sleep again!* she thought, and swore the glow grew brighter. She squinted hard, and — was it? — if her eyes did not deceive her, food lay upon the table. A sudden waft of leek and lilac bloomed across the night.

My nose deceives me. But her eyes did not. The light draws the eye. And the light illuminated Virginia creepers as they tightened their grip on the stone cabin walls, squeezed it, strangled it, cut off its pulse. Cut her off from her head, her heart, her home. The very walls constricted where the vines made their noose. Her breath came in fast, sharp huffs; her feet halted their pacing, her feet seemed to leave the ground. A lightness, a levitating, a thrill of exultation.

Do my ears deceive me, too? She heard music, a soft tinkling sound, an old off-key piano. The notes smelled of soil, of dry leaves, of huckleberry pie. *My eyes will not deceive me.* Large, rough hands touched the candle holder. Placed there just for her, she knew! Was certain. The shadows danced faster on the walls, the vines crept across space toward her, slithering like snakes, rising like waves. Coming for her. To choke her, to wrap tight around her neck. A feral scream ripped through her throat. She stamped and she thrashed, her eyes wild and frightening things.

And she stood and she watched with a gaze of steadfast fury. Fists

222

clenched tight, blades of grass tickling the bottoms of her feet.

And the candle again grew brighter.

— NINTH NIGHT —
the candle.

She must go. *The light draws the eye. The light draws me like a beacon.* Her ears roared with thundering waves and her hands gripped tight around her nightdress. With one great thrust of motion, her journey began. She stumbled among the brambles, the bracken, the moss. With the lunge of one foot and then another, she came closer to her defiled cabin, the vile evil lurking within. *The lies, the lies, the lies,* she muttered.

The ivy seemed to flutter and breathe on her approach. And then she saw the symbol, a white mark upon the wall, an outline like the planchette of an old spirit board. She stopped and she stared. *The mark of the witch,* she thought. But it is the light that draws the eye. The power of the candle overwhelmed her. *I must go nearer. I must see the truth of it.* And she stood before the window, the great blazing, glowing candle reduced by proximity to a tiny quavering thing. And beyond it, so easily, she saw the intruders of her cabin. They sat there, cozy and smiling, like they'd done nothing wrong. Wearing strange clothes, showing too much skin, and the drape of the fabric all wrong. From the past, from the future, from some supernatural realm?

Tap, tap, tap, her finger went on the glass. Her gaze bore into them, watching them almost jump out of their skin. Her gaze was steady as she watched them whisper. *My eyes will not deceive me.* They were fearful, this she knew. She spoke to them, scolded them, pointed her finger in accusation. *"This is my cabin, my home. Mine!"* Their eyes grew large, and a hand grabbed at an arm for consolation.

She moved to the door. Above the knob was a strange pad with numbers on it. What was that? It was not here before, some strange contraption. *Dark magic, evil thing.* She wriggled the handle, but the door didn't budge. *"Let me in!"* she roared. *"This is my cabin! My home!"* She grabbed the handle, shook the door as hard as she could. *"You have my husband. You have my pie and my crushed velvet blanket!"* The smell of lilacs grew thick in the air. She shook the door, she kicked it, she heard a shriek inside. *Witch!* she thought. *I will make those shadows dance for you!*

She stood again before the window, having floated there on waves.

She danced and thrashed and raged and huffed. She listened to the voices. Fog, just fog, she heard them say, all the while their voices trembling. *My eyes will not deceive me.* She peered through the veil of her rage and found the night clear, riddled with stars and lit by the bright waning gibbous moon, the ground free from a shroud of fog. And then she shook from her toes to her fingertips, her hair lifting from her shoulders and quivering, shivering like rattles and dancing like snakes. *Why won't they leave? Why don't they listen to me!*

She picked up a stone and hurled it through the window. When the glass shattered, soup and huckleberry and lilac hit her like a wave. The woman screamed. But she screamed louder still, scolded them, cursed them, yelled through the window, *her* window. *"Get out of my home! Show me my husband!"*

The man stood up, put his arms on the woman's shoulders, and pressed her deeper into the couch. He whispered something she could not hear over her own hoarse screaming, over the scents of the secrets held within her home. The man took great stomping steps toward the window, pulled the candle from its holder, and threw it through the hole in the glass. It went straight through her. *"Noooo,"* she muttered it. *"Noooo,"* she wailed it. *"Noooo,"* she screamed it, pacing back and forth, pulling her hair out at the roots. She stood still and looked at the wide-eyed couple in the window. *My eyes will not deceive me.*

It went *through* her. But for a moment, it lit up her soul. *A light to keep the ghosts out, another to fight the shadows, another to watch them dance.* She chanted it, stomped her feet, grew louder, screamed it. Her hair floated about her neck, the vines reached out to her, wrapping around her ankles, tethering her to the earth as her feet left the ground. *"This is my home!"* In the window, she saw her husband. *My eyes will not deceive me.*

Dry autumn leaves caught fire behind her. Then so did she. No pain, no heat, only light. And she realized: she was the vigil she had kept.

She was the light that draws the eye.

She was the candle glowing bright in her own window.

And for a moment, she burned bright and solid.

The Light that Draws the Eye

ASHES OF THE SILVER FLAME

A SHORT STORY BY
ABIE DAVIS

CONTENT WARNINGS

This story contains themes that may be distressing to some readers, including:

Moderate violence

Dedicated to those who never stopped believing in magic.

Ashes of the Silver Flame

I arrived in Greyhaven under a bruised sky.

Last night's storm still echoed in my bones. The town, Greyhaven, stank of brine, fish guts, and the sour reek of rotting seaweed.

Now, dawn light unveiled the wreckage: splintered piers, bobbing flotsam. The sea-swell had battered the harbour mercilessly. A splintered mast jutted from the shallows near the pier. It was all that remained of some unlucky fishing boat.

A fine spray of salt hung in the air. The world was wet and grey. Even the colors had drowned in the storm.

This was it, the ragged edge of Aeloria's Stormcoast. What a fitting name.

For all its name, Greyhaven was no safe haven at all – merely a battered outpost clinging to the Stormcoast while the sea tried endlessly to claw it back.

Pulling my threadbare cloak tighter, I limped on. Each step sent a dull ache through my knees – a lingering gift from a life on the road and too many hard falls.

I must have looked like a vagrant emerging from the mist: mid-forties, unshaven, hair tangled with salt, clothes little more than rags.

One of the dockworkers eyed me warily, as one would a stray dog. Another spat and went back to hauling broken planks. To them, I was just another drifter blown in by the gale.

Fine by me. Anonymous was safe. Anonymous kept me one step ahead of the past.

A gust of briny wind cut through my cloak, and I tasted salt on my tongue. It stung my throat. Greyhaven's narrow coastal lane lay ahead, muddy with seawater and debris.

Sailors cursed as they untangled ropes and righted capsized dinghies. A few children ran about, chasing driftwood like toy boats, their laughter a brief brightness in the gloom until their mothers called them back to help.

Overhead, the clouds hung low and dark, reluctant to leave. With each step, I hunched my shoulders and pressed on, leaning on my wooden staff.

At the far end of the dockside lane, a stone seawall had partially collapsed where the waves had breached. Townsfolk gathered there in clusters, inspecting the damage and muttering.

I kept my distance. The last thing I needed was conversation or pity. People here had troubles enough of their own.

As I passed a shuttered shrine by the roadside, I noted it had once borne the sigil of some sea-god – now the paint was peeling and the small offering bowl lay empty save for rainwater. Fading faiths, indeed. Greyhaven's gods had gone as silent as mine.

My hand strayed to the pendant hanging under my tunic – a small amulet of tarnished silver shaped like a flame. Cold metal, slick against my palm. The symbol of Seravai, goddess of wild magic.

Once, that pendant marked me as her priest. Now it felt more like a millstone dragging me into the deep.

I clenched it instinctively as another tremor of pain twisted inside me, the familiar ache of memory. Mila's face flashed before me – my daughter's bright smile the day I gave her a wooden toy ship, the way her dark eyes danced like sunlight on water.

I hissed through my teeth, forcing the recollection back into its coffin. Not now.

I released the pendant, letting it fall against my chest beneath the cloak, hidden from sight. Better it stayed hidden; symbols of the old faith weren't welcome in towns like these, not since the storm of wild magic scorched the world.

Not since the goddess abandoned us.

I moved on, skirting around a toppled cart, its driver shouting curses at no one. Each curse was an old prayer in reverse – calling damnation where once someone might have implored a deity for aid. But the gods weren't answering, so damnation was all they had.

No gods, no magic, I thought bitterly. Only survival.

§

The waterfront opened into a small market square of cracked cobblestones.

Stalls had been overturned by the storm. A few merchants were salvaging what they could – a man in a soaked turban struggled to lift a crate of oranges upright, muttering about losses; an older woman wrung seawater from a bundle of cloth that might once have been fine silk.

I momentarily paused at the square's edge, an old urge to help tugging at me. It would be nothing to lend a hand to that old woman with her heavy, sodden fabric...

But I stopped myself. Others quickly stepped in to assist her, and I took the chance to slip by unnoticed. Keep moving, Tomas.

As I passed, I caught a glimpse of my reflection in a puddle: a gaunt, weather-worn face, stubble peppered with grey, eyes haunted by the storm inside. I looked away.

The puddle rippled under a drizzle that had begun to fall, blurring the reflection into nothing. For an instant, I didn't recognize the hollow-eyed wraith staring back at me as myself.

On the far side of the square stood a long wooden warehouse, one wall facing the sea. It had taken a beating; the plaster was cracked, and a corner of the roof sagged.

Several workers were already atop ladders, trying to hammer things back into place. Through its broad doorway, I saw barrels and crates strewn across the floor, the goods likely soaked if not ruined. A portly man with a ledger yelled at some laborers to be careful with the remaining cargo.

A crack of thunder made me flinch and look up.

The storm was spent, but an angry black cloud still hung over the bay, trailing fingers of lightning. As I paused, a heavy raindrop splattered on my cheek, rolling down like a cold tear. I brushed it away with a callused finger.

Then came the sound that would change everything: a sharp *CRACK*, not of distant thunder, but of wood splitting nearby, followed by screams. I whirled toward the noise by instinct.

One of the storm clouds had spat down a final thunderbolt, and it found its mark. Mila's scream, ten years gone, flashed bright as the lightning.

The old warehouse I'd just passed moments before now belched black smoke from its far side. The lightning strike had shattered the upper wall. Even as I watched, part of the roof collapsed inward with a roar.

Debris rained down – planks, shingles, shards of burning timber. Workers who had been repairing it shouted alarmingly, scrambling down their ladders as the structure groaned ominously.

For a heartbeat, I stood frozen.

Splinters and ash swirled in the air, and a few figures staggered out of the ruin, coughing and covered in soot. The portly man with the ledger was kneeling in the mud outside, wailing about his warehouse. Others rushed to help him up or beat out embers on their clothes.

Amid the chaos came a panicked cry: "Help! Someone's trapped!"

A dockhand stumbled out carrying a limp form; he laid his friend gently on the ground and then turned to dash back, shouting that more people were inside.

Smoke poured from the gap where the wall had been, and I could see flickers of flame inside. The lightning had done a thorough job.

I gripped my staff hard enough that my knuckles ached. Instinct, training, habit – whatever it was, every muscle in me tensed to run forward, to help.

My boots stuck. Old fear. Then the child screamed again, and the past shoved me forward.

People rushed past me toward the wreckage. Two fishermen dashed in with wet blankets to beat down flames.

A young woman, maybe a weaver by her apron, ran over carrying a coil of rope. They were strangers to those trapped, yet they went. And here I stood, a coward in a tattered cloak, trying to melt into the background.

Another cry, higher-pitched – a child's voice – echoed from within the shattered warehouse.

My heart clenched. I saw villagers exchange stricken looks at that sound. A few hesitated near the entrance, smoke billowing out as flames crackled.

"There's a child in there!" someone shouted.

My chest tightened. Smoke, fire, screams... it was slicing too close to memory. I tasted copper as I realized I'd bitten my tongue.

A small, terrified wail came from within the ruins, and that sound cut through me sharper than any blade. I imagined Mila in there, alone and afraid.

My vision blurred, the edges of the present moment melting into the past for one terrible heartbeat – my little Mila reaching for me...

The pendant at my throat grew suddenly warm against my skin, a pulse of heat I hadn't felt in years. I gasped and yanked it out from under my tunic.

The silver flame symbol glimmered faintly as if caught by unseen light. It hadn't glowed since... since the Binding, since the day everything went to hell.

Help, daddy… help! Mira's voice echoed in my head.

My hand closed around the pendant.

A surge of emotion swelled within me – grief, fear, and something else, something like hope struggling to breathe. No. No, not hope. Anger. *Why now? Why in the gods' grieving ashes would you answer now?*

Another child's sob snapped me back to harsh reality.

A little child was trapped under that wreckage, and each passing second could steal their last breath.

Near the warehouse entrance, two men had gathered, arguing anxiously – one wanted to go in, the other held him back, both terrified. The townsfolk had no miracle, no magic to save the day, just as it had been for me and Mila – no divine intervention, only mortal hands.

Damn it all.

Before I had fully decided, I found myself moving. My legs carried me forward through the crowd. I tore off my heavy pack, tossing it aside to move unhindered.

The rain picked up again, cool needles against my face as I pushed past a burly sailor who'd retreated coughing from the smoke.

Inside the collapsed warehouse was chaos.

Flames licked broken beams. Tar stung my nose; smoke clawed my throat.

I crouched low, pulling my damp scarf over my mouth.

"Hello!" I rasped, voice cracking from disuse and smoke. "Where are you?"

A faint whimper answered, off to the right, behind a pile of collapsed timber and half a dozen toppled barrels. I clambered over a fallen beam, staff clutched in one hand.

The heat was intense; sweat sprang on my brow immediately. In the flicker of firelight, I saw a tiny hand protruding from under a broken table and wood slabs. Gods.

"I'm coming!" I called, praying the child could hear. Another weak whimper. The little hand moved slightly, then went still.

I fell to my knees beside the wreckage, heaving aside smaller planks and debris. Beneath were the remnants of a fallen storage shelf, pinning the child.

I saw a small figure in a sooty yellow dress curled under the table, dust and ash coating her dark hair. She looked about five years old. Her eyes were closed; she might have been unconscious – please, not dead.

My arms strained as I tried to shift a heavy beam across the wreckage, trapping the table in place. Too heavy. I planted my staff as a lever and heaved, gritting my teeth.

The beam shifted a fraction with a groan of nails. Smoke swirled around me; I coughed hard, nearly retching. The heat was searing my lungs. This damned beam wouldn't budge enough.

Outside, I heard faintly someone shouting, "Is anyone still inside?" and another voice, "That beggar went in!"

I barked a cough that might've been a bitter laugh.

The pendant against my chest seared suddenly, a flash of heat that made me cry out.

Let me help, Daddy.

My hand, slick with sweat and blood from a scrape, slipped from the staff. A jolt of something – power – rushed up from my gut to my heart and out through my free hand as I instinctively flung it against the beam.

For an instant, the world went white.

A sound like a great *whoosh* roared in my ears. My palm blazed with heat. When my vision cleared, I saw the heavy beam had been flung aside – tossed as if by a giant's hand, now crashing to the floor with a thunderous thud.

It left a trail of silvery flames dancing along its length, flames that vanished after a breath, leaving only ordinary fire clinging to the wood.

Wild magic – raw and unbridled – had answered my call. After so long... a mix of dread and grim exhilaration twisted in me.

In the aftermath, my vision swam. A copper tang flooded my mouth, and bile roiled in my gut. My legs buckled underneath me as a feverish tremor seized my limbs, and I doubled over retching into the ash–streaked floor. Every breath felt like splinters in my lungs.

With the beam gone, I scrambled forward, shoving aside the table and broken shelf that had shielded the child. I reached the girl and carefully gathered her into my arms. She was limp, but I felt a faint rise and fall of her chest.

Alive, thank the gods.

The fire was spreading, hungrily devouring old rope coils and sailcloth stacks. I shielded the child's body as best I could with my arms and turned back the way I came, hunched low.

My exit was now a corridor of flame; smoke clawed for our lungs.

Heat blistered my skin. The girl moaned softly, stirring in my arms –

236

alive, and starting to come to. We were running out of time. The smoke would kill us even if the flames did not.

My eyes watered as I looked desperately for another way. There – a gap in the wall where the lightning had struck, partially open to the street. If I could climb through.

Clutching the girl tightly, I smashed my staff against the weakened boards blocking that gap. They gave way with a crack, and fresh air flooded in – a blessed cool gust from the storm outside. I hauled us both toward it.

"Cover your face," I rasped to the girl, not even sure she could hear or understand. With one arm around her and the other bracing the edges of the gap, I shoved us through the narrow opening and out into the rain.

We tumbled onto wet cobblestones a few yards from the warehouse's seaside wall. I hit the ground on my back, skidding on the slick stone. Pain lanced up my hip.

The girl rolled from my grasp onto her side. A chorus of gasps rose from the knot of townsfolk that had gathered at a safe distance. They had likely thought me dead, or the child lost.

I sucked in great gulps of salty, smoke-free air. Every inch of me ached, but I was alive.

More importantly, the girl in the yellow dress was alive. She coughed – a thin, weak sound – then she started crying, a reedy, terrified wail that was the sweetest sound I'd heard in ages.

Tears of relief stung my eyes, hidden by the rain on my face.

A few people rushed forward now that we were clear of the burning structure.

"He got her!" someone yelled.

My palms were blistered and black with soot. As I steadied myself, I realized the silver pendant was dangling openly on my chest, its once-bright flame symbol now dulled with tarnish and ash. I quickly shoved it back under my shirt before anyone noticed.

My mind was reeling with what had happened in there – what *I* had done. A bolt of wild magic, responding to me as if the old days had never left. As if Seravai still listened. But that was impossible.

Sure, the magic had hurt me, wrenching itself out of me to shift that heavy beam. My limbs trembled from exhaustion, and after images still swam across my vision.

Despite the pain and my disbelief, I recognized the touch of magic.

My heart thundered almost as loud as the fire behind me. *Why now?*

Rain was coming heavier now; villagers ran for cover or formed a bucket line to douse the flames. A rail-thin man with a greying beard rushed through the crowd – a look of sheer gratitude on his soot-streaked face.

"My daughter – is she –?"

The woman holding the girl turned so he could see. The child – Lira, I would later learn – was still crying, but very much alive. She reached out her arms, and the man swept her up, clutching her to his chest.

"Thank you," he sobbed, looking over his daughter's shoulder at me. "Thank you, stranger. I thought – I thought I'd lost her." He wore the rough boots and salt-stained tunic of a fisherman – a common man, brought to his knees by uncommon gratitude.

I stood awkwardly, rain plastering my hair to my skull, feeling more exposed than ever. I didn't know what to say. The girl was safe; that was all that mattered.

I gave a curt nod, my throat raw from smoke and shouting. The father looked like he might fall to his knees in front of me next, which made panic rise in my gut.

I... I couldn't handle this. Not the gratitude, not the eyes suddenly on me like I was some hero. I was no hero. If they knew the truth about me...

Before he or anyone else could approach further, a loud cheer went up from the onlookers who had gathered at a distance.

"He saved the girl!" someone cried jubilantly. A few others took up the cheer.

They looked at me with something akin to awe in their exhausted faces – people battered by storms and hardship yet suddenly alight with hope.

A middle-aged woman in the crowd made a trembling sign of the sun on her chest and whispered, "A miracle."

Others shushed her quickly, darting fearful glances around – even hope was a thing to be careful of under the Order's gaze. To them, I must have seemed like a miracle worker – a ragged outsider who walked into the fire and came out with a child in his arms.

I couldn't bear those eyes. A cold dread slithered in my stomach. Miracles draw attention.

As if on cue, I spotted movement beyond the crowd.

Two figures were striding purposefully down the lane toward the smoldering warehouse, clad in dark cloaks despite the rain.

They moved with that telltale confidence of authority – everyone they passed cast their eyes down or aside, even in the midst of chaos.

One was a broad-shouldered man with a shaven head, the other a younger woman with a scar across her cheek. Under their rain-soaked cloaks, both wore the dark mail of the Order.

I glimpsed a crossbow slung over the man's back, and a longsword hung at the woman's hip – they came armed and ready. Each wore an iron brooch clasping their cloaks, fashioned in the shape of a black sunburst. My blood ran cold.

Inquisition scouts.

Here. Of all the forsaken luck, the Order's dogs had arrived, doubtless drawn by the commotion... or by the telltale flare of wild magic amid the storm. Their kind could smell sorcery like sharks scenting blood.

Heart hammering, I tugged my hood up, shadowing my face as best I could.

The crowd was still between me and those scouts, but they were closing in, scanning faces and assessing the situation.

I heard the man bark to a villager, "What happened here?" and the trembling reply, "L-Lightning strike, sir. That man – he pulled a child out..." The villagers' eyes flicked in my direction.

Damn it. My feet began to move before my mind finished cursing. I backed away, keeping my head low.

The last thing I saw as I slipped into a narrow alley between two stone storehouses was the Inquisitors pushing through the throng, heading straight for the charred shell of the warehouse – and for the knot of people still gathered around it, including the grateful father and his daughter.

The girl was safe. They had no reason to linger on me if I disappeared now.

As I melted into the shadows, I caught a snippet of the Inquisition woman's voice, sharp and suspicious: "Who is he? Where did he go?" The rest was lost in the crackle of the dying fire and the rumble of thunder overhead.

I was already gone, vanishing like smoke into Greyhaven's maze of alleys before they could lay their eyes or hands on me.

§

For hours, I ran blindly through the twisting backstreets.

I cringed inward as each splashing footfall echoed in the narrow confines. "I'm going to get caught if I keep this up," my breath wheezing, heart pounding.

I forced myself to slow and move more carefully, hugging the walls. My lungs burned from the smoke I'd inhaled, and I stifled a coughing fit against my sleeve.

At one crossroad, I glimpsed a lantern's glow and ducked behind a rain barrel as heavy boots splashed past. The Inquisitors' voices drifted through the dark: angry, frustrated.

"Spread out," I heard the man snarl. "He can't have gone far."

I waited, heart hammering, until their steps receded. Greyhaven was a warren of crooked lanes, and I knew I could lose them if I kept to the deepest shadows.

I limped down an alley toward the old temple quarter as the adrenaline ebbed. At last, when I was certain I'd shaken any pursuit, I allowed myself to breathe and take stock of my surroundings.

§

Night had fallen by the time I found refuge in the ruins of Greyhaven's old temple.

Rain seeped through the gaps in the half-collapsed roof as I slumped against a cold stone pillar, chest heaving from the chase.

I had fled through winding alleys until the shouts of the Inquisition scouts faded behind me, leaving only the drum of my ragged breath and the distant patter of rain. My legs trembled with exhaustion.

Every bone and old wound in my body ached – a bitter reminder of the *magic* I'd unleashed and the toll it took. I tasted blood where I'd bitten my tongue during the escape, and my skin still stung with fresh burns from the fire.

For a long moment, I simply crouched there in the shadows, shivering. A withered husk of a man, hiding in a broken temple of a dead goddess – how fitting.

Water dripped onto my brow from a fractured beam above, tracing down my face like cold tears. I let them fall. I was too numb for pride or comfort; only weariness and guilt remained.

§

As my eyes adjusted to the darkness.

I surveyed the once-sacred place my panicked feet had carried me to. Weeds choked the courtyard beyond the archway, and moonlight glinted off toppled stones.

At the center loomed the shattered idol of Seravai: once the goddess of wild magic, now a rain-slick ruin.

Her statue had been decapitated and broken at the waist, the top half lying in pieces around the pedestal. Vines crept over the fragments as if trying to bind the goddess back together.

The sight made my stomach twist with a concoction of anger and heartbreak.

I forced myself upright, leaning on my staff for balance, and limped toward the crumbling altar at the statue's feet.

The altar slab was split, blackened with soot and old ash. Charred timbers were strewn about, remnants of when the Order had put torch to this place years ago, snuffing out Seravai's sanctuaries after the Binding.

My boots stirred up swirling motes of ash with each step. *Ashes of the Silver Flame* scattered and cold.

In the silence, my gaze fell on a faded scrawl painted across a toppled marble panel leaning against the wall. The crude symbol of the Order, a black sunburst, had been drawn there and slashed in red.

Beneath it, nearly obscured by moss, were the words: **"WHERE WERE YOU?"**

The question struck me like a physical blow.

I staggered and caught myself on the altar's edge, heart pounding. Some forsaken soul must have scrawled that after Seravai's fall. After our world was abandoned to silence. *Where were you?* I whispered it again in my mind as lightning flared faintly outside.

A bitter laugh escaped my throat.

Slowly, I sank to my knees before the ruined altar. Rainwater and grime soaked through my travel-worn pants, but I didn't care.

My fingers closed around the small pendant hanging at my chest—the silver flame symbol of Seravai. It dug hard into my palm. I realized I was shaking, whether from cold, adrenaline crash, or the corrosive emotions raging inside me, I could not tell. Perhaps all of it at once.

Staring up at the mutilated statue of the goddess, I felt something in me fracture. The question on the wall tolled in my head, relentless: *Where were you?*

"All those years I begged you for a sign," I rasped into the darkness, voice low and raw. My words echoed off sagging beams and stone, dripping with venom and grief.

"I prayed until my voice broke. I would have sacrificed *anything...* *everything...* to save her. And you did nothing."

My whisper reverberated, gaining strength. I bared my teeth and hissed through them, pressing the pendant so tightly that the sharp edges bit into my skin.

"Was it retribution, Seravai? Because we tried to bind you? Is that why you took her from me?" My volume rose without meaning to, bouncing back from the ruined walls.

I forced it down again to a harsh, hate-filled whisper.

"They called us heretics! Hunted us like animals for believing in you. Maybe we deserved it. Maybe I deserved it. But *she* didn't. Mila was innocent. She was only seven... only seven years old."

My vision blurred with hot tears.

When was the last time I had wept openly? I couldn't remember. I had grown adept at numbing myself with cheap ale and denial. Anything to keep the pain at bay.

But now, alone in the dark with the ghost of my goddess, the floodgates opened. My shoulders jerked with silent sobs as words tumbled out, a decade's worth of anguish and fury spilling into the void.

"I loved you," I snarled bitterly, shaking the amulet in my fist as if to jolt life back into it. Rain and tears mingled on my cheeks, cold and stinging.

"I gave my life to your service! I kept faith when others wavered. And when your priests twisted your nature—when they tried to *chain* you—I... I stood by and let them. Like a coward, I hoped they knew better. I watched them doom us all. And you—" my breath hitched on a sob, "you did nothing to stop it!"

My shout rang through the crumbling sanctuary, fading into the distant rumble of thunder.

No answer came from the broken stone or the empty sky beyond. Only the wind sighed through the exposed rafters, a forlorn whistle. The goddess I once worshipped with all my heart was gone. Maybe she never was there at all.

Gradually, my ragged breathing slowed. The outburst left me hollow, an extinguished husk collapsing under the weight of years. I realized I was hunched forward, kneeling in the mud before the sundered altar like a penitent before a tomb.

A bitter half-chuckle escaped me. Penitent. Yes, perhaps I looked insane, raving at a dead goddess in a forgotten ruin, begging absolution from silence. Perhaps I *was* insane.

Gasping in the damp air, I slumped and rested my forehead against the cold stone altar. The solidity of it grounded me a little. I closed my eyes, utterly spent.

Rain dribbled down from the open roof, pattering my back and neck. My tears had stopped, leaving tracks in the grime on my face. Now there was only a vast, aching emptiness inside my chest.

After a long moment, I drew a shuddering breath and opened my eyes. In the dirt by my knees, dark soot stains formed the outline of old burnt offerings, long since turned to cinders.

I lifted the little silver-flame pendant, unfurling my stiff fingers. Even in the darkness, I could see the faint gleam of its polished surface. I had worn this symbol of Seravai since my youth, through faith and *apostasy*, through every triumph and every tragedy.

I thought of casting it aside right then, flinging it into some dark corner and leaving it in the dust. But I knew I wouldn't. For all my fury and grief, I could not yet sever that final connection.

The chain chafed at my neck, heavy with unspoken meaning. I slipped the amulet back under my tattered cloak, resting it against my heaving chest.

Lightning flickered beyond the shattered roof, illuminating the temple ruins in a stark white flash. Soot-stained mosaics glistened wetly on the walls, depicting coiled serpents and blooming flowers, symbols of the wild goddess's domain, now cracked and fading.

With the wild magic snuffed out, those images felt like carvings on a tomb.

All of Aeloria had languished under a pall since that night. The wonders and terrors of old were gone, leaving a world as hollow as I felt.

Many called it peace or penance—an end to chaos—but to me, it was a sorrowful silence. As if the land itself were holding its breath, waiting for something: the return of magic... or the final death of hope.

In the void left by Seravai's fall, the Order's power had spread like a blight. Town by town, their inquisitors enforced curfews, tribunals, fear.

They filled the vacuum with iron laws and flaming pyres. Broken shrines like this one littered the realm. They were all monuments to a faith chased to the corners of the world.

I closed my eyes and exhaled slowly. Memory flooded in like a tide, cold and inexorable. Despite my exhaustion, I knew sleep would not come. When I closed my eyes, I only saw the past, that night replaying in vivid detail behind my eyelids. I could smell the hot ash and blood, hear the thunder of collapsing stone...

I was there again, in the Grand Sanctum of Seravai in Elesar, ten years past, on the night it all ended.

That night, a decade ago, I found myself back in the Grand Sanctum of Seravai in Elesar, the night it all went to hell.

The marble floors gleamed under flickering torchlight as twelve of us stood in a wide circle around the great wooden statue of the goddess.

Our voices droned in a low chant, repeating the Binding Hymn repeatedly until the words lost all meaning. My heart thudded with dread beneath my ceremonial robes.

High Priest Aedran paced at the circle's center, silver-chased chains coiled in his arms. Four lengths of black iron, each inscribed with runes of binding and blessed by every archbishop of the Order.

They were tools of audacious hubris, meant to symbolically cage Seravai's essence and bring wild magic to heel. I remembered how my gut twisted with doubt even then. *Could* any mortal truly chain the wild goddess?

Every instinct screamed that this ritual was wrong.

But I did nothing.

Fear held me in place. Fear for my little girl, waiting innocently one floor above. Aedran's threats had been thinly veiled earlier that day.

"You won't be our guests for long," he had said with a patronizing smile. "Just help us tame the wild goddess, and you and your daughter will return home. Unless it takes longer... in which case we'll have to find a more *permanent* arrangement."

I caught the cold gleam in his eye as he glanced at Mila by my side. The message was clear: my daughter would pay the price if I refused to cooperate.

What could one disgraced flame-priest do against the full might of the Order? I was alone, a coward clinging to the hope that Mila would be safe if I obeyed.

So, I stood by like a spineless accomplice as they prepared to violate my goddess' very soul.

We intoned the final verses of the hymn. Aedran stepped forward, each movement deliberate as a snake.

"Steady," he murmured, though his voice trembled. With ceremonial gravity, he draped the first chain around the statue's shoulders. The metal links clanked unnaturally loud in the hushed sanctum.

A chill rippled through the air. I swallowed hard, my throat bone-dry, and continued chanting.

Another priest—Brother Kalvis—brought the second chain, looping it around the statue's torso. As he did, the brazier sputtered in the statue's wooden hands.

This brazier was the very heartfire of Seravai, an eternal flame said to be lit from the first spark of creation. Usually, it burned a gentle gold.

Tonight, for an instant, it flared a violent *blue*. Gasps rose from the watching acolytes who lined the walls. My stomach lurched. Was that a warning... or just my terror playing tricks?

Aedran shot us a sharp look. We pressed on with the ritual, voices rising to drown our mounting dread. Sweat beaded on my brow despite the Grand Sanctum's chill.

My eyes kept darting up to the shadowed arches of the ceiling where, directly above, Mila would be waiting in our little guest room. I'd tucked her in hours ago, assuring her I'd be back soon, that everything would be fine.

Brave girl. She tried so hard to smile and believe me. My heart clenched at the memory of her face, so trusting. I tightened my grip on the staff in my hand and forced my trembling lips to keep forming the words of the hymn.

The third and fourth chains were lifted into place by Aedran's assistants, encircling the statue of Seravai completely now, like dark iron snakes binding a living tree.

The moment the final link fell against the wood, a sound like a distant sigh echoed through the hall. My chanting faltered. For a heartbeat, all was still.

Then a fork of lightning lashed across the domed ceiling, impossibly, *inside* the temple. It was as if a thunderstorm had torn through reality above us. In the same instant, the brazier's flame erupted upward in a pillar of searing silver fire.

"Back!" someone screamed.

Chaos detonated. The nearest priest to the statue—old Father Briant—was engulfed as the silver flame whooshed outward. He didn't even have time to cry out; one breath he was there, the next a living torch collapsing in a shriek of fire.

The rest of us broke formation, panic shattering our holy pretense. I threw myself back as the iron chains around the statue glowed red-hot and then white, straining and warping. With a horrible molten *drip*, the links began to liquefy, puddles of blazing metal splattering onto the altar and floor.

I stared in horror as cracks splintered through the wooden statue, fissures spider-webbing across Seravai's serene carved face.

High Priest Aedran stood transfixed, eyes wide and reflecting the inferno. This was not the controlled suppression of wild magic he had promised the Order. This was an explosion, raw, vengeful power unleashed tenfold.

"Seravai, mercy!" I heard myself cry as chunks of burning wood rained down. I raised my arms uselessly to shield my face. A colossal *boom* followed, an unseen force blasting out from the statue like an exploding star's shockwave.

It hit me full force, flinging my body aside like a rag doll. I sailed through the air and slammed into a marble pillar. I heard a crack and a red-hot agony flared in my side; one or more of my ribs had just broken.

I hit the floor in a heap, gasping, unable to draw breath for a moment. All around me the Grand Sanctum was coming apart. Flames crawled up the tapestries lining the walls. Stone and timber cracked and tumbled from the trembling ceiling.

Panicked acolytes and clergy ran in every direction, their prayers turned to screams. The very air was alive with a deafening, high-pitched whine, magic unbound, whipping through the chamber like a tornado.

The world itself seemed to convulse. I dragged myself up to my hands and knees, choking on smoke and pain. My broken ribs grated with each shallow pan.

Through the churning haze of dust and embers, I saw Aedran, illustrious High Priest of the new Order, lying crushed beneath a fallen beam, his sightless eyes reflecting fire. He had wanted to play jailor to a goddess, and in the end, he died a fool's death.

"M-Mila," I coughed out, barely a whisper. A spike of panic cut through my shock. Mila was still upstairs, likely asleep or cowering in fear as the temple collapsed.

I had to reach her. Nothing else mattered now.

Ignoring the agony knifing through my chest, I staggered to my feet. The chamber tilted and swam in my vision. I clutched my side with one hand and used my staff with the other, limping toward the archway that led out of the sanctum.

Others were stampeding for the main doors, but those had blown off their hinges entirely. I glimpsed the night sky through the gaping entrance, lit by mad flashes of silver lightning outside. Seravai's fury wasn't contained to the temple; it was spreading through the city.

A young priest nearly bowled me over in his desperate flight. I grabbed his arm, intending to steady him, or beg for help, but I recoiled as I saw his face.

The flesh was... *shifting*, as if unseen hands pressed and moulded it like clay. His eyes bulged, one dilating while the other shrank. He gurgled wetly, lips twisting in a soundless plea as wild magic coursed through his body, warping as it went.

Before I could react, another thunderous crash from above sent chunks of plaster raining down between us. The unfortunate young man stumbled away into the chaos, half-mad with terror and disfigurement. I forced myself onward, tears of smoke stinging my eyes.

The corridors beyond the sanctum were dark and filled with choking fumes. I knew the way by instinct, up a curving stone staircase toward the modest guest room we'd been given.

Mila and I had arrived only the day before, brought by the Order from our village under guard. *Just a formality,* they had told me. *Your daughter will be comfortable while you assist us.* I should have known better than to trust their assurances.

Each step up the winding stairway felt like a mile, my injured side screaming with each jolt. A section of the wall had collapsed, exposing the staircase to the night air. Through it, I could see Elesar beyond the temple grounds.

The city was descending into nightmare: bolts of silver lightning arced from building to building, setting rooftops ablaze. I heard distant explosions and an eerie, keening wail that did not sound human. The Binding had failed catastrophically, unleashing a storm of wild magic on everything around.

At last, I reached the landing and threw myself down the hall toward our room. The door was ajar, hanging loosely from a splintered frame. I stumbled in, half-blinded by smoke.

"Mila!" I screamed, coughing.

There. On the floor by the little bed. A small figure in a soot-stained nightdress. My heart stopped. I rushed to her side and fell to my knees, nearly collapsing as another flare of pain lanced my ribs.

Mila was lying motionless on her back. For one terrible second, I thought she was dead. There was blood trickling from her nose and ears, staining her pale cheeks. But then I saw her chest give the faintest rise. She was alive. Oh gods, she was alive. Relief and terror warred in me.

I gathered her into my arms, cradling her head.

"Mila, Mila, look at me," I begged, brushing singed brown hair from her face. She wasn't responding. Her eyes were open, but blank, staring through me. Her small body felt unnaturally rigid, every muscle taut as a bowstring.

Worse, tiny arcs of silvery light skittered across her skin like miniature lightning dancing over her arms and neck. I realized with dawning horror that raw magic was coursing through her frail form, the same wild power that was tearing the city apart.

She stopped breathing.

"No… no, no, no." A frantic litany babbled from my lips as I fumbled to lay her flat. Training took over where panic threatened to paralyze me.

I pressed trembling fingers to her neck. There was a pulse, faint and fluttering like a dying bird. She was slipping away.

I will never forget the sight of my little girl that night: her face smudged with ash, eyes staring at nothing, silver sparks crawling over her like some living web. It was an abomination. A child's body wasn't meant to channel such power.

That damned ritual was killing her.

"Hold on, my love. Stay with me, just stay…" I pleaded as I tore the amulet from my neck and pressed it into her small hand. Her fingers were so cold. Hot tears blurred my vision, but I forced myself to focus. If there was ever a time for a miracle, it was now.

I placed my hands over her heart, the way I had done countless times when tending sick villagers back home. Summoning every shred of training and faith left in me, I began to chant the healing canticle. Words of supplication, of light and life. Words I had thought holy.

A faint glow ignited beneath my palms, gentle and golden.

"Come on," I whispered, voice shaking. The glow bathed Mila's still face. "Please, Seravai... please... save her. Take me if you want a life. Take me instead! Just don't take her, please..."

I poured every ounce of magic I had ever been blessed with into that healing spell. Warmth flowed from my hands into her chest. But the moment the magic touched those writhing silver sparks on her skin, it recoiled.

The golden light scattered across her in droplets, sliding off without effect, like rain on oiled glass. I tried again, feverishly switching to a purifying rite, then another prayer of mending. Anything, everything I could recall through my haze of panic.

My hands glowed, but nothing I did could penetrate the wild magic consuming her. It was as if some invisible barrier surrounded her, rejecting all hope of salvation.

"N-no... please...!" I sobbed, desperate. Mila's eyes fluttered once. For a heartbeat, they seemed to focus on me. In them I saw agony... and the faintest flicker of recognition.

Perhaps she knew I was there at the very end. Her tiny hand tightened almost imperceptibly around my silver flame pendant. A single, soft sigh escaped her lips. I watched, numb and disbelieving, as that hateful silver light danced in her eyes one final time... then winked out.

A lone silver *spark* drifted from her parted lips, her last breath made visible. It floated upward and landed on the pendant she clutched, then faded to nothing. Her fingers slackened. The charm fell from her hand onto my chest.

Mila was gone.

A raw animal howl ripped its way out of my throat. I cradled my daughter's lifeless body to my chest and screamed like a man being flayed alive.

Perhaps I was.

My soul was certainly being torn apart piece by piece. Around me the world was ending. Gouts of fire and light consuming the night, the temple collapsing, but I no longer cared.

Let it fall. Let the whole cursed city burn and bury us.

I rocked back and forth on the bloody, smoke-stained floor, pressing Mila's head to my shoulder, tears pouring down my face as I begged any god or devil to trade my life for hers. Take me. *Take me!*

They didn't.

I don't know how long I knelt there, keening and cradling her. Minutes? Hours? Time lost meaning.

I was dimly aware of the roof above finally giving way, flaming timbers plummeting all around. A slab of stone struck my back and I hardly felt it. Pain was nothing; I was already broken.

The last thing I remember of that night was the feeling of a gentle rain on my face as I stared upward. The storm had moved directly over the city, and through the gaping, ruined ceiling I saw torrents of water and silver lightning pouring down from the heavens.

A sheet of white flame and rain descended upon us. I closed my eyes and held Mila tight as the fury of a vengeful goddess crashed down.

And in that blinding light, everything went dark.

§

The nightmare faded by degrees.

The roar of collapsing stone gave way to the gentle drip of water on the shrine floor. I wasn't in Elesar anymore. I was here, in Greyhaven's ruined temple, kneeling in the dark, my arms wrapped around myself as if I were still holding my child.

"Mila…" I breathed her name into the silence, and it left my lips like a prayer and a curse all at once.

The only answer was the distant roll of thunder and the whisper of rain through broken beams. My entire body was shaking uncontrollably. Whether from the memory or the chill seeping into my bones, I could not tell.

I wiped at my wet cheeks with a muddy hand, smearing tears and rain.

I had survived that night.

Some days I still don't know why. When dawn broke over the charred ruins of Aeloria's capital, a squad of the Order's soldiers found me half-buried in rubble, miraculously alive with Mila's body limp in my arms.

Perhaps they thought me too far gone to bother with at first. A broken man in every sense. By the time I regained my wits, they had far bigger fires to put out across the city and beyond.

In the confusion, I slipped away before they could decide what to do with the heretical priest who had helped unleash this catastrophe. Maybe

I *should* have let them execute me; a quick death might have been kinder. But instead, I became a fugitive, a lingering pawn in the goddess's cruel game.

In the weeks that followed, people flocked to Order for assurance, peace, and protection. They formed the Inquisition, a zealous scourge tasked with hunting down anyone tied to wild magic or Seravai's clergy.

My fellow priests, those who hadn't died that night, were rounded up and burned or driven into hiding. As for me, I became a ghost on the roads.

I discarded what remained of my old life and even my name. Tomas the flame-priest effectively died in that sanctum along with his daughter. What walked out was something else: a hollow man carrying nothing but guilt and the *ashes* of failed faith.

For ten years I wandered, avoiding towns, speaking to no one unless I had to.

Guilt was my only companion. And guilt does not make for pleasant company. I offered no more prayers to any power. I sought no comfort in temple or church.

Most nights I found it in the bottom of a bottle instead. Wine, ale, whatever could dull the edges of the pain for a few hours. It never lasted.

I'd wake from nightmares of Mila's face, only to find the same sorrow sitting heavy in my chest. A living ghost. That's all I was. A dead man who hadn't had the decency to stop breathing.

§

It took a long time before my shaking subsided there on the shrine floor.

Slowly, I pieced reality back together: the faint smell of wet stone and mildew, the ache of my bruises and burns, the distant call of a gull from the harbour.

I was here, now. Mila was gone. Safe from pain, beyond fear, beyond the reach of any Order or goddess.

At some point, the drizzle had ceased without me noticing. Only droplets from the eaves plinked into shallow puddles. The silence of Greyhaven pressed down like a weight. By the watery moonlight filtering in, I could tell midnight had long come and gone. I might have knelt here lost in memory for hours.

I drew in a slow breath, steeling myself. One thing was certain: come morning, I would have to leave this town far behind. The Inquisition would not give up after a single skirmish tonight.

They would scour Greyhaven once they realized their scouts had failed to find me. More of them would come, maybe dozens, and I refused to let any more innocent people get hurt on my account. The sooner I vanished, the safer for everyone.

Groaning softly, I planted my staff and forced myself to stand. My joints protested after so long on the cold stone, and a spike of pain in my side reminded me of the evening's exertions. I sucked in a breath and steadied myself.

My head swam from exhaustion. Using the staff like a walking stick, I hobbled toward what used to be the temple's grand doorway, now just a gaping opening filled with night.

As I limped out into the open-air courtyard, I found the storm had truly passed. The clouds were breaking apart, revealing patches of star-strewn sky.

The air smelled of wet earth and lingering smoke from the distant warehouse fire, but all was eerily calm. Too calm, like the breathless lull before some unseen tempest.

I had only taken a few steps beyond the fallen arch when that uneasy quiet was shattered.

§

A sudden scream ripped through the stillness, raw and urgent.

I froze, every muscle tensing. It was a man's voice, shouting in panic or pain somewhere in the warren of streets beyond the temple grounds.

A second later came a crash of metal clattering to the ground. Then another voice, deeper and angry, barking words I couldn't make out.

I felt the hairs on my neck rise. Even after years, I knew violence when I heard it.

For an instant I wondered if my mind was playing tricks. After reliving that night, maybe I was hearing echoes from the past. But no… these sounds were real and close by. Perhaps a street or two over, near the ramshackle cottages by the docks.

Then I heard it: a child's high-pitched cry, piercing the darkness.

My blood turned to ice. It was a sobbing wail of pure terror, and I recognized the voice at once. It was the same little girl I had pulled from the fire earlier. Lira. Even through her cries, I was certain it was her.

A sick feeling clenched my gut. Gods, no. Not again.

The image of Mila's small, rigid body flashed across my mind overlaying Lira's face. Hadn't that child suffered enough for one night? Hadn't I done enough damage by intervening?

Heart hammering, I slipped from the temple courtyard into a narrow alley, moving toward the sounds. I kept to the deepest shadows, instincts honed by years of hiding guiding my steps.

Part of me begged to stay out of it. Hadn't I learned my lesson about getting involved?

But I couldn't ignore Lira's sobs any more than I could ignore Mila's memory. The gods wouldn't be so cruel as to put another child in mortal danger before my eyes... would they?

I crept down a winding side street, each step measured and silent. The cries and voices were clearer now, drawing me like a moth toward flame. I hugged the wall of a timber cottage and peered around its corner into a small open square lit by a few guttering lanterns.

What I saw made my teeth clench in fury.

Several villagers were gathered at the edges of the square, hovering in nervous silence. Their eyes were fixed on a scene unfolding in front of one of the modest homes.

The door to the cottage stood ajar, lamplight spilling out onto muddy ground. There, in the center of the lantern light, a bearded man knelt in the mud with his hands locked behind his head.

I recognized him: Lira's father, the same man I'd seen sobbing thanks after I carried his daughter from the blaze. Now his face was bloodied, one eye swollen shut, as he knelt defenseless before his attackers.

Lira herself was a few paces away, clutched protectively in an older woman's arms, perhaps a neighbor. The woman was pale as death but doing her best to comfort the child, who was wailing uncontrollably. Lira's tiny fists clung to the woman's apron, her eyes squeezed shut in terror.

Towering over the kneeling father were two figures in dark leather armor, each marked by the black sunburst of the Inquisition on their breasts. My stomach twisted.

The same pair of scouts I had encountered earlier tonight. I had hoped, prayed even, that I'd lost them for good in the maze of Greyhaven's docks. They had been more tenacious than I gave them credit for.

Or perhaps the townsfolk themselves had pointed the way. Either way, the hunters had found their prey's trail again.

The female Inquisitor stood closest, her scarred face contorted in a vicious scowl. She had discarded the heavy cloak she wore earlier; now I could see a studded cuirass and a short sword in her fist. The blade's tip hovered inches from Lira's father's throat.

Her partner, a brawny bald man, lingered a step behind her. He held a loaded crossbow casually aimed at the small knot of neighbors who had gathered. The implication was clear: no one was to interfere if they valued their lives.

"I'll ask once more," the scarred woman hissed, her voice low and lethal.

"Who was he? The sorcerer who pulled your girl from the fire. You spoke to him. Where did he go?"

Despite the fury simmering in her tone, I detected a taut eagerness beneath it. They were like wolves on a hot scent. My heart thundered in my ears as I watched Lira's father struggle to speak through split, swollen lips.

"I-I told you," he stammered, shaking visibly. "I don't know! He was a stranger. He saved my Lira and vanished into the night. I've never seen him before."

His one un-swollen eye flickered over to where his daughter sobbed in the neighbor's arms.

"Please… she's scared. Let us be. We've done nothing—"

The Inquisitor's response was a swift boot to his gut. The man crumpled forward with a choked groan, only kept upright by the woman's iron grip on his collar.

A ripple of shock and anger went through the onlookers. One young fisherman stepped forward as if to protest, but the bald Inquisitor levelled the crossbow at him with a cold stare. The would-be hero shrank back into the trembling crowd.

My hands tightened around my staff until my knuckles burned white. I felt a red haze creep into the edges of my vision as the female Inquisitor yanked Lira's father back up by his hair.

He gasped, coughing, struggling just to breathe.

"We have witnesses," the woman said, her voice dripping with malice. "People saw you thank the sorcerer. Saw you speak to him. You're lying to protect a heretic. And do you know what that makes you?"

She leaned down, almost gentle in her menace, and answered her own question: "A traitor. An accomplice to the highest form of sedition." She spat the last word like poison.

She pressed the sword's tip under his chin, forcing his head up. "We could execute you and your entire family right now, and it would be *lawful*."

A collective murmur of horror swept through the villagers. One of the women let out a quiet sob. The bald man smirked as he swiveled the crossbow slowly, reminding them all to stay back.

§

Rage coursed through me, hot and acidic.

I realized I was shaking again, but not from fear this time. This was all because of me. These good people had endured a fire and nearly lost their child tonight and now the damned Order was ready to murder them in cold blood because I had intervened.

Because I had used magic I shouldn't even possess. My reckless attempt to do the right thing was about to bring the hammer of the Inquisition down on them.

No. Not this. I would not allow another innocent family to be destroyed in front of me.

Once in my life I had stood by and done nothing, and it had cost me everything. I would not watch passively as this man was butchered and his daughter possibly harmed, all due to my actions.

There was no time to think it through, no careful plan to be made. If I hesitated even a moment more, someone was going to die right here and now.

Before I fully knew what I was doing, I stepped out from the alley's mouth and into the open square, my staff in hand.

"He told you the truth," I called out, voice ringing across the lantern-lit space.

Every face whirled toward me, the onlookers, the Inquisitors, Lira's father swaying on his knees. The two hunters reacted with startled confusion that melted at once into vicious satisfaction.

They had been searching for a rogue miracle worker, and here I was: a gaunt, bedraggled man leaning on a wooden staff, my cloak still smeared with soot and blood. I might as well have painted a target on my forehead.

The bald Inquisitor wasted no time. He pivoted, bringing the crossbow to bear on me instead. "Halt! Who in blazes are you?" he snarled, levelling the bolt straight at my chest.

I raised my free hand, palm out, in what I hoped looked like a pacifying gesture. My heart was thundering, but I fought to keep my voice even.

"Just a traveler," I said loudly. "A traveler who happened to be in the right place at the right time. I saw the fire and did what I could to help. The girl was trapped, and I got her clear, that's all."

The female Inquisitor's eyes narrowed. She kept her sword at the kneeling man's throat, but her attention was now fully on me. I could feel the hatred emanating from her like heat off a forge.

"Helped, you say," she mocked. "We know *exactly* what you did, witch."

She gave the father a hard shove, knocking him to the mud, and started advancing toward me. Her boots squelched in the muck, the lamplight gleaming on the crimson insignia on her chest.

"On your knees, now," she barked, eyes alight with triumph.

I didn't move. Behind her, Lira's neighbor hurriedly dragged the child back into the cottage's doorway, whispering frantically to hush her. Good. At least the girl was out of immediate harm's way.

"I'm unarmed," I lied calmly, taking a few slow steps forward. In truth, a small rusted knife hung at my belt beneath my cloak, but it was laughable against trained inquisitors.

"I don't want any trouble. There's no need for violence. Let the man and his daughter go—they've done nothing wrong. Your quarrel is with me."

My words only provoked a mirthless snort from the bald soldier.

"No need for violence," he says. After using sorcery in front of a crowd?" He spat on the ground. "Drop the staff, heretic, or I'll skewer you where you stand."

He kept the crossbow trained on me, finger on the trigger. The woman was circling slowly to my left, sword pointed at my heart.

I quickly realized they intended to capture me alive if possible. Far better for them to haul in a witch for public execution than to kill me here and deny their superiors a spectacle.

But I also saw that if I so much as twitched the wrong way, the bald man would happily put a bolt through my chest and call it a day. Either way, my life was measured in instants now.

My mouth went dry, but I steeled myself. Fine. If this was to be my end, at least I could ensure these townsfolk were safe first.

"I'll come quietly," I said, voice steady. "Just promise to leave them alone."

"Shut your mouth," the woman growled. "You're in no position to bargain."

I inched further from the alley entrance, deliberately drawing their focus away from the bystanders. Mud squelched under my boots. My mind was racing.

Should I try to fight? I was half-crippled with exhaustion and injury; they were fresh and armed. In a fair fight, I had no chance. But nothing about this was going to be fair.

The inquisitors began to fan out, one on either side of me. The bald man's crossbow never wavered. The scarred woman focused on me, clearly ready to cut me down if I made any move.

My gaze flicked past her for an instant, toward Lira's father. He was sprawled where he'd fallen, gasping for air. Our eyes met and I saw a mix of despair and regret there, as if he blamed himself for drawing me back into danger.

I offered him the smallest nod and a tight, sad smile. It wasn't his fault. This was my choice.

"All right," I said quietly. "You've got me. I'll kneel."

Slowly, I began to lower myself, letting my weight lean on the staff as if in surrender. The woman took another step forward, within striking distance now. The bald man kept a few paces back, giving himself a clear shot. They thought they had me cowed.

In truth, my mind was coiled like a spring. Not in years had I attempted anything reckless.

But seeing Lira's tiny form quivering in that doorway, seeing her father beaten and these jackals ready to slaughter them... something snapped the final restraint in me. Maybe it was suicide to fight.

But if I was fated to die tonight, I would damn well go out on my own terms.

I bowed my head, drawing their eyes to the motion, feigning submission, then I struck.

With a snarl, I surged up from my crouch and swung my staff in a tight, brutal arc. The iron-shod tip whistled through the air and cracked against the bald man's crossbow.

I felt the jarring impact as wood splintered. The bolt he'd been ready to lose went flying harmlessly into the mud, his shot spoiled by my blow.

"Bastard!" he roared, stumbling back a step with the ruined crossbow in hand.

I had no chance to follow up; the female scout lunged at me with a gleam of steel. I barely twisted aside. Her sword slashed a shallow line across my upper arm instead of plunging into my chest.

White-hot pain lanced through me, but I gritted my teeth and drove my elbow into her face as she rushed past. The crunch of cartilage was satisfying. She yelped, staggering, blood spurting from her smashed nose.

I turned to swing my staff at her again, but the bald inquisitor was already upon me with a furious bellow. He had dropped the crossbow and drawn a broad hunting knife from his belt.

I interposed my staff just in time to block a stab aimed at my gut. His blade scraped along the wood with a shriek. He barreled forward, using his weight to slam me back.

We went down hard in the mud, his full bulk crushing me. The impact knocked the wind from my lungs. I lost my grip on the staff as we hit the ground; it skittered out of reach.

In an instant the man was on top of me, pinning me in the muck. Rainwater and filth soaked through my cloak. I struggled, but he was younger, stronger, and armored.

He let out a feral grin, straddling my hips, and raised his knife high.

Time slowed to a heartbeat. I caught a glimpse of the female Inquisitor a few yards away, on one knee, wiping blood from her nose with murderous eyes.

I saw Lira's father trying to rise, dazed, and the neighbors staring in shock. But most vividly, I saw the knife poised in the bald man's fist above me, its steel slick with rain and reflecting the lantern light.

This was how it would end, then: stabbed in the mud like a rabid dog.

Perhaps I deserved no better. I felt strangely calm at the thought.

But as the knife began to plunge, survival instinct overtook fatalism. I got both hands around his wrist just as the point drove toward my face.

Blade met flesh with a jolt of force. With all my strength, I just barely managed to hold the man's thick wrist back. He snarled and bore down, trying to drive the knife home.

The tip hovered a hand's breadth from my right eye, quivering as I fought him. My arms shook with effort; he was immensely strong, fueled by righteous fury and hatred.

Slowly, inch by inch, the dagger crept closer, my grip slipping in the mud and blood.

"No..." I gasped through clenched teeth. My muscles were burning, vision blurring from strain. He was going to overpower me.

Hot droplets of his spittle hit my cheek as he leaned his weight into the blade, growling, "Die, heretic!"

I let out a desperate cry, somewhere between a sob and a roar.

No, leave my daddy alone! I was frozen as the voice, Mila's voice, echoed in my mind.

What was happening? Was I going crazy just as I'm about to die?

Don't let him, dad... Mila's voice whispered through my thoughts.

My mind scrambled for any advantage, any last trick. And in that moment of mortal peril, the thing I feared most, the *magic*, answered my call.

A sudden heat flared in my left hand, the one still clutching the length of my staff (or what portion of it I could reach on the ground beside me).

It grew rapidly, painfully hot as if I were gripping a branding iron. Out of the corner of my eye, I saw a glow, faint silvery light tracing along the carved runes in the wood of my staff.

Runes I had etched there in devotion so many years ago, back when I still believed my goddess heard me.

My heart lurched. Not now. Please, not now, I thought wildly.

I didn't control this power; I didn't even understand it. It had burst forth earlier during the fire and saved Lira... but what if it consumed me next? What if it hurt these people I was trying to protect?

I had no time to weigh the risk. The knife was grazing my brow, a thin line of blood trickling into my eye.

With a final, desperate yell, I let go of the inquisitor's knife arm with one hand and thrust my palm toward his chest.

Wild magic, born of terror and wrath, *surged*. My vision went white for an instant as a concussive blast erupted from my outstretched hand. It struck the man atop me like the kick of a giant horse.

His eyes flew wide in shock. One moment he was crushing me into the mud, the next he was lifted clean off and hurled backwards with bone shattering force. I heard rather than saw him hit the stone wall of a cottage several yards away.

The sickening crunch that followed told me I needn't worry about him any longer. He crumpled to the ground in a heap of limp limbs and did not stir again.

I rolled onto my side, chest heaving. My head swam and a wave of nausea nearly doubled me over. The burst of magic had sapped what little strength I had left.

Every joint in my body felt like water, and a pounding headache pulsed behind my eyes. I coughed and spat, tasting iron. Blood was flowing from my nose, a crimson drip pattering into the mud.

My body was punishing me for calling on the goddess's cursed gift.

But it had saved my life. The bald Inquisitor lay twisted and motionless by the cottage wall. Whether he was dead or merely broken, I neither knew nor cared at that moment.

A ragged gasp drew my attention back to the female scout. She was still on one knee where I'd seen her last, a few yards away. Her eyes were huge, *fearful* now, rather than cruel. She had witnessed what I'd just done, seen me unleash that invisible force.

Even among the Order's zealots, few had likely seen wild magic in action since Seravai's fall. To them, it was an abomination, a demon's trick. And I had just confirmed every worst story they told about me.

"You... damned witch," she coughed, wiping blood from her lips. Her sword was lost somewhere in the dark, but she drew a long dagger from her hip.

Even injured and afraid, her fanaticism was undimmed. With a hoarse scream, she pushed to her feet and rushed at me, blade low, intent on finishing this at any cost.

I scrambled up, planting my boots under me and grabbing my staff with both hands. My shoulder throbbed where she had slashed me earlier; warm blood trickled down my sleeve.

I felt utterly drained, unsteady. But I managed to raise the staff in time as she closed the distance.

She lunged, sweeping her dagger toward my belly. I twisted with a grunt, the blade skittering off the side of my coat instead of sinking into flesh.

Summoning the last of my strength, I swung my staff two-handed. It connected solidly with her forearm. The dagger flew from her grasp with a splash into a puddle.

Before she could recover, I reversed momentum and slammed the oaken shaft against the back of her skull with a dull *thok*. The force of it jolted up my arms.

The Inquisitor's eyes rolled back. With a feeble gasp, she collapsed face-first into the mud at my feet and went limp.

I stood over her, chest heaving, staff still raised in a shaking grip. Lantern light and shadows spun nauseatingly around me as I tried to catch my breath. It was over.

Both inquisitors were down, neutralized. Silence crashed down on the square, broken only by my rasping breaths and the distant drip of water from the rooftops.

For a moment, nobody moved. Then a low sob of relief came from the cluster of villagers. The danger had passed.

§

I bent at the waist, bracing myself on my knees.

Black spots swarmed at the edge of my vision, and I feared I might faint. My body felt like it had been trampled. Every muscle quivered, and a pounding headache pulsed behind my eyes. I swallowed repeatedly, trying to keep the bile in my stomach from rising.

The magic I'd unleashed left me feeling like a wrung-out rag.

But I was alive. More importantly, Lira and her father were alive. I had managed to protect them... for now.

With effort, I straightened. The onlookers were beginning to cautiously approach. I saw the neighbor woman rush forward from the cottage, still holding Lira tight against her hip.

Other villagers gathered around the injured father who remained collapsed in the mud, groaning softly.

Lira's father, dazed but conscious, crawled toward the fallen female inquisitor. For a moment I thought he intended to pick up her dagger and finish her off as she lay unconscious. He would have been well justified.

But he merely spat a mouthful of blood onto the back of her head and turned away, stumbling toward me.

He stopped a few paces off, eyes wide with disbelief and... something else. Gratitude, maybe, tinged with awe. He took in the sight of me, doubled over, filthy and bleeding, barely standing, and his battered face crumpled with emotion.

"You... you came back," he managed hoarsely. It was not a question so much as an astonished acknowledgement.

I gave a weak, weary smile. Or perhaps it was just a grimace.

"I'm sorry," I rasped, voice raw. I glanced at the cut across his brow, the bruises already darkening on his cheek. "They targeted you because of me. I never meant—"

He shook his head fiercely, then winced as the sudden motion caused him pain.

"You saved my Lira. Twice now. We'd be dead if not for you." His one good eye shone in the lantern light. Before I could react, he lurched forward and seized my mud-stained hand in both of his. He pressed it to his brow, a gesture of reverence I'd seen peasants give priests in better days.

Startled, I tried to pull back, but he held on with surprising strength. His voice trembled with fervor.

"Seravai herself sent you to us, I swear it. You're a blessing, sir... a miracle."

That word stabbed through me like a dagger of ice. I stiffened and gently extricated my hand from his grip.

Miracle? If only he knew the truth. I'm no miracle worker, just a broken tool through which the goddess might be acting if she was acting at all. And I wanted no part of that.

"No," I said more harshly than intended. "The goddess had nothing to do with it." The denial came out like a growl. The man looked taken aback, hurt even, by my tone.

I softened slightly, mustering a weary explanation. "I'm just a man— one who wasn't willing to let another child suffer."

He looked unconvinced. Honestly, I wasn't sure I believed my own words either. The things I'd done tonight defied any logic or ability I thought I had.

But I would rather cut out my tongue than praise Seravai for any of it. Not after what she had allowed to happen to Mila... and to the world.

The man opened his mouth as if to argue, but then thought better of it. Instead, he nodded, accepting my version for now. Behind him, some villagers were cautiously tending to the unconscious female inquisitor, tying her hands with rope and removing her weapons.

The bald man still hadn't moved at all; a couple of braver souls crept over to examine him, grimacing at what they found.

Lira's father followed my gaze.

"The big one's dead," he muttered. "Snapped his spine like a twig when he hit that wall." There was a note of grim satisfaction in his voice.

I simply grunted, unsurprised. A distant part of me was relieved I wouldn't have to face that brute again.

The neighbor woman now approached, coaxing Lira forward by the hand. The little girl's face was blotchy from crying, but when she saw her father standing and me beside him, her eyes lit with recognition.

She broke away from the neighbor's grasp and ran toward us on unsteady legs.

"You came back!" Lira cried, echoing her father's words with childish wonder. She barreled straight into me, wrapping her small arms around my legs.

I went rigid in surprise. My instincts screamed to gently push her away. Surely I didn't deserve the trust inherent in that embrace.

I wasn't some hero from her bedtime stories. But how could I refuse? Awkwardly, I rested a hand on her trembling back. She felt so tiny, so fragile. A lump rose in my throat.

Memories flooded with the simple touch of a child's arms around me. For an instant, it felt like I was holding Mila again, feeling my little girl cling to me like she used to when frightened of thunder late at night.

The innocent trust in that gesture was almost more than I could bear. It was a knife twist of pain and a balm all at once.

"I'm sorry I scared you," I murmured to Lira, patting her shoulder gently. She looked up at me with those wide brown eyes, and in them, I saw not fear but adoration. My heart lurched.

"You're bleeding," she said softly, pointing to my shoulder where the cut from the sword had soaked a good portion of my sleeve dark.

I managed a faint chuckle.

"It's nothing, little one. I've had far worse." I carefully lowered myself to one knee so I could meet her eye to eye.

Gods, everything hurt when I moved, my ribs, my side, my head, all competing with the new gash on my shoulder for attention. I swallowed the pain and mustered a reassuring smile for her.

"Lira, I need you to do something very important now."

She sniffled and nodded, listening intently.

"I need you to take care of your papa," I said. "He's had a very rough night, and he'll need his brave girl to look after him. Think you can do that?"

Lira wiped her nose with the back of her hand and stood a little straighter as if I'd just knighted her. "Yes," she said solemnly.

"Good girl." I brushed a stray lock of hair behind her ear, revealing a sooty smudge on her cheek. Without thinking, I spat on my fingertips and gently scrubbed the dirt away like I might have done for my own child once.

She held very still, patient under my tending. The simple act undid me. I had to blink rapidly to keep more tears at bay.

Suddenly she threw her arms around my neck, hugging me fiercely.

"Thank you," Lira whispered, her breath warm against my ear.

I closed my eyes. My throat felt tight as a vice. For a moment I couldn't speak at all. I returned the hug as gently as I could, patting her back.

This sweet, innocent warmth, how long had it been since I felt anything like it?

My soul felt like a threadbare cloak, and this child's gratitude was sewing pieces of it back together in ways I didn't know if I deserved.

After a long moment, I pried her loose with a trembling hand.

"Be brave, little one." I ruffled her hair softly. She gave me a teary smile and stepped back to her father, who put a protective arm around her shoulders.

The crisis truly over now, the neighbors hurried forward, peppering Lira's father with concerned questions and checking his injuries.

Someone wrapped a shawl around Lira to warm her. The older woman who'd held her scooped her up again, fussing and embracing her like a granddaughter.

A few of the stout fishermen who had tied up the female inquisitor were now debating what to do with her.

"String her up in the square as a warning," one man muttered, to a chorus of agreement and uneasy laughter. Another suggested quietly that it might be better to dump both bodies in the harbour and feign ignorance when more Order came asking.

The others grimly nodded; it was likely the wisest course for them.

I realized I should leave. Now. The longer I lingered, the greater the chance reinforcements would arrive and catch us all. My job here was done, at least as much as it could be.

Already my vision was starting to tunnel from fatigue and blood loss. If I didn't find a place to tend my wounds and rest soon, I might keel over on the spot.

I stepped back, swaying slightly. The movement caught Lira's father's attention even amid the flurry of townsfolk around him. He pushed through and came up to me, placing a rough hand on my good shoulder.

He leaned in, speaking low so the others wouldn't overhear.

"You need to go," he urged, confirming what I already knew. His voice was raw but earnest.

"There'll be more of them by sunrise, I'd wager. We'll..." he hesitated, then continued firmly, "We'll take care of these." He tilted his chin toward the unconscious woman and the corpse in the shadows. "Leave no traces. Buy you some time."

I felt an immense rush of gratitude to this man. A stranger whose life I had upended twice in mere hours. Despite everything, he was willing to shield me now, at no small risk to himself. How could I possibly thank him for that?

I gripped his forearm.

"I'm sorry," I repeated again softly. "For everything. I never meant any of this to fall on you."

He offered a weary smile through his bruises.

"You gave me back my daughter. Twice. We'll hear no apologies from you." He glanced over his shoulder at Lira, who was watching us with concern from the neighbor's arms.

"You should get moving. I reckon you know the roads better than most."

I nodded. There was nothing more to be said. He was right. I needed to disappear, now.

Before I turned to go, the man squeezed my arm.

"Listen," he whispered urgently. "There have been... rumors lately. Whispers that perhaps the wild magic isn't gone for good. A healer in Karun Vale who cured a dying man with a touch. Strange ghost lights over the ruins of Arkelai. Little miracles the Order can't quite stamp out." His eyes searched mine, hopeful.

"Maybe tonight was one more. Maybe Seravai is not truly dead. Maybe... maybe the Silver Flame is lighting again, even if just flickers."

I stared at him, unsure how to respond.

My immediate impulse was rejection. After all the horror Seravai's 'return' had caused in my life already, I did not relish the idea of her wild magic seeping back into the world.

And yet... a part of me, buried under cynicism and grief, wanted to believe it. To think that maybe, just maybe, some good could come back to this broken land after all.

But I couldn't afford such hope, not anymore. So I just managed a noncommittal shrug.

"I've heard the whispers too," I admitted quietly. "But I wouldn't pin my hopes on ancient gods. We have to look out for each other now because no one else will."

He looked a little disappointed, but he nodded in understanding.

Behind him, the villagers were already moving with efficient purpose. Two men had hefted the limp female inquisitor under the arms and were dragging her toward a nearby shed.

Another was fetching tools, likely weights or chains to sink the corpse of the other one when they hauled it to the water. These people knew exactly what needed to be done to protect their own.

It was not the first time the Order had brought violence to their doorstep, I sensed, though perhaps the first time the villagers had won, however briefly.

Lira wriggled out of the neighbor's hold again and ran to her father's side. She clung to his leg, eyeing me anxiously. I gave her a gentle smile.

"Take care of Papa, now," I reminded her softly. She nodded and wiped her nose, trying to put on a brave face.

It was time. I inclined my head respectfully to Lira's father.

"Thank you," I said simply. The word felt inadequate for all he and his people were doing, but he understood.

"And thank you," he replied, his voice thick. "May the gods—" he caught himself, then corrected, "May fortune protect you, friend."

With that, I pulled up my hood with a trembling hand and turned away, leaning heavily on my staff. My legs were like lead, but adrenaline still lent me enough strength to shamble into the alley from which I'd emerged.

I didn't look back. It was better that way. With each step I took, I faded from their world and they from mine, as if our paths had only briefly intersected in this dark square and now diverged forever.

Perhaps in time, the Order would come asking questions here, but I trusted these hardy Greyhaven folk to guard the truth. They had survived worse; they would survive this.

As for me… I would carry on surviving as I always did: alone, in the margins, unseen.

§

The cold predawn air was beginning to stir, carrying the scent of brine from the harbour as I left the square behind.

Dawn was approaching, and with it a new hunt. The Order would never stop pursuing a man like me, a renegade priest bearing the last embers of forbidden magic. And I would never stop running from the ghosts behind and the hounds ahead.

My ribs throbbed with each step. Blood oozed stickily from my shoulder wound, and I felt lightheaded from fatigue and blood loss. But I welcomed the pain; it meant I was still alive, still paying penance in this world for my failures.

As I limped down Greyhaven's empty streets, the eastern sky grew lighter with the first hints of dawn. In that dreary half-light, the town's silhouettes looked like black skeletons, charred by the night's fires.

Another day would soon begin under the Order's sun-cross banner. For Lira and her father, perhaps it would be a day of hope and gratitude that they still had each other. For me, it would be another day of exile and uncertainty.

I paused once at the top of a bluff that overlooked the bay. Behind me, Greyhaven lay quiet, its people beginning to retreat into their homes to wait out what remained of the night.

Before me, the open road and wilderness beckoned. I reached into my tunic and pulled out the silver flame pendant one last time, letting it catch the dim, newborn light of dawn.

The little charm was stained with soot and specks of blood. In my palm, it felt cold, inert.

Just a piece of metal. For ten years it had hung around my neck, a symbol of a goddess I had loved and then hated... and perhaps still couldn't fully let go of.

I thought of Lira's father's hopeful words. Maybe the wild magic was returning. That maybe Seravai had not truly abandoned this world forever.

A part of me wanted to snarl and cast the pendant into the sea right then. To be done with gods and destiny and false hope.

But another part, perhaps the part that moved my legs into that fire to save a little girl, refused to let go. Perhaps the truth was that I didn't trust Seravai... but I couldn't entirely stop *believing* in her either, in some form.

I closed my fist around the pendant.

"I am not your tool," I whispered hoarsely. Whether I meant the words for the absent goddess or the encroaching Order, I wasn't sure. Maybe both.

"Whatever power is left in this world… it's not yours alone. It's *mine*, too. My curse, my burden. You can't have it back."

And this pendant, my curse, was all I had left of Mila.

There was of course no answer from the dawn sky. Mila's voice stayed silent. I hadn't expected an answer. Not now.

With a weary sigh, I tucked the emblem away against my chest and turned my back on Greyhaven.

As the sun broke over the horizon behind me, painting the low clouds in forlorn hues of pink and grey, I set off down the coastal road.

A tattered wanderer against the coming day, carrying nothing but the scars of the past, and the faint, unwanted glimmer of magic that lingered in my soul like the last *ashes of the Silver Flame*.

BEAUTIFUL EVIL THING

A SHORT STORY BY
KELSEY CLIFTON

CONTENT WARNINGS

This story contains themes that may be distressing to some readers, including:

Blood and gore

Death

Violence

Allusions to sexual violence (but no descriptions or portrayals)

This is for every man
who wonders why we choose the bear

And for every woman
who wishes she could become one.

Beautiful Evil Thing

The first thing he knows is that his face is buried in dirt, and it smells like pine and blood.

Old blood and *old* pine, old enough to sink into the bones of the earth and withstand storm and fire alike. There are other smells, some wild and musky, others clean and sharp, but he can't parse them out beneath the overwhelming power of the first two.

The second thing he knows is that the forest is *screaming*.

It *is* a forest, his instincts say, both like and unlike the piney woods of the Gulf where he grew up. Insects chirp from every direction, and night birds call, and wolves howl way off in the distance. A hound bays in return, somewhat closer.

The third thing he knows, when he opens his eyes, is that he is not alone.

He yelps and scrambles up, his limbs at wrong angles and his eye line too low to the ground. He stands, and that's better, but he can't hold his balance for long before crashing back down to all fours. But it's the *wrong* all fours: Four paws planted solidly on the ground, covered in coarse brown fur and capped with wicked black claws. He knows those paws, has seen them in movies and documentaries for years. But still, the knowledge won't settle at the bottom of his murky, addled mind.

"You make a very handsome bear."

He looks up at the voice and finds the girl still crouching in front of him. She's slim and delicate, just the kind of girl he'd push up against in a crowded bar, trying to catch a whiff of shampoo or sweat. Her arms are folded over her white knees, the skin glowing like moonlight in the dim forest. A sun riding high over an ocean wave is tattooed on one forearm, while a wooden wand wrapped in white-flowered vines covers the other. Shaggy strawberry blonde hair falls over pale eyes as she examines him.

"Yes, you're much better this way," she decides with a nod. "Quieter, for one."

He's confused and afraid, and both of those things make him so very angry. A snarl builds in his chest, but it dies when the girl raises her hand, choked by a tightness that goes bone-deep.

"I should have explained the rules." She stares at him with those fey eyes, unblinking. The phrase *manic pixie nightmare girl* springs to the front of his mind. "The only one allowed to talk here is me."

The hound bays again, this time a little closer.

"You're wondering if this is all real," the girl continues, as if they're meeting over drinks. "Or is it a dream? Will you wake up in twisted sheets, sweating with unspent rage and fear? Or are you still at the bar, passed out in a pool of your own sick?"

The bar. That's right, he had been at some new bar on the corner, The Palace. She was the bartender who flirted with him, her tank top cut low and her shorts barely covering her ass. She even took a shot with him, something thick and syrupy overflowing a gold shot glass. That's the last thing he remembers.

A sharp canine winks out at him from her smile. She rises, and as she does her image flickers. For a moment she's the slut who ran off on his dad when he was a baby—

Then she's his whiny bitch of an ex-girlfriend—

Then she's that hot Instagram model, the one he likes to wank to after he calls her out for being an attention whore—

And by the time she stands at her full height, it is abundantly clear that she, like him, is not human.

She's resplendent now, unnatural sunshine pouring out from her rich red-gold hair. It tumbles artfully over a perfect unibrow and ferociously blue eyes lined in black. The lines of her face are stronger, her jaw square instead of dainty and pointed. A white Grecian dress edged in swirling red patterns hangs off her wide-shouldered frame, nipped in at the waist by a golden belt that reveals even wider hips. Her whole presence presses against him like a hand on his neck.

He was afraid before, but now he is *terrified*. He means to roar, to warn her back, but the fear fills him up, throwing out any wild suggestion that might appease her. So instead he approaches slowly and licks the fabric of her dress in supplication. He asks for mercy.

But she is implacable, the wild sea and blistering sun made flesh. "Somewhere on this island, there is a hunter," she says. "If you wish to go home, you must make your way past him and reach the shore. If he finds you like this, he will do everything he can to kill you." She is terrible in her beauty as she looks down at him. "But if you ask, I will change you back into a human."

Relief blooms in him.

"A human *woman*," she warns. "He might help you, if you take that form...or he might not."

The feeling withers and rots as the full danger of such a choice hits him. He wavers, chuffing softly as he backs away.

"You understand, then," she says, holding his gaze. "For all your words and actions to the contrary, you do know the things a man might do to a young woman he finds alone in the woods. At least this way, you might outrun him. And if he catches you, you might make him pay for the privilege of killing you." Her head tilts, a bird of prey sighting on him. "I can think of many women who would choose to meet him as a bear."

He wants to scream, to beg, to demand *why*. Why is she doing this at all? Why *him* when there are worse men out there by far? He hasn't *hurt* anybody, not really. A few comments, that's all. A palm here and there on an ass as he walked by. He's *harmless* for God's sake, a nice guy most of the time, but nobody in this bullshit woke world can take a goddamn joke.

The damned hound bays for a third time, this time close enough to startle the nearby woods into silence.

She leans closer to him, bloody hair flashing in the moonlight. "If you've made your choice, I would start running."

So he does.

He bolts away from the sound of the hound. The trees are large and spaced out, but he is not made for weaving between them. At least he barely feels the brush as he crashes through, other than the prickle of pinecones between his toes. Sneakers would be better, but jeans worse— and that's if she gave him jeans at all. If she didn't make him wear leggings, or a dress, or worst of all, only his own fragile skin.

He stops in a grove of squat, wide trees, different from the stately pines he woke up under. Which trees grow closer to the water? Is he heading towards the beach, or deeper into the island?

He raises his nose, questing for sea air, and the woman is at his side. "You brought this on yourself, really," she remarks lightly, running pale fingers down the trunk of a tree. "You should know better than to accept drinks from a stranger."

He chuffs at her and takes off again in the same direction. But at every turn, there she is, an icon forgotten deep in the woods. "Don't be so ungrateful," she tells him in passing. "In my youth, you would have been turned into a pig."

That's when he knows who she is: Another impossibility in a night overflowing with them. A witch, a villain, a seducer of men. Ruin as sure as the rocks that lurk just below the water's surface.

"They've told such tales of me over the centuries," she remarks as he stops at the edge of a shallow stream to catch his breath and still his shaking legs. His body is powerful, but it tires sooner than he expects. "Even when they forgot my name, I was still *kalon kakon*, the beautiful, evil thing that haunts your dreams and drives you to do terrible, wicked deeds. As if your wickedness was ever my burden to bear."

Partly to slake his thirst and partly to put some distance between them, he steps closer to a still part of the stream to drink. The smell floods his nose and he realizes the rocks half-submerged in the nearby water aren't rocks at all—they're a girl, her bloodless limbs naked and the wide moon of her head cratered and gaping. Her visible eye is pointed towards him, and something wriggles in the watery cavern of her mouth.

"That one chose less wisely than you," the woman remarks.

He tries to stumble back, but a hand on his head forces him to stay still. "*Look at her,*" a voice hisses, and it isn't the slim dream girl or the nightmare woman but a third thing, a creature with one tooth for every moment of misery and fear she has ever witnessed. A voice to eat the world and spit out the bones. "Look at every violation. You can't count them, can you?"

He can't help struggling, though he knows it's useless. The hand on his head tightens, drawing blood.

"Your stories tell you I changed men into beasts, but do they tell you why? Have you never *wondered?*" The light from her is scorching now, hot enough to singe fur and blister skin. "The first time men came to my island, I welcomed them in, and this is how they left me. They repaid my hospitality with violence. The magic I taught myself after that was only ever meant for protection—but you do so love to make villains of women who only wish to be left alone."

Hot breath spills over his snout as she leans closer to him. "And since you would not leave me in peace, you will not know it either."

He whimpers, unable to tear himself away from either the terrible sight or the terrible voice. The wriggling thing in the girl's mouth emerges and disappears into the water in a flash of slick skin. He would swear she is looking right at him.

"After all these years, I do have one regret," the voice with teeth murmurs in his ear. "I regret the mercy I showed by only changing them and never myself. I should have met them as a bear instead of a woman. I should have ripped their chests open and feasted on their hearts."

As quickly as it appeared, the hand is gone. He bolts in the first direction he sees, terrified of what he might witness if he dares to look back at her. Other bodies appear as flashes in the gloom: A Black woman with her legs twisted up beneath her, clothes ripped and bloody. An older olive-skinned woman with an arrow in her back, one hand still clawing desperately for the next tree. She makes a sound as he passes, but he can't stop. That scent of blood and pine is choking him.

He runs and runs until his legs falter and he stumbles, skidding to the cool earth with a heavy *whump*. A moment, he thinks. He'll rest here only a moment, free of the horrible presence of dead and dying women.

It takes him far too long to realize that the forest has fallen silent.

His nerves are razors drawn across a violin, the warning red-hot and immediate. Stumbling up to his feet, he turns in a circle, staring into the gloom hanging between the trees. Nothing stirs.

On the second circle his nose twitches on a new scent: Leather and something sharp, metal maybe. Unwashed human skin.

The hound bays from just beyond the closest trees, and he knows nothing except the need to flee. He wheels and scrambles away in the opposite direction, mindless of the brush he barrels into and the rocky formations he clips, which draw blood in bright lines.

At last he breaks into open ground, where his huge strides can eat up the distance. He shouldn't look back, he knows he shouldn't, but he can't help a single glance.

From the trees behind him, only a hundred feet away, a shadow is emerging. The snarling shape of a black hound first, its long muzzle open and snapping as it strains at its lead. Next is a worse sight by far: A broad-shouldered man, the details of his face blurred but the heat of his gaze unmistakable.

His mind goes white with fear, a single long, screaming note that blocks out everything else. He is grateful—*stupidly* grateful—that he chose to stay a bear.

The other side of the meadow is approaching swiftly. Over the *thud* of his paws tearing up the ground and the furious barking of the hound, he thinks he can hear the faint whisper of waves. The beach is just beyond those next pines, he *knows* it, and if he can just reach it, he will be safe.

Those are the rules.

The first arrow takes him ten feet from the trees.

Searing pain, and his back leg is collapsing. He roars and goes on, hobbling as fast as he can. A second arrow buries in his gut, tearing something vital. He goes on anyway, because to stop is death. Those are also the rules.

He staggers into the trees and sees immediately that he was right. Ahead, moonlight gleams on waves between the pines. Hope pierces deeper than the arrows.

The woman is walking beside him, stately and content in her power. "How have you liked being a lesson instead of a person?" she asks. "A cautionary tale for unsuspecting young men against the dangers of the world? People are so *complicated*, with all their nuances and feelings. They work much better as allegories."

He whimpers, one last plea for mercy. He's learned his lesson, he *has*. He'll learn whatever lesson she wants him to learn, if she'll only let him make it to the safety of the beach.

"Turn and fight him off," she tells him amicably. "How will they ever believe you otherwise? Surely if you didn't want this, you would fight back. Or better yet, you would never have been out here alone in the first place. What is that phrase they all use these days?" Those awful canines glitter at him as she smiles. "You must have been asking for it."

He's through the trees somehow, at the top of a gentle slope. At the bottom is glorious sand, and the slow curl of wine-dark waves.

But heavy bodies are crashing through the trees behind him, and his back legs are no longer working, and the world is wavering. He tries to crawl; if he can just reach the slope, he can roll down to the bottom. It will hurt, but he will survive. Any hurt is worth surviving.

She is waiting for him at the slope's edge, blood-gold hair whipping wildly in the sea-bright wind. "A tragedy," she sighs. "Another promising young man cut down by the witch Circe. He had his whole life ahead of him."

He is so close, but the footsteps are closer and the sound of the sea is fading. Her voice is the last thing he hears before the world goes black—

And he wakes.

He comes up fighting, clawing at the hands trying to help him up from the bar's sticky surface. It takes a moment to realize where he is, longer to calm the instincts still screaming inside his frayed body. The body is his own again, thank God, and there's no sign of the dream girl—just a chunky blonde behind the bar with an ugly frown cutting her face, and the bouncer currently hoisting him up.

He shrugs free and stumbles outside into the hot moonlight. Still panting, he puts a hand against his heart, grateful to be alive and here and himself again. He'll never drink again, he privately swears, at least not mystery shots. They aren't worth the vivid nightmares that still feel like eyes on the back of his neck.

A chills creeps down his spine. Around him, the parking lot is still—no humans, no birds, not even insects. Nothing at all to stir the heavy air.

In the distance, a lone hound bays.

THE END

BOY SCOUT CAMP

A SHORT STORY BY
ROBIN HAYNES

Boy Scout Camp

My son is a great kid. He is trustworthy, kind, cheerful, helpful, friendly, brave, and all those other things Boy Scouts are supposed to be. He really is those things, and all the time, not just when he's with his scout troop. He's made me a very proud dad.

I work hard at being the best dad I can be. Now, I'm sure I would love my kid no matter who he turned out to be; that's the way it is with dads — and moms too, I suspect. But it seems to me I have the best kid in the world. I gather there are others who feel that their kids are the very best, and I admire that sentiment, even though they are sadly misguided in that assessment. I would never want to make them feel bad. It's only right that they should feel a prejudice for their own. I'm just content to know that my kid actually is the best.

My commute is long. The city just didn't seem like a good place to raise kids. So we got a place in a tiny village out in the country, where he could breathe fresh air, go to good schools, and live a life just a little more innocent than the kids who are raised in town. Unfortunately, the result is that I'm up and out the door before the rest of the family is awake. And by the time I get home in the evening, there isn't time or energy to do much more than have some dinner and get ready to do it all again the next day.

I try to take advantage of the weekend for us to have some quality father-son time. Of course, he has a life also, and he often has plans on the weekend. I tell myself that at least he knows I'm there for him, even if he's rushing out the door to meet his friends down at the stream. Friends are important, and he deserves that time to go and be Tom Sawyer for a while. My wife gives me all the news, so I know what's going on in his life, and hers as well.

So when Frankie asked if I would spend a night with his troop at summer camp, I felt like I had to oblige. I certainly didn't want to miss an opportunity.

Frankie's Boy Scout troop is what they call a "wilderness" troop. When they go camping, they don't use the official Boy Scout camp, with cabins and real bathrooms. Oh, no! One of their Assistant Scoutmasters has some land up around Lookout Hill. Frankie's proud of the fact that they pitch their tents in the woods, dig their own latrine, and build a log bridge across the stream so they can take their swimming lessons in a pond.

Now my idea of "roughing it" is a hotel with no cable TV. My grandfather used to say he wanted to put his knees under a table. That skeptical view of the outdoorsy life is a family tradition, and this apple definitely did not fall far from the tree. I can't imagine how my son came to love abandoning civilization and tromping off into the woods, but he seemed to spend quite a bit of time drooling over catalogs full of sleeping bags, pocket knives, and windproof fire starters. It was the stuff of my nightmares. Nevertheless, duty called, and if my son wanted to share with me something that was that important to him, I wasn't about to let him down.

The week of summer camp was suddenly upon us, and we delivered Frankie and all his various gear to the meeting point. He proudly donned his backpack and bounded off to join his fellow scouts, clearly expecting that a good time was to be had by all. As I watched him with his friends, it was clear they were all excited about the coming adventure. I almost envied him the camaraderie, but then I remembered that I would be joining them in a few days, and a sense of impending doom fell over me.

I have no idea whether it is universal in the Boy Scouts, but it was a tradition in Frankie's troop to invite one of the dads to come up to summer camp each day. Not all of the dads are able to participate, but I was one of the lucky few. I would go up for dinner, stay the night, and then participate in the scouts' activities the next day. I was fortunate enough to draw the Friday night-Saturday slot; so I wouldn't have to take off work. I would also have a day to recover before I had to go back to work. However, it did mean that I had the whole week to anticipate the ordeal, like a condemned man looking forward to his execution. My wife did her best to distract me and keep me cheerful during those final days, but every once in a while, I'd remember what was coming, and the pall would descend once again.

In the blink of an eye, the day was upon us. I left work early so I could get home in time to change into something a little more rugged than my office clothes. After a quick hug and a word of encouragement from my wife, I headed up to the area where the boys were camping.

Boy Scout Camp

I parked where I had been instructed, took a deep breath, and bravely marched off into the forest primeval.

I was greeted at what turned out to be the camp's perimeter by two young scouts, who looked to me as though they should still be eating soft foods and hiding behind their mothers' aprons. But they seemed to know what to do when I asked for Mr. Jones, the Scoutmaster. These two cherubs guided me through the jungle to the leadership tent, where I found the adults.

Stan Jones is a thoroughly nice guy, but he's a man's man, exactly the sort of fellow you'd expect to be heading up a troop of boys who were orienteering their way through the wilds of New Jersey. I pictured him hacking his way through dense forest with nothing but a hatchet and a compass. Stan and Lou Carter, his Assistant Scoutmaster, greeted me like a member of a secret order, which was gratifying. To be fair, Stan never made me feel put down, but I always felt the twinkle in his eye, as though on some level he was making fun of me.

I would be bunking in the leadership tent once it was lights out, but in the meantime, they sent someone to find Frankie so that I could join him and his patrol for dinner. I could tell that Frankie was glad to see me, but he was being very grown up and blasé for the benefit of his compatriots.

Preparations for dinner were well underway when we got to the area where Frankie's patrol had grouped their tents. The menu consisted of a troop specialty called "hamburger a la foil" and potato chips. I told Frankie privately that I had brought up with me a bag of his favorite chips, and maybe even a candy bar for dessert. He allowed as how he would stash that treasure in his tent for later and have the regulation chips for dinner, along with his fellow scouts.

I gather the boys loved their hamburger a la foil. To me it tasted of aluminum and despair. I guess that's just another indication of what a tenderfoot I am. Dessert, however, was another matter entirely. The boys, who by this time were all experienced wilderness chefs, concocted something they called "campfire brownies," which were truly delicious. I gather they were excited to show off their skills, but I was deeply grateful that they allowed me a ration of this delicacy. This camping thing might not be so bad after all.

After dinner, the boys' time was their own. Frankie and I sat by the fire for a while and talked. Of course, I asked him how the week at camp had been going, and he regaled me with tales of his achievements.

"I earned my First Aid merit badge a couple of days ago," he said. "And if I pass the swimming test on Sunday, I'll get that one too."

"Have you been having swimming lessons?" I asked. He had taken some beginning lessons, but he was not a strong swimmer.

"Yeah, Mrs. Acosta has been teaching us, and I've been practicing a lot. It's been really hot, and the mosquitoes can't get me in the water."

I couldn't think of a better incentive to learn to swim.

One of the other boys stopped and said to Frankie, "We're gonna play Capture the Flag up in the hollow. Do you want to come?"

Frankie looked unsure. It seemed to me he wanted to go but felt bad at the idea of leaving me on my own.

I quickly said, "Hey, go play. I'm pretty beat after work. I'll go up and hang out with Mr. Jones at the leadership tent. We're going to have all day tomorrow to do stuff together."

Frankie smiled but said, "Are you sure?"

"Absolutely," I said. "I'm looking forward to seeing all the stuff you guys do, and I need to get some rest so I can keep up. Go ahead." He was gone in a flash.

It took me a while to find my way back to the leadership tent via the labyrinth of trails among the various patrols. What with its being the middle of summer, daylight lasted until quite late. That was great because it gave the boys plenty of time for Capture the Flag before they had to hit the hay. For me, however, it simply meant that I had to stay awake while Stan and Lou waxed poetic about what a great week of camping it had been. It dawned on me that these guys actually thought of this week at camp, which seemed to me an ordeal imposed by some medieval torturer, as a kind of vacation.

Not a moment too soon, it was time to retire for the night. I was eagerly looking forward to laying down my weary head. In just a few moments, however, I realized the difficulty I faced. My cot came equipped with a down sleeping bag. As I mentioned earlier, it was a hot midsummer night in western New Jersey. Within a few moments of zipping myself into the sleeping bag, I was dripping sweat. Clearly, no sleeping would happen like that.

The solution seemed clear: I would simply lie on top of the sleeping bag. I was covered with the bare minimum required by modesty, exposing a great deal of my skin to the air. The sides of the leadership tent were open, which would allow any movement of the air to be felt inside.

Boy Scout Camp

Conditions might not be ideal, but I should at least be able to sleep. So I extricated myself from the down sauna and prepared to doze in relative comfort.

There are two kinds of mosquitoes in New Jersey, the big ones and the little ones. The only real danger from the little ones is that they'll pick you up and carry you off to the caves where the big ones live. No sooner had I closed my eyes than I heard the telltale whine of a flying bloodsucker near my ear. Within seconds, I was gesticulating wildly, trying to fend off the aerial attack. It was to no avail, however. Every inch of my exposed flesh was under attack. In a last-ditch effort at self-preservation, I put on all my clothes. Somehow, my two tent mates were sawing logs as though they were impervious to the heat and the bugs. Suffice it to say that almost no sleeping happened in my bunk that night.

Dawn came early, but frankly, it was a relief to me. At least I could get up and move around. As the boys began to stir, I found my way back down to Frankie's patrol, where breakfast was happening. Fortunately, there was a simple option of some cereal, and I chose that.

Once breakfast was taken care of, I had a horrifying realization. Somehow, I had gotten through the previous evening and the whole night without even learning where the latrine was. I can only attribute my lack of internal action to the enormous tension under which I had been holding myself. But now, the pressure would not be put off any longer.

I discreetly alerted Frankie to my need, and he gave me directions. Practically doubled over by now, I made it to the latrine, where I paused longer than I would have thought possible. Firstly, the boys had constructed a flimsy-looking scaffold of branches, which they had used to suspend a toilet seat over an open pit filled with things too horrible to describe. Also, what privacy it afforded was provided merely by some bushes and a bend in the trail.

I realized I had no choice, but the thought of some impressionable Boy Scout's coming around the bend as I sat suspended above that nightmare pit with my pants around my ankles was almost more than I could bear.

I did manage to complete the task without interruption and make it back to Frankie's tent without incident, but I will never be quite the same again.

The rest of the day was a complete blur. I managed not to fall down any ravines or grab onto any poison ivy. I was, in fact, quite lucky. Frankie was so focused on showing me all the things he and his friends did that he paid almost no actual attention to me, and so didn't notice that my eyes were all but closed for most of the day. As it got closer to time for me to escape, I gushed to him about how proud I was of him and how impressed I was by everything he and his patrol mates did.

Parting wasn't too bad, since I would be back the next day with his mom to pick him up. I assured him that we would come in time for the award ceremony.

We did make it back to the camp in time for the awards and got pictures of Frankie receiving his two merit badges. Stan, with the usual twinkle in his eye, announced a special award that he then presented to me for having survived a day at summer camp.

We gathered up our son and headed home. On the way, Frankie talked breathlessly about how great the whole week had been and how he couldn't wait for next year, when we would do it all over again. I looked over at my wife, who tried valiantly to suppress a giggle.

Boy Scout Camp

GUIDED BY THE LOST

A SHORT STORY BY
LIAM P BOYLE

CONTENT WARNINGS

This story contains themes that may be distressing to some readers, including:

Alcohol use disorder

To my son Drustan.

Guided by the Lost

Asplitting headache throbbed above his eyes. It was the anniversary of Gabriel's disappearance. The pain of the loss was still there even after five years. Usually this had him getting black out drunk, but he had avoided this the night before. Maybe the grief was finally getting better. But what did that mean for Gabriel, his son, the sweet little boy who spent an entire day bringing him and his wife pretend coffee and chicken soup when they were both sick with the flu at the same time? The child who made his heart leap the first time he came home from work and heard the words "da home" from a tiny body. He could still see his son's cherubic face, and golden brown hair with the pure white patch by the nape of his neck.

The tears started again. The ability to weep had left him a long time ago, no matter how low he felt. Thinking of Gabriel was the only thing that could actually make him cry. He didn't even cry during the divorce from Katrina. She had blamed him for their missing child; he had gone to the store without her, taking Gabriel. He'd turned his back for the briefest moment when loading groceries in the car, and then his son was gone. The incident had left him paralyzed. Children getting snatched from grocery store parking lots—that was supposed to be an urban legend.

Walking into the bathroom, he turned on the hot water for a shower. He still had to work today. There was no getting out of it. He got through the shower on autopilot, mind numb, body aching from age and abuse. Scott was not taking good care of himself these days. He turned to the mirror to wipe away the steam to shave and stopped. There on the mirror, drawn through the condensation, were words. They read: "I can tell you where he is."

What the …?

There was no one but him in the tiny studio apartment he had gotten after the divorce.

Quickly, he wiped the mirror, erasing the words. He stepped out of the bathroom and looked around the apartment's single room. Empty. Walking to the door, he jiggled the knob, checked both the deadbolt and chain were all still locked, just as he'd left them. There was no sound but the whisper of his own breath.

He started walking back towards the bathroom to finish getting ready for his day. Was he finally losing his mind? Was this what going insane felt like? He took a breath. *Pull yourself together, you still have to work.* He looked around the apartment again, still empty.

He shook himself free of his nerves and continued with his morning ritual, but his hands were unsteady as he shaved and brushed his teeth. Returning to the main room to get dressed, he saw a piece of paper on the night table that had not been there last night. He didn't remember it being there this morning. A child's pencil script had scribbled: "I can tell you where he is. - A."

He looked around the apartment once again. Still empty. He looked under the unmade bed. No one. The small closet? Empty of everything but his clothes. It was a one-room apartment. There was literally nowhere for anyone to hide. There had been no deliveries, no visitors, no one but him with his sober mind.

None of this made sense.

He walked into the kitchen and poured himself a cup of coffee. He turned around and immediately dropped the mug to the floor. Standing before him was the translucent image of a young girl, maybe nine years old. The same age Gabriel would be now.

He screamed as hot coffee and the shards of the broken mug pelted his feet and legs. *"Fuck!"*

The apparition remained unmoving.

Unwrapping the towel from around his waist, Scott mopped at his mess. He could sweep up the broken bits later.

He felt his chest constrict, and heart began to hammer. He shuddered as a chill ran through his body. "Who are you? What are you?"

A soft voice finally spoke, although the apparition's mouth didn't move. "Put some pants on, silly. I can show where he is. He's finally close enough for me to show you."

He threw on his jeans as quickly as possible. "Show me where who is?" he asked the specter.

"My brother, Gabriel."

He fell to one knee as the specter spoke. Gabriel was his only child, but Katrina had originally been pregnant with twins. One of them suffered from *Vanishing Twin Syndrome* in the womb. He and Katrina had only found out about this in retrospect after they thought she'd had a miscarriage in the early second trimester. Only one twin miscarried, the other remained a viable pregnancy. Supposedly, Gabriel's patch of pure white hair was a remnant of the miscarried twin. But how could this thing–ghost, specter, hallucination… he wasn't sure–know that?

He and Katrina hadn't announced the pregnancy to their families when they'd learned they were expecting. They had just picked out names after weeks of debate. It was only after the miscarriage that they had told anyone about the pregnancy, and they had never mentioned the vanishing twin. He and Karina never even brought it up to each other anymore.

"Hurry, get dressed. Gabriel needs us." The specter stayed floating as he grabbed a work shirt from the closet and then a pair of socks from the plastic storage bin he used as a dresser. After slipping on his shoes, he dialed his work's call-in number and left a message to say he couldn't make it in today, hoping that the absence wouldn't cost him his job.

Finally, he turned and addressed the apparition. "How do you know about Gabriel, and how do you know where he is?"

While the image of the apparition didn't change, she answered him with a clear voice, "He's my brother. I didn't make it to being born, but he did. Parts of me are still in him. He needs us. Just follow me."

The apparition moved to the door. He grabbed his keys off of the nightstand and followed her out the door.

This was insanity, following a ghost to find his son, missing now for five years. He followed the ghost of his unborn daughter–Alyssa–, out of the building, the surrounding scenery a blur.

He had doubts about ghosts and the paranormal, but this was something extraordinary. Whether or not he was crazy, Gabriel missing was a fact. He would follow a demon if it meant seeing his son again.... So, he continued. He walked for hours, heading out of the city into the surrounding forests. The organic smells of trees and leaf litter replaced the smells of car exhaust and trash. Still, the ghost of Alyssa led on. She urged him to hurry. Finally, they reached a steep embankment at a turn in the road. The guardrail was broken, like a large vehicle had smashed through it.

"We're here." The apparition turned to face him again. "Tell Gabriel I love him, but it's not time for us to be together yet." With that, she faded from view.

Scott walked to the broken guardrail and looked down. There amongst the trees was an overturned minivan. He climbed down the embankment carefully. He turned his body sideways and leaned back to keep a hand touching the ground as he made his way down the steep slope. Earth skid under his feet along the path of deep skid marks from a vehicle. He floundered to keep his balance.

Reaching the overturned van, he saw two unmoving adults in the front seats, covered in blood. There appeared to be no one else. Listening closely, he heard crying nearby.

"Gabriel!"

He called as he tried to pinpoint where the sound came from, and headed toward it. He walked about twenty feet from the crash site, and saw a small boy sitting by an oak tree, his hands around his knees, crying.

"Hey, hey kiddo, what's your name? I'm here to help." He tried to keep his voice friendly as he walked closer to the child. The kid looked to be about the right age. He had the right golden brown hair… Could it really be Gabriel? Scott needed to be closer to tell. He needed to see if the boy had the birthmark, the patch of pure white hair by the nape of his neck that Gabriel had been born with.

The child stopped sobbing to speak, "My name's Gabby. Can you help me? I think Nancy and Jack are hurt."

"Nancy and Jack, are those their names? Don't worry, I'll get us help. Can you come here so I can see if you're hurt?"

Gabby slowly got up and hesitantly walked closer. As soon as Gabby came close enough, he pulled him into a hug. "It's going to be okay. I'm going to call some people to help us. Let me turn you around so I can make sure you aren't hurt."

The boy let him do so, and he saw the spot on the back of Gabby's head, the telltale patch of white hair no larger than a coin. It was him; it was his son.

"Who are Nancy and Jack? Are they your parents?" he asked the child, his son.

Gabriel wiped the tears from his eyes. "No, they said my parents were gone, but Alyssa always said my parents were still alive."

As joyous as this moment should be, Scott felt another chill go through him at that statement. "Who is Alyssa?"

The child sobbed again before answering, "She's my sister. Nancy and Jack said she couldn't be real, so they took me to a doctor about it. We were on the way home."

He pulled his phone out of his pocket and dialed emergency services.

As he was talking to the dispatcher, Gabby spoke again. "Did Alyssa find you? She said she was going to find my real dad."

He dropped his phone and broke into tears in front of the child. "Yes, yes, she did. I've missed you for a very long time. It's going to be alright now."

Gabby grabbed him in a hug and stayed there while they waited for the police and ambulance to arrive.

LEHOL

A SHORT STORY BY
LILY KRAJACICH

CONTENT WARNINGS

This story contains themes that may be distressing to some readers, including:

Blood and gore

Violence

Lehol

1: Delicacy

He cut her arm, exposing everything within. She screamed. Blood dripped down her skin, the chair, onto her bare legs. He dug his fingers into her flesh. He felt her muscles, grazed the bone. He shook in excitement at the sounds she was making, at the way the tendons and muscles felt when she moved. He wanted to dig deeper. His fingers were in between her radius and ulna. He could feel the flesh past that, could feel the armrest it lay on. She pleaded, crying. He smiled, removed his hand. He stood staring at her wrecked face. At the mascara running down her cheeks. The way her mouth moved as she begged for her life. *No body, no crime,* his classmate used to say. *No body, no crime,* he repeated in his head. He read it tasted like chicken, or maybe it was pork. Which was it, chicken, or pork? It was vital he knew. He needed to prepare the way he would cook chicken, or the way he would cook pork. What would the organs taste like? Could he make a stock out of the bones? He needed to know. He needed to know. He needed to know. He pulled out every bit of flesh he could from the slit in her arm. He held the strings of meat in his hands. No body, no crime. Could he eat the veins? She's covered in hair; he'll have to shave her before he prepares it. He couldn't eat her brain. He read somewhere it causes madness or death—he couldn't remember which. He'll say his sister died and she wanted her brain to be donated to science. She always thought she had OCD.

He wiped the blood from his hands on his face. "What do you think?" He asked her. She continued to cry, testing his patience. "What do you think?"

"Please," she cried. "If you let me go, I promise I won't tell anybody."

"Did they tell you you're pretty," he brought his hands from his face, "when you cry? You're not. I don't know what man would be attracted to a squealing pig." He looked at her body, picking the bloodied knife off the floor. The eyes. Could he eat her eyes? He imagined they were like tomatoes when eaten. If he bit into them a certain way, would they pop? Maybe if he cut them up he could stomach it. "Hey, tell me, are you okay?"

309

"What?" She said. She saw he was serious in asking. "No, I'm not okay," she answered.

"I wonder if the shock or the blood loss will kill you first." He smiled, it faltered. "What do you think?" He grabbed her breast and started to cut. Slicing through the tissue. She screamed, cried, the pain she felt was making him excited. Her breast came off in his hand, and he looked at it. "I did you a favor. See here?" He held her breast up for her to see, unaware that she had passed out. He pointed to a lump. "You'd have to get them removed at some point."

Blood pooled down her naked body, seeping into the wooden chair under her, dripping onto the concrete floor. He put the knife on a table, the breast in her lap, and told her he would be back soon. He walked up the wooden stairs to the ground floor. Over the sink, he licked most of her blood off his hands before scrubbing them clean.

He found pleasure in imagining her mutilated body and relieved himself each time he did. He read the news in the following days, telling the dead woman no one had reported her missing. He could very well bury this body, but it was already engrained into him: No body, no crime. He could only stall for so long before she would go bad. He moved her limp body to a table, putting the breast he'd cut off into a labeled container. He cut her hair short and shoved the tufts into a bag. He could use this as kindling in the coming months. He shaved her head, her body, every piece of hair needed to be removed. He put on gloves and an apron before he started dismantling her.

He began with her hands. He plied off her fingernails and placed them in a trash can. He cut as much meat off the bones as he could. It found its home in its own labeled container. The bones were put in a large tub. He continued this process for every bit of her. Organs, meat, and bones were all placed in the large tub or in their own containers. He watched as she slowly became nothing, no longer a recognizable person. He washed as much of the lingering flesh off her bones as he could. He kept the bones down in the basement, deciding he'd retrieve them when needed. There was more bone than he knew what to do with. Maybe he could sell some of it as stock, claim it as beef. People will believe whatever the stores tell them. He brought the containers full of her to his fridge. At some point, he'd have to cook her. Eat her.

She was a pig to him. He'd cook her up like pork. Marinade her. Grill her. Braise her. Broil her. His mouth was watering just thinking of it. He'd have to experiment, test out different spices, different ways. He started preparing a marinade. He reckoned the thigh meat would be perfect. It was plump, juicy, not too fatty. He pulled the container from the fridge, feeling ravaged. He wanted to shovel handfuls of the uncooked meat into his mouth. He restrained himself just barely. He didn't know if eating uncooked human flesh would cause him harm, and he didn't wish to find out.

He thought of himself while he mixed up the marinade. Something long ago. His father had asked him why he had killed the cat. He didn't know the intricacies behind the *why*, he only knew it had hissed at him. It had pissed him off, and he stepped on it until he felt the spine break simply because it had made him mad. It wasn't their cat, his father had explained to him, that he couldn't go around killing the neighbors' pets. But his father had then asked him something that threw him off guard: if a dog had barked at him, would he do the same? He had answered his father no because dogs were stupid, he couldn't blame a dumb dog for being an idiot. Cats, on the other hand, had intelligence and needed to be held accountable.

"What if one of your schoolmates yelled at you?" His father had asked. "Would you do the same?"

He had stared his father in the eyes and answered, "Humans are more intelligent than cats and must be held accountable."

His father had let out a sound between disappointment and curiosity. "Do you understand that you can't go around killing animals and your schoolmates?"

"I do," he had said.

"Then why did you kill the cat?" His father had asked. "Why would you kill your schoolmates?"

"Because no one else will." He had answered.

He didn't like his brain. It worked in ways considered abnormal. That's what all those doctors had told him, at least. He believed them in the way any impressionable boy would. They held more power over him, and he understood that. He didn't like that they held more power over him, but he had to sit quietly. Maybe they'll slip up, he thought. Say something he could get them fired for. That must have been one of the ways his brain didn't work normally. He thought the concoction of pills they forced him to take were to sedate him. He refused at first, told his parents he would never take them. They had to watch him swallow those pills. He practiced rolling them around in his mouth. He was able to make it seem like he had swallowed them. He'd flush them down the toilet first chance he had. He believed that was normal.

He put the marinade in a bag, then added the thigh meat. He rolled the meat around in the bag, coating it in every inch of the marinade. He placed it in the fridge. Overnight, the meat would soak in the marinade, giving birth to flavor he could only imagine. He wanted to taste it now. He had to be patient, as much as he hated it. If he slept, night would come sooner. He was too excited; he wouldn't be able to sleep. He needed to do something to take his mind off everything. Read. Watch television. Scroll the internet. He could watch those videos on the blacklisted sites he enjoyed so much. The ones where they tortured people, animals, lower life forms on camera. That's how he got his inspiration. Eating her, however, was all his classmate's idea. He wanted to watch those videos, see how others did it. He was an amateur by their standards. He had only just started.

Watching those videos through the night, he never considered targeting the things they cared about. Emotional and mental torment could be powerful. A woman who valued her appearance above all else could be destroyed by cutting her hair, peeling off her nails, and smearing her makeup. Women who care about animals could be defeated by murdering one in front of her. Compared to the ones who were physically tortured, they made different sounds. The sounds of a woman distraught over her favorite things was sadder than one who got cut, or flesh gouged out. They cried more emphatically. He thought of making videos to post to these sites as night turned into morning. It was easy to find the first woman so he figured he could do it again.

He wanted to eat her, and his stomach agreed. He must be patient. Cereal for breakfast, salad for lunch, the delicacy for dinner. Was it always this hard to control himself? Impulse, impulse, impulse, he was always impulsive. He didn't think twice about killing the woman. He was only mildly disgusted by the idea of eating her. But that had been removed as he convinced himself it was needed. That was the only thing he could think about. He *needed* to eat her. He *needed* to eat her *now*.

Control yourself, that's what they always told him. He couldn't do what he wanted at school. He couldn't do what he wanted at home. It wasn't until years later that he could live with few rules; rules dictated to him by society. He broke those rules. He was free. Free to live how he wanted, do what he wanted, eat what he wanted. And he wanted to eat her. Eat her until he himself was a pig. He couldn't wait past eleven. He made it to an early lunch. He didn't want the neighbors to smell his meal. He didn't know if they'd bother him or if they'd call the cops. It was better to be left alone. He cooked the marinated meat in his oven, unsure how long or how it would look. He treated it like pork, like the pig she was. He couldn't wait for it to cool. He cut into it, his mouth watering as juices spilled out. He burned his tongue on the unique flavor. He shoveled the meat into his mouth. He was never addicted to anything. Now that was beginning to change.

2: Normalcy

Isaiah had to sit through family dinners every Monday night. It was his parents' way of keeping tabs on him. Making sure he was taking his medications. Making sure he was going to his doctor. Making sure he was a normal member of society. It was stifling to him. Especially now that he had tasted something delicious. Steak, pork, chicken, lamb, they all smelled disgusting to him now.

Normal, that's all his parents wanted him to be. Normal, normal, normal. He was fed up with *normal*. His sister was "normal," the perfect child. She caused no problems for their parents. He hated her like a selfish brat. Unlike him, she could skip these weekly dinners, and it irritated him. He had things he needed to get done, just as Sarah had things to get done. But Sarah, the ever-perfect Sarah, having grown up in fear of her brother, was allowed to abandon family time. She was always able to. Run to her room when Isaiah was present. Run to their mother when Isaiah did *anything* that bothered her. If only he could be his abnormal, she would understand why he acted the way he did.

He didn't want to talk, he never did. Not now, when his mother was off somewhere, and his father stared at him. He wanted him to stop. He wanted him to eat the nauseating food on his plate. Do *something* but stare at him. His father's gaze brought Isaiah unnecessary questions, unnecessary probing. Girlfriend, job, overall life. Then he would ask about appointments, prescriptions, changes. He hated it almost as much as he hated his sister. He drank water like a traveler in a desert. He didn't touch his food. He *couldn't* touch his food. The sweating gaze was becoming too much to bear. He wanted his father to get on with it. To berate him for being abnormal. To let him go home. To let him eat something edible.

What even was normal, he asked himself. Who decides? Who sets the guidelines? The doctors were his first guess. They told him, told his parents that he was abnormal. Who made him that way? Was it society or his parents? Did he piss off God in the womb? He found it funny, the concept of God. If there were a God, then it would've stopped him from eating that woman. It would've stopped him from doing anything considered abnormal in his life. Maybe his life was just one cruel joke by God. He decided God could go to Hell.

His father inhaled slightly, moving as if he had just come out of a daze. "Your sister is getting married."

"Why?" He asked.

His father took a sip from his glass. "Do you understand the concept of romantic love?" He asked. Isaiah thought he was patronizing him, but he sounded genuinely curious.

"It always seemed..." he trailed off, thinking of the right word. "Troublesome."

"How so?" His father responded.

He paused, trying to figure out how to explain his muddled thoughts. "You have to spend time and energy *caring* about someone else. For what? To not be alone?"

His father let out a sighed laugh. "You never bothered to care about anything but yourself." He paused, then added, "She doesn't want you at her wedding."

It didn't surprise him that she felt this way. She didn't want him at any of her soccer games in elementary school. She didn't want him at any of her middle and high school swim meets. She didn't want him at her high school graduation or college graduation. It was that fear in the back of her mind: What if Isaiah lost it? Did something that couldn't be fixed? The neighbor's cat was her friend, and he took it away from her. What else might he take away from her? Per her knowledge, he had never killed a person, but that nagging thought, *what if he kills her fiancé?* Made her wary of him. He took what she deemed was rightfully hers. It wasn't his fault, her mother told her, he's not right in the head. He's not *normal*. That's all it ever came back to: normal.

He was sick of his parents' ideas of normalcy. He tried "normal", and it failed. It failed superbly in his mind. What a beautiful fall from grace. He imagined Lucifer's fall from grace was just as beautiful. Beauty, that's all anyone cared about, beauty and money. He learned early that people thrived on money and that everything and everyone had a price. He asked those doctors how much it would cost for them to tell his parents he was cured and didn't need pills. At first, they said that's not how it works, but he pressed on. They finally gave him an answer, close to five hundred thousand dollars. Where would he, a young boy, get that kind of money? He'd have to steal it, he reckoned. Consequence was not something he understood then. He barely understood it now. Why is he not allowed to live the way he wants? Wasn't there a piece about everyone being free and having the right to pursue happiness? His happiness was looked down on, pushed aside. Where was his right? Some could argue his happiness would take away from another's. Maybe he could get around that by finding someone whose happiness was rooted in wanting to die. They giveth and he taketh away.

"Why don't you come back and live with us?" He asked. "You might feel more comfortable here."

"I'm not a child anymore," Isaiah said, his voice even. "If these weekly dinners are all I have to deal with to be left alone, then the pros outweigh the cons."

This house brought him confusion, infuriation, not comfort. He got scolded for burning ants with a magnifying glass. He did it because he was bored and told to play outside. He was playing, but not in the way his parents had wanted. There were millions of ants, why should he be scolded for killing off a few? His mother said it wasn't the ants they were concerned about, but the grass. The grass could catch on fire. It hadn't, had been his defense. He made sure it didn't. Only after the cat incident, he had to be watched outside. Even his taste in books was considered troubling. He liked books about unsolved murders and serial killers. His parents wanted him to read, and said something about it helping his brain grow, yet he wasn't allowed to read the things that interested him. He was caught dissecting a rat in the garage, and his father disciplined him. He thought they were varmints, that's what his father had said. Varmints didn't deserve to live were his father's exact words. He didn't understand why doing what his parents had asked him to do, doing what he thought was okay, got him in trouble.

Yet Sarah did everything she was asked of her, and she wasn't reprimanded. She played outside when she was told and wasn't scolded. She read books when asked; her books were never taken away from her. It was okay for her to set out rat traps and poison. He thought of taking that poison and putting it in her drinks. He'd do it slowly. Just enough to affect her, but not enough that it would kill her outright. He'd keep adding it until she was sick to her stomach. Until she died right there at dinner. He'd feign shock, sadness, be the concerned younger brother. His parents would never know it was he who killed her. Why did she get all the praise, and he was shunned? They fought once, no one knew where he had acquired a pocketknife. He didn't feel anything but sweet rage in that moment; however, Sarah claimed, after the shock, that he was crying. He had cut her cheek trying to make his hunting last. She had a scar now, she had to get stitches. That was the first time he was told he was abnormal. It was normal for siblings to squabble over petty things, but it wasn't normal for the squabbling to turn violent. It wasn't normal for it to almost end in the death of one of them.

At first they thought the power of God could cure him. They were fools to think that. What afflicted him was not of the soul. What afflicted him was of the mind. It was clear to them soon after. When faith didn't work, they spent thousands of dollars on doctor appointments and pills. Doctor appointments that he didn't feel he needed. Pills he refused to take. He was fine. There was nothing wrong with him. Normal was just a concept that differed from person to person. Differs from region to region. Country to country. Was anybody truly normal?

3: Philosophy

"There's a story," he started, "about a satyr."

"Why are you telling me this?" She asked.

He looked over at her where she was hanging and continued with his story. "Apollo was jealous of the way the satyr played, so he challenged him to a contest. The Muses judged the contest, and the satyr won. Apollo, being the god of music and not liking having lost to a mortal, punished the satyr. That's how it always goes: mortals being better than gods and getting punished for it. Well, Apollo hung the satyr upside down and flayed him." He had a sharp, thin wire in his gloved hands. He hoped it would do what he wanted. "Be grateful all the blood isn't running to your pretty little head."

"You don't need to do this," she said.

He shook his head. "No, I do."

"Why?" He hated the word "why," because it forced him to explain his actions. Maybe there was nothing to explain. He did things because it

316

felt *good*. He did things because he *wanted* to. There was no grand scheme. There was no master plan. There was *nothing*. He did because he could.

He never answered her, just got to work. The wire made a cut on her thigh, and he pulled it down. Slowly, he made a cut, a tear, a peel. She wasn't screaming at first. By the time he had peeled to her knee, she let out a cry of pain. He wanted to hear her scream, hear her plead, hear her sob. He let the flap of skin hang as he pulled at the tendons, meat, and muscles inside her leg. "Doesn't this hurt?" He asked, starting to feel dissatisfied.

"Of course," she answered quietly.

"Then why aren't you screaming, crying, or pleading for me to stop?"

She was quiet for a minute; he could barely hear her breathing. "I've accepted my fate. Made my peace with God."

"This isn't a church," he said. "God isn't here."

She squirmed a bit, finding a better position for her wrists within the confines of the rope. "He's all around. It's okay, you can continue. I don't mind." He felt pitiful towards himself. He didn't want encouragement. He wanted screams. He wanted tears. He wanted *something* that wasn't silence. He uttered the question he hated; that one word that dredges so much to the surface. "You're not alright," she said, "in the head. I hope by doing whatever it is you're planning on doing to me, you see how broken you are. And you go and get help, and repent."

He started to feel anger. What was it with women and righteousness? Why did they feel they could fix everyone they ever met? He couldn't be fixed. God couldn't fix him, and he wasn't convinced God was real. Imagination. He must lack that. Imagining gods is something normal people could do. It was just a cult. One big imagination cult. He watched the blood drip down her leg. The flap of skin hanging uselessly, reduced to a banana peel. He felt devoid of anything. What was he doing? Why? Why? Why? He'd run out. He needed more. He couldn't go back to being semi-normal. He drove too far to turn back. He continued, in silence, to flay the woman. He wasn't excited, happy, angry, sad. He wasn't anything.

He left her hanging after she'd bled out and he'd peeled most of her. He locked the basement door and sat. He's all around, her words were getting to him. He isn't real. Was anything real? Was Isaiah real? He touched his arm, making sure he was real, alive, awake. If He could see him, He'd tattle. Sarah used to tattle. Tattling got him in trouble. He didn't want to get in trouble. If He were real, he'd tell Him not to tattle. But He wasn't real, so he couldn't. He needn't get worked up over real and unreal. How did he *know* He wasn't real? No one could *see* Him. Some people on television claimed they could see Him, and they were praised for their faith. Some people said God made them commit crimes, and they were cast down and confined. God could only be good, they all claimed. But they also claimed humanity was made in His image, so why were humans evil?

He stood. At some point, he'd have to go back down in the basement and dismantle her. His mood was ruined by her words. By her morals. He never met her before he killed her. Her words shouldn't be bothering him as much as they did. Something about her reminded him of someone. Someone he probably saw on television. He shouldn't be bothered by it, by her words, by her better-than-thou aura. She was nothing now. Felt nothing now. All she could do was haunt him. The first woman didn't haunt him. If anything, it brought him joy to remember her body.

It shouldn't bother him this much. He must stop thinking about her words. He didn't need help. He never thought he did. It didn't bother him when his parents brought him to doctors, thinking they'd help. It must be because she's a stranger. He felt he fit right in, but she saw through him. Who else might see through? Who else might find out he's not normal? Who else might push their infuriating religion onto him? What if he ran away? Left everything but the most essential items. His parents would report him missing by next week when he didn't show up to dinner. Didn't respond to their texts or answer their calls. He could be dead in a ditch, without worry. He'll go to Hell and be happy. Happy. He never felt the mildness of happiness.

Lehol

HAINT BLUE

A SHORT STORY BY
CARLA HENNES

CONTENT WARNINGS

This story contains themes that may be distressing to some readers, including:

Emotional abuse

To my family at Screamtown

Haint Blue

"**C**an I borrow some coagulated blood?"

Cassie took the bandage snipper from her throat and turned to the open trailer door.

"Mehron or Woochie?" Cassie asked, naming two brands of stage blood.

The zombie nurse shook her head, dislodging a plastic cockroach from her wig.

"Mehron, if you have it. I'm allergic to something in the Woochie."

Grabbing the 3-oz bottle from her makeup table, Cassie tossed it. "No getting sick in October, Lizzie. We're short on actors in the graveyard."

Crickets thrummed in the background, amid the pounding of last-minute repairs and babbling animatronics. A chill breeze snaked across the grounds of the haunted house attraction.

"I won't get sick." Lizzie's voice got softer. "I've got another IVF next week."

Cassie left the sharp ammonia scent of latex and stepped into the fresh air outside the door. "Lizzie, if you need to leave early for the border run, let me know. I'll cover for you."

Lizzie tugged the ripped sleeve of her scrubs back onto her shoulder. "It's only two hours to the state line. The clinic's right across the river. I can sleep while my wife drives."

Cassie hugged her friend, transferring some coffee grounds and chocolate syrup stains to her costume.

"You and Mary will make great parents. I know it. No matter what that crazy governor thinks of lesbian parents. There's nothing unnatural about wanting to have a kid," said Cassie. "God, can you imagine if Todd and I had a spawn? Talk about unnatural."

"He would have tried, if he thought it would make you stay." Lizzie scowled. Disgust wrinkled the white paint and maggots on her face.

Cassie's dial-a-pill pack had moved to a different shelf on the medicine cabinet. Had he tampered with her birth control? She never told him about the new IUD. The little clinic had taken cash when she lied about insurance, his insurance. A phone call for an appointment that had opened up, then a road trip across the state border, and a missed cast call at the haunt. It had been three years to this day, but a Friday when Todd had been distracted with grading papers.

Stupid, stupid, Lizzie must think I'm so stupid, going back to Todd again and again.

Lizzie broke the awkward silence. "You can stay on our couch as long as you need to, Cassie. You don't have to go back alone to the apartment for your stuff."

"How am I going to afford a new place? I don't have anything lined up after Nightmare Farm closes in November. I don't even know what rent costs!"

Let me handle the rent, Cassie. No one expects a theater major to understand finances. A few more semesters and Dr. Slava will make me his assistant. He'll take us all to Berlin with a huge research grant when he has a working prototype.

Lizzie rolled her eyes. "You'll figure it out. What about that year-round haunt in Vegas?"

Cassie picked at the corpse-blue paint on her bare arm. "I'd never get that. Who'd believe I could manage a real team? I can't even keep Todd from sabotaging my haunt family."

Lizzie held Cassie's shoulders, forcing her to meet her eyes. "If he shows up at the gate, he's not getting in. Security knows what he looks like."

"In a mask?" Cassie tugged a stray hair out of the drying latex, ignoring the pain. "Last week, he sweet-talked his way on site with a new prop, talking like he knew the Nightmare Farm owner." Collecting odds and ends from the university labs, Todd would wire them up, showing off his engineering skills to his adoring girlfriend. Most junk in the mad scientist's room came from him. "After dumping the prop, he showed up at the flaming coffin scene."

"Oh, Cassie—"

"He didn't know about the trick door, so I snuck away before he could start any of his arguments." She hunched her shoulders as though she could repeat the vanishing act.

Tapping Cassie's chin, Lizzie said, "You're smarter than you think... And you missed a spot while slitting your throat."

Cassie grinned and snapped the scissors at her. "Begone, foul demon!"

Haint Blue

§

Cassie swept through the black hallway on her final walkthrough, stepping over trigger markers. An actor settled a water bottle on a shelf and closed a pop scare door within the thin plywood walls. A shaggy werewolf, with a rattling noise maker of nails in a can, tested a sticky drop window. Locking yellow eyes with Cassie, the teenage girl grinned with large fake teeth. Luna threw back her head and howled, her tail thumping against the fire extinguisher in its bracket. Echoes of the howl responded from the rest of the house. Patting the tufted ears, Cassie moved on to the next room in the maze.

The mad scientist's room came alive with twitching tubes and bubbling beakers. A Cold War-era Geiger counter clicked ominously, while lasers shot through the heavy fog. Breathing shallow through her nose, Cassie passed the gurgling fog machine as it cycled through another billow of white mist. An animatronic scientist torturing a student would goose the patrons through the lab coats hung over the exit. Sometimes they panicked into the actor's door and got lost in the backstage area, forcing the actors to herd them back into the maze.

A massive bank of electronics filled the far wall with a projector the size of a car door. Buttons, switches, and flashing lights covered the rest of the box, with labels in Cyrillic. Todd's professor had been a refugee from Ukraine, working on quantum multiworld theories in the Physics department. Obsessed with the universes created by Schrodinger's theories, Dr. Slava had been one step away from a stable prototype to produce windows into the alternative timelines where the cat had lived. Named after the scientists who had laid the theoretical foundation, the Everett-Rosen-Carroll projector hovered on the edge of the possible. All they needed was a little more funding. Cassie brushed aside the charred flap that covered the date input on the familiar box. No wonder Todd wanted to get rid of it. The scar pattern revealed the version of the ERC prototype – the disastrous demonstration run by Todd.

Summer sun had poured in the lecture hall windows, drowning out the projected view of an alternative university. Todd's audience sat on the student benches. A general with his aide lurked in the back while an investor from a tech company sipped a latte in the front row. Cassie had provided the cool drinks and strategically closed the curtains as Todd began his spiel.

"Pick a point where the universe divides, a point where the cat is either dead or alive," Todd said, pushing back the long hair from his face. "With the ERC, you can see the other path. Schrodinger's thought experiment suggested that until the cat was observed, it was both dead and alive. Later scientists, such as Everett, expanded on that quantum state, theorizing that each time an observation was made, determining whether the radiation had decayed or not, each time a new universe, a new timeline, spun off from that inflection point."

Todd paused to enter the date he applied to the university into the panel. Painfully bright lights projected from the ERC, reproducing a copy of the university campus outside the closed curtains. The whine of a full power run-up jabbed like a needle in Cassie's ear but didn't stop this time. The projection changed as the sapphire blue sky turned to green-gray clouds and a siren bit the air.

"Turn it off, turn it off!" yelled Todd.

Cassie tugged on the dead weight of the heavy cable.

"No, you idiot, turn it off, not—"

The mark one experiment had ended with an explosion that blew out the windows, destroying Todd's dreams of securing a grant for his mentor. Dr. Slava had died soon after, ending the promise of research in Berlin. Without a mentor, the university shunted Todd to another adviser who hated him.

What if, what if, she'd had a baby? What if she'd had a baby and gone to Berlin with him? Trapped with a child she didn't want in a country where she didn't speak the language, without any outlet for her acting. Or trapped with a baby and no Berlin, a slowly intensifying frustration from Todd as his career sputtered and died. For Lizzie, a baby meant an unreachable joy, but for Cassie, an anchor dragging her down.

A shudder from the fog machine brought her back to the haunted house and the flicker of lights across the ERC device. Dr. Slava usually chose the inflection point where he boarded the overnight train from Lviv. Cassie chose a more personal inflection point. She punched in the date when she'd gotten the call from the clinic about the IUD appointment, which she'd almost let go to voicemail. Turning on the device, Cassie stuck her hand in the light, and ripples danced across her fingers. The projector overlaid the other half of the room with a lighter copy, blue twilight shining through holes in the other timeline's ceiling. Pulling her hand out of the light, Cassie slouched toward the darkness of other people's nightmares.

§

"One, two, three, four, go!" Cassie pointed the patrons to the haunted house. The open doorway gaped with hanging strips of garbage bags. Lights flashed from around the first turn. A tween's piercing scream confirmed an actor had taken advantage of the strobe's distraction to jump out behind her.

"Start walking, meat muffins," snarled Cassie, lunging into the first girl's personal space.

With an eep and a giggle, the girl, a brunette with perfectly manicured stabby nails, stepped through the door. At the end, a tall lunk in a letter jacket poked at his girlfriend, who wiggled forward. Seconds before he disappeared inside, Cassie leaned in and stage-whispered, "Watch out for the ceiling zombies."

"Huh?" His momentum carried him inside. "Wait, what ceiling zombies?"

With a peal of hideous cackling, Cassie counted off the next staggered entry.

An evil clown tumbled out of an actor's door. "Cassie, I got a follow." Never interact with troublemakers, she had trained them. Follow them until you can report. The black-eyed harlequin pointed to a group of basketball-jerseyed teenagers at the exit. "Assholes were flinging props around." She grinned. "Mean one got shocked in the mad scientist room."

Ah, hell. If the vandals had damaged the device…Maybe instead of exploding, it would actually work.

"Keep on their tail. I'll call it in." Cassie gave the clown a light push. She keyed the mic under her shredded top. "Cassie to Security. Vandal follow headed to the corn maze. Clown tailing."

In the seconds while she waited for an answer, she sent another group through the black flaps of the entrance. Finally, a distorted voice crackled back.

"Copy, Cassie. Hank to corn maze."

Cutting through the mini-doughnuts, spray paint, and sweaty actors, a scent of char jolted her attention. She spun, sniffing, but the source evaded her. Cassie cursed under her breath and backed into the entrance strips. She picked up the chain for a sign with Closed written in reflective tape and clipped it across the entry.

"Aw, man, really? I paid big bucks for this dorky show," said the man at the front of the line.

"If it's nothing, we'll re-open in a minute," Cassie replied, then strode deeper into the house.

Distracted, she swept through the first trigger, and lights pounded her senses.

"Ahhhhgh oh, sorry, Cassie," said the haunted Kewpie doll.

"Do you smell anything?" Cassie asked.

The girl tapped the doll mask. "All I smell is my pizza dinner."

"Head for the exit but be ready to reset if it's someone vaping again."

The head bobbled and the doll disappeared out the actor's door. Cassie walked on, more careful to avoid breaking the sensor lights. Masked by the soapy fog, Cassie struggled to identify the smell: wood smoke, plastic fumes, or skunky CBD vape.

"Madre de Dios, no, no puedo…"

Three patrons huddled by a cabinet in the cannibal kitchen. An older woman muttered as a young man in Candy Skull face paint pulled her arm. At the obvious exit, a chained refrigerator bucked and hopped, with bloody fingers reaching out around the closed door. In the more open space of the mildew-painted kitchen, the smell resolved to wood smoke.

Cassie opened the actor's door on the other side of the shuddering prop. "Fire!" She waved at the group. "Come on, out the next door marked Emergency Exit."

The woman moaned another prayer. Cassie locked eyes with the young boy at the woman's side. "Fuego. Sigue andando, nunca pares. Fuego!" The boy nodded and scampered past, while the woman followed with outstretched arms in a useless attempt to catch him.

Cassie brought the radio mic to her mouth and sent the message that would terrify Security. "Cassie to Security. Fire in the house. Repeat, fire in the house."

"Quit effin around, Cassie. I found your clown's hoodlums," replied Hank.

Cassie ground her teeth. "You can't have pissed off all the ladies at dispatch. Make the call."

"Copy. Fire in the house. Call the FD and coordinate evac." A moment of silence passed before he continued with a break in his voice, "Kyle, get the friggin house lights on."

Cassie followed the thickening smoke down the hallway, ignoring the jostling fridge. Tendrils of fumes twisted into her lungs. Stumbling, she flopped spread-eagled against something warm, soft, and furry. Convincing screams blared from the speaker in pitch black. A limb squirmed under her hip. Abruptly, the speakers stopped, leaving her ears ringing in the muffled quiet. Dim lights pierced the smoke.

"Uh, Cassie, why are you on top of me?" mumbled Luna.

Cassie rolled to thud on the bare floor. Grabbing behind her pointy ears, she tugged off the wolf's head. The girl's face was pasty white and shone with sweat.

Lizzie would know what to do. A real nurse, not a flake like her. She couldn't stop hearing Todd in her head, calling her a flake, a useless liberal arts major, a dork no one else could love, an idiot who would only make mistakes.

Cassie shook her head. Lizzie trusted her, and so did the other actors. Follow the plan - evac step one was get everyone out.

She reached back into the wolf's hiding spot. Flipping open the top of the bottle, she dashed water over Luna's face. "Shake it off, Luna, you need to get out. There's a fire."

Luna's eyes focused. "Getting the hell outta Dodge, yes ma'am!" Luna snatched her wolf head and dove for the exit.

The dusty fire extinguisher hung on the back of the actor's nook. Had anyone remembered to charge it this year? Had Hank managed to get the fire department? He'd have to convince them to send a truck out, overcoming the rural volunteers' distaste for the rowdy crowd.

A high-pitched wail echoed through the walls. Cassie stared at the dead speaker. No music, no growls, no groans. A real child's scream.

She grabbed the fire extinguisher and ran.

Crackling hungry sounds grew louder with gnawing bright maggots glowing through the walls. The house lights flickered and died at the end of the hall. Wracked by a full-body cough, Cassie brought her arm to cover her face, batting away the dangling earpiece.

"Daddeeeeeeee!"

Wisps of charred cloth stung her face as she charged into the remains of the mad scientist's room. Flames engulfed the plywood wall opposite the ERC device, spreading to the mannequins by the exit. Their melting faces rendered both teacher and student into featureless sludge.

"Daddeeeee!"

Under the table? Behind the dryer vent hoses? Where was the kid hiding?

Her gut twitched, and acrid smoke followed her breath, triggering another round of coughing. Her itchy eyes streamed with tears, and she blinked through blurry vision. The professor's device threw patterns of light and shadow against the far wall, sputtering and sparking around a fist-shaped hole.

The weight of the fire extinguisher dragged down her arm. Cassie hefted it up and found the pin by feel. The metal ring cut into her fingers as she pulled it free. Flying off her finger, a brief tinkle died away amid the cackling flames. She rubbed her sleeve across her face, smearing char, tears, and fake blood. Her knees swayed, and the extinguisher thunked on the floor.

Give up, give in. Let someone smarter make the decisions.

The ERC projector painted an imperfect copy of the room. Todd was an idiot to leave it here. Maybe he knew more about physics, but she got shit done, too.

Cassie raised the canister and squeezed the handle. After a jolt uselessly blasted the floor, she aimed at the flames. Choking on the ammonia smell, she coughed, then opened her eyes. Amid the fine yellow dust, glowing ember eyes glared at her, but no flames.

"Dadddeeeeeeee!"

Cassie spun. The whining device no longer showed a copy. Peering into a parallel world, the device worked, but the fire still raged in that alternate timeline. Curled in a ball under the dryer vent hoses, the image of a little boy shimmered and flickered.

She stepped closer. "Can you hear me?"

The boy's tear-streaked face popped up.

Dear God, he looked like Todd. Baby-fat rounded his face, but there was no mistaking the stormy-blue eyes.

"Get away from the fire," Cassie yelled.

The boy curled tighter and shook his head. "Daddy said stay put. Don't wander, don't run away like Momma."

Another impossible choice. Would she have made the right one, escaping but leaving the child with a neglectful father? Or would Todd find another way to explain why Momma didn't come home from the hospital? Cassie shivered despite the heat, feeling an echo of footsteps across her grave.

"Do you remember Momma?" she asked.

"Blue," the child blurted.

"What?" Baffled, Cassie wrinkled her face.

"Haint blue," continued the child. "I was scared to sleep in my room. She painted the ceiling a special color of blue. So the ghosts would think it was sky and fly away."

Cassie sank to her knees. Her Southern grandmother told her the same story when she slept on hot nights on their porch. She had set the inflection point, and this child was hers. The little boy was her child with Todd in that otherworld, in the timeline where she didn't get an IUD.

"Honey, you don't need to be scared of ghosts." The smoke in the flickering images thickened. "But you have to leave." He deserved a parent who loved him, even if that couldn't be her or Todd.

Urging him forward would send him into the flames, but sideways a few steps would take him to the actor's shortcut, a route to Lizzie's scene.

"I need you to be brave, honey." A bitter smile twitched her face. Could she be brave? Brave enough to shut Todd out of her life, out of her mind, for good? Brave enough to take the risk of rejection from the Vegas haunt? Soot covered her hands, dirty from running towards the fire. Why did she think she wasn't brave?

"Crawl away from the flames, honey. Press against the wall until you find a place where it swings open. Keep crawling."

The little boy shuddered. "Can't move. Daddy angry."

"Momma wants you to be safe. Go find Momma's friend. Tell Lizzie..." Did the other-Lizzie even know Cassie? Know what had happened to the other-Cassie? "Tell Lizzie you need a new Momma."

A groan tore through the fire-eaten wall. Frightened eyes stared at her. She'd spent hours sketching Todd's handsome face with those beautiful eyes. She'd loved him once, wanted to love him still, but the man she loved was dead and buried by who he became.

"You can trust Lizzie. She can hide you from angry Daddy." Sharing beers after the haunt closed, Lizzie had slurred through a song she sang to calm her patients in the pediatric ER. "She knows Momma's lullaby - the Water's Wide." Cassie only sang the first verse, skipping the later verses about love betrayed.

The boy turned, starting to hum. Cassie licked her dry lips and sang.

The water's wide, I can't cross o'er

The child's pale legs crawled.

And neither have I wings to fly.

Smoke swirled as he opened the actor's door.

Give me a boat that can carry two.

The door closed behind him.

And we shall cross, my love and I.

Cassie wiped another smoky tear from her eyes. Safe, he was safe with Lizzie. She stared at the blank wall as the light died away and the device faltered into silence. A persistent buzzing sounded from her shoulder.

Cassie picked up the fallen earpiece and mashed it into her ear.

"Cassie, do you copy?" Lizzie's voice bounced through the line. "Cassie, where are you?"

Cassie keyed the mic. "Cassie here."

Her thumb fell away from the button. Where was she? Right where she was needed. By November, long gone from Todd and building a new life.

Haint Blue

UNDER THE NEW MOON

A SHORT STORY BY
BECKY HANSEN

Under the New Moon

Dot turned off her kitchen light, opened the door, and entered the blackness of the night.

She hobbled down the two steps to the sidewalk and tried not to grunt as her arthritic knees creaked and bent. Her black coat was buttoned to her chin, and Bill's old hat was shoved down over her ears. The cul-de-sac was quiet on the moonless night, and she waited a few minutes while her eyes adjusted to the darkness. She thought to go back into the house for a flashlight for a moment but decided against it as she gradually made out the houses in her circle. They were all dark, except for a glow from the in-ground low-level lighting on the walkway leading through Cecilia's garden. Dot's grip tightened on the newly-sharpened scissors in her pocket as she thought about how much time Bill had spent working on Cecilia's house and those stupid lights.

Dot turned and strolled along the sidewalk, her pain subsiding after a few steps. It was Tuesday, so no one had their garbage cans out, and the sidewalks were clear. In the distance, she heard a wailing—coyotes, perhaps? Maybe it was a dog. She wasn't sure. She passed Joanne and Ed's house and stopped at Cecilia's walkway. The lights dimly outlined the pavers to the side yard, and Dot turned into the garden. She took the scissors out of her pocket and looked around at the tulip bed - Cecilia's pride and joy. Well, when the photographer comes tomorrow, he won't stay.

She started on the right-hand side and bent over to quickly cut the flower off the first tulip. She thought the bloom would flutter to the ground, but instead it fell like a head of old lettuce thrown into the garbage. She looked at the delicate white petals as they lay on the ground, and wondered if she should pick them up. She cut the bloom off the next stem and watched it fall silently on top of the first. The third and then the fourth blooms were cut. Soon she had beheaded all the white tulips. Dot straightened up, and her back creaked. She took a minute to rest and stepped back to admire her work. The petals made the weed-free garden look rather messy, she thought. What a nice bonus.

She wished Bill had spent half the time in their own yard that he had spent helping Cecilia. It had all started right after Cecilia's "divorce" party. Since when do people celebrate their failures? That was exactly what she asked Bill when they got the invitation. But he had been happy for her. "For god's sake, Dot, her husband was a jerk. She SHOULD be celebrating."

He talked her into going, and just as she had predicted, she had a miserable time watching everyone talk about Cecilia's husband, the weather, their gardens, and "did you hear about Joan So-and-So or Joe What's-his-Name"? Such petty conversations and such petty people. But Bill had enjoyed it so much that she had to drag him away at midnight.

"Did you see the books in her bookcase? They were all romance books. Barbara Cartland. Not a decent book in the house."

Bill had just laughed at her.

After that party, Bill went to Cecilia's a lot. Helping her unclog her sink. Going to Home Depot with her to pick out a refrigerator.

"Oh, Bill," she would ask in her sing-song voice, "can you give me a quick hand with my couch, my oven, my windows…"

Dot despised Cecilia's helplessness and couldn't understand why Bill fed into it. A lifetime ago, when he had proposed to her, he had told her that he loved her strength and independence above all else. He told Dot he would never ask her to change, and that their marriage would be a true partnership. She had said yes immediately, and they were married in a ceremony that did not include the word "obey" in any of the vows.

Bill was true to his word, and they had a quiet and fulfilling life together. They both taught English at the local community college. They spent evenings reading and marking papers side by side, the quiet occasionally interrupted by one of them reading out loud the tortured attempts at poetic beauty from one student or another. How often had they laughed until the tears came!

The divorce party came soon after they retired from teaching. Bill started spending too much time at Cecilia's house, helping with a project. At first, Dot thought it was a good thing that he had something to occupy his time. But when she found herself alone so often, she challenged Bill. He dismissed Dot's observation that Cecilia needed to learn to live alone and do things herself.

"She's not as smart as you, Dot, she needs help." And then Bill put those ground lights in her garden and replaced her pavers. That work took the better part of two weeks, and when he was done, the garden had been transformed into a beautiful maze of lighting, paths, and seasonal blooms.

Dot's grasp on the scissors tightened as she remembered the day they got Bill's Stage 4 prognosis, during a doctor's visit he had put off until he had finished Cecilia's garden. Stage 4. She felt the prick of the blade against her palm, and the pain brought her back to the present. She looked at the next row of tulips, the black ones. She never understood why anyone would want a black tulip. Dot bent over and quickly worked on them, cutting them and grinding the blossoms into the ground with her boots.

She looked at her watch. It was 2:30. She knew the photographer from Yankee Magazine would be there at 7am, to catch the morning sun on the flowers. Cecilia had cornered Dot at the Food Lion yesterday to tell her about it.

"My little garden! Can you believe it, Dot? I'm so excited! I was weeding all morning!"

She had followed Dot around the market, starting at the dairy case, telling her about the article they would write about her garden. Not once did she mention Bill, although it would have incensed Dot even more if she had. Dot abandoned her cart to escape her, feigning a stomach illness that was not too far off the mark.

A car's engine broke the silence. She shuffled to the wall, her back flat against Cecilia's house as the car approached. The headlights were visible as they turned into the cul-de-sac and headed toward her. She tried to crouch, but the pain in her knees returned. Instead, she slowly slid down into a sitting position. She held her breath as the arc of the headlights drew closer. She was sweating, but didn't dare move to loosen her coat or hat. The car slowed down before reaching Cecilia's, turning into Joanne's house.

Dot briefly wondered where her neighbors had been so late on Tuesday. She remembered an incident when Joanne had called the cops about a stranger in the circle, and it turned out it was someone's house sitter. Being caught by the police had never occurred to her, and she lowered her head into her arms as she thought about the humiliation it would bring. She finally started to breathe normally as she heard the grating sound of the garage door opener. When she looked up, the car had disappeared, and the house lights were on.

She watched the progression of lights turn on, then off, and waited an extra five minutes after the house was once again all dark. She struggled to get up and used the side of the house to help her rise. She limped back to the flower bed.

The car had delayed her mission, and she moved quickly, ignoring the pain in her back and knees. She worked from row to row, following the color pattern: Cutting off the yellow, then the red, the striped, and finally, the delicate Lavender Triumph tulip, Cecilia's favorite. She didn't leave those petals on the ground but slipped them into her pocket.

Dot backed away from the garden. All 120 tulips were gone. The garden seemed to shimmer, as the lighter petals on the ground reflected the garden lights and shone like pearls.

"That will not do," she murmured to herself.

She followed the line of lights until they ended right next to the transformer box. She stabbed the ground with the scissors, digging around the last light. She found what she sought and pulled the wire to the box. She held the scissors against the cables and tried remembering what Bill told her about them. Can she cut them without getting shocked? She wasn't sure and put the scissors back in her pocket. She yanked as hard as possible and pulled the wires from the box. The line of lights went out.

There was one last thing she needed to do. Dot turned and headed for Cecilia's front door. She took the Lavender Triumph blooms from her pocket and picked the petals off one by one, dumping them in a pile right outside the front door.

Dot checked her watch. It was a little after four. She turned her back on Cecilia's house and strolled back to her place, savoring the calm that had settled in. She walked with a lightness she hadn't felt in months. Her pain had subsided, and she almost smiled. When she reached her porch, she settled her bulk on the steps and looked up at the stars. They were so bright without the moon, and she easily found the group that made up Cassiopeia, the Queen. She could almost feel Bill's arm around her as he told her about the stars that made up that constellation.

"One of those stars will turn supernova in the next millennium. It could be tonight, it could be a thousand years from now. Maybe you and I will see it!"

To her surprise, the tears that were held back in the weeks since his death came easily, and she cried silently. The sky had brightened when she finally threw the scissors in the garbage pail and returned to the house.

Under the New Moon

About StoryForge

These are but a fraction of the stories available on StoryForge. There were dozens more submitted, from short stories to poetry, to full-length novels. Stories from every genre you know and many you've never seen before. There aren't many options for brand new ideas to get published.

Traditional publishing is nearly impossible to break into. But it's free. Self-publishing is very expensive. But it's open to everyone.

StoryForge is a new way of publishing that's free and open to everyone.

Making publishing accessible is the goal of our founder, Sabrina Rucker. Her work was denied again and again – nineteen rejections in total. One agent loved Sabrina's work, but couldn't think of a publisher who would take it. Praised, but blocked, Sabrina couldn't see a clear path forward. So she made one.

StoryForge gives every writer the opportunity to get published – for free. We keep your project moving forward by focusing on the most important part: You. Need a break from writing? You can decorate your personal library to be the perfect magical retreat. Need someone to talk to? We have a bustling community with Circles dedicated to all sorts of topics. There's something for everyone, and a safe space to be who you are. StoryForge helps you find readers who'll give great feedback on your work-in-progress.

Readers can discover stories from new, uncensored voices. That can be hard to do in an industry that prioritizes playing it safe. StoryForge's strategy lets us take risks on new ideas that other publishers pass over. We have over two dozen genres, and a tagging system to help readers find exactly what they're looking for. If they want to get in on the action, readers can comment on specific paragraphs or leave a note at the end of the story.

We're developing a gamified system that keeps track of your work as a reader, writer and editor. Soon, you'll be able to level up your stories, earn achievements, and get credit for all your hard work.

Writing doesn't have to be lonely. Getting published doesn't have to feel hopeless. You can learn more about how we highlight new voices at storyforge.com.

The stories in this anthology can all be read in their original form on app.storyforge.com.

www.ingramcontent.com/pod-product-compliance
Lightning Source LLC
Chambersburg PA
CBHW030242120726
47903CB00005B/1589